CHARITY

A DARK RETELLING OF BEAUTY & THE BEAST

VIRTUES FAIRYTALE
BOOK ONE

ALEXANDRA K MARTIN

Copyright © Alexandra K. Martin 2023

This novel is entirely a work of fiction. The names, characters, and incidents portrayed in it are the work of the author's imagination. Any resemblance to actual persons, living or dead, events or localities is entirely coincidental.

Cover Art: ©DAZED Designs 2023

Editor: Melissa Plant

Formatting & Design: ©DAZED Designs 2023

"Tell me every terrible thing you ever did, and let me love you anyway."
-Edgar Allan Poe

FOREWARNING

Please be aware that this is a Dark Contemporary RH fairy tale retelling, with adult content, and it is recommended for the mature audience. It contains some darker elements that could be triggering, please keep this warning in mind going forward.

Enter at your own risk...
    *Insert evil laugh

This for all the sinners, the saints, and those of us that are a bit of both. Live your best life and be honest with yourself along the way. Always remember, life's too short to waste it on regrets, so only make choices you can live with.

CHAPTER 1

FOXY

"Why is this my problem?" I yell at Alonzo through the phone perched between my cheek and shoulder as I change the brake disks on one of the cars I have to take care of today. "You know where I stand on all the crap, and I'm not getting involved, no matter how much you beg. You should have figured it out by now. If Mami and Papi can respect my decision, then why can't you?"

Alonzo sighs heavily like I'm the one being unreasonable here. I made it very clear growing up that I wasn't going to be a part of the 'family business.' If they want to live a life of crime, then that's on them. I have my own dreams, and Cartel life is not one of them. I just want to fix cars, fuck, and drink. Is that such a big ask? No, it's not.

"Who do you think asked me to call you?" my brother asks quietly, surprising me. "Plus, it's not what you think. We're not asking you to do any illegal shit, just help out around the garage for a couple of months while Mario and I deal with some business in El Salvador. Nothing underhanded. I promise."

That's what they always say, but somehow I end up mixed into their other pursuits. If I knew that it was just for fixing up a few cars here and there, I'd be happy to help out. Family is the most important thing, after all, except for where business is concerned. If I give my family even one inch in that regard, they take a damn mile.

As if on cue, Alonzo adds, "Aren't you sick of living off-air, Foxy? I know you're stubborn, but it's ridiculous living the way you do when you could be neck-deep in cash if you'd just swallow your pride occasionally. It's not charity when you work for it, and we have plenty of things you can help with outside the Garage."

"Fuck off, Alonzo," I swear, losing my patience with him and this pointless conversation quickly. "Remind me to send you some pride-filled cookies when you're in jail. I'm tired of having the same fight over and over again. For once, can you respect my decision or just leave me the hell alone."

My fingers slip as I pick up the brake disc, and I accidentally touch it in the wrong place, leaving a dirty fingerprint. *Mierda.* How am I meant to focus, when I have this shit to deal with?

While I carefully wipe it down, I hear a shuffling sound and then my mami's voice as the phone gets passed over. "Mija, we don't ask you for much, but we're about to be seriously short-staffed and need you to help out. Mechanics only, your hermano is trying to mess with you, baby. We don't expect you to do anything that makes you uncomfortable, plus Papi would love to get your help around here. We all know you're the only one as blessed as he is with an engine. You can teach Juan and Antonio a thing or two, and maybe help me get their heads pulled out of their asses. The two of them are nothing but trouble these days."

Argh, if I say no now, I'm going to be pulled into one of her long-winded guilt trips, and I'm really not in the mood for that right now. "When do you need me?" I grumble out between clenched teeth and sit on the nearby trolley seat, giving up on focusing on my actual job, so I can deal with this, all the while knowing there's no way out of this.

"Gracias, mija." Her voice instantly perks up as my mood drops significantly. I guess I'm going to lose my job in Sinhaven over this because I can't imagine them being alright with me taking off for a few months. *Puta.* "You can be here by Monday, can't you?" Mami asks, and I almost choke on my own spit.

"Monday? Are you fucking serious?" My voice rises loud enough that two of my colleagues look up from their own vehicles. Talk about giving me no time, that's in four days.

Mami goes off on a tangent instantly about me swearing at her, and I have to pull the phone away from my ear as she threatens to kick my ass if I talk to her like that again, and I have no doubt that if I'm not careful, the second I get there a chancla will be flying at my head. If it's not already on its way here.

With a long spiel of apologies, while rolling my eyes at her over-the-top response, I manage to calm her down and very reluctantly agree to go back to Beastville to help out at the garage until my two older brothers get back from El Salvador.

I hang up, finish off what's left of the brakes, clean my hands off, and call Allure. I'm done for the day anyway, and I'm really hoping my main bitch is going to have my back and come out with me tonight to help drown my sorrows. If she thinks that her kids or the Hunter brothers are coming, she's shit out of luck.

It's been four years since mi hermana became a mami to the cutest twins ever, and let's be honest, the only kids I can stand being near. Her unconventional relationship with three sexy-as-sin brothers is a thing of beauty. While the idea of committing to anything, other than a pet, makes me want to swallow razor blades while swimming through acid, I couldn't be happier for Allure. I mean, why have one dick, when you can have three. Score.

* * *

AFTER EXPLAINING MY PREDICAMENT, ALLURE happily drops everything and shows up at my place in less than half an hour with a tub of ice cream, a box of tissues, and a giant-sized bottle of tequila. God, I love this woman.

"Do you want me to come down and stay a couple of days with you?" she asks me as she sits at the dining table, while I grab us two bowls, spoons, and glasses, pointedly ignoring the rent reminder stuck to my fridge door. "Callum said to tell you that two days is the maximum before he comes over and steals me back. It's not like the kids don't have three dads to keep them occupied."

Placing the stuff on the table, Allure quickly takes her glass before I get a chance to fill it, and I quirk a brow at her. "Why did you bring tequila if you weren't planning on drinking any with me? I need some serious drunk talk." I fill my own glass beyond the appropriate mark for straight liquor then suddenly stop, an unwelcome thought entering my mind and my head snaps up to see Allure's guilty look and I know I'm right. This pendeja is pregnant again. "Are you fucking kidding me? ¿Cómo me vas a decir que estás preñada otra vez? Me estás mintiendo, ¿verdad?"

Not even slightly fussed by my outburst, Allure proceeds to laugh at me instead like the spawn factory that she is. I mumble, "Está pendeja de verdad..." before slamming down my whole glass, simultaneously loving and hating the fiery burn.

"Come on, you can't be that mad. I know you love my babies, even if you deny it," my traitorous sister giggles, while topping up my drink for me again. "We were going to take you out to dinner next week to tell you, but I guess now is as good a time as any, Tía Foxy. It's just the one this time, though. I already checked, and we're happy about it, so I need you to be happy for me too. I even brought you strawberry ice cream, even though I hate it. You know how seriously I take my ice cream flavors."

I grit my teeth, take in a deep breath, and shoot my glass once more before turning to the person who means the most to me in this world and telling my inner bitch to calm the fuck down. "Congratulations, I'm very happy for your parasite." My tone is flat, but she knows I'm joking; it's a part of my unique charm, after all.

Her melodious laugh fills the room, and I can't help but to smile back at her. "That didn't hurt too bad now, did it?" I playfully flick some ice cream at her.

Every day I'm grateful for this human being; we are absolute opposites and I wouldn't have it any other way. Allure is the light to my darkness that keeps me in check, and I am the strength and caution to her wayward trust and naïveté that always seems to get her into trouble, or at least it used to before she found the Hunters. Sometimes I wonder if I still have a place in her life now, or if it's just me desperately holding onto her light.

Choosing to dispel those negative thoughts before they consume me, I get up and pour Allure a water because my fridge is damn near as empty as my wallet. "Here, bish, have some non-alcoholic tequila and pretend that you're gonna get as fucked up as I am tonight."

Pride is a poor person's sin, because I refuse to take any of the hands reaching out to help, especially if it's my family's brand of money. They can keep their greed, and I'll keep my pride. Luckily, mi hermana respects my decision and always has my back because she's just as stubborn as I am when it comes to handouts.

Like the queen she is, she shoots the water down as if it's really tequila and asks, "Alright, what are we packing first? I'm gonna need another bartender because I'm ready to get lit."

CHAPTER 2

FOXY

Driving down my driveway in Beast, my Fox Body Mustang, as it roars the way I love, I look down the long drive to the infamous family home, the Hernandez Compound. Not only is this the place where I grew up with my parents and four older brothers, but it's also at the very heart of their successful cartel.

When I was really young, I thought the way that we lived was the same as the way everybody else lived. It was only when I began school that I started to realize that things were a little bit different from other households, especially when I became inseparable from my best friend and sister of choice, Allure. Her family life was very different from my own, with her sweet, straight-down-the-line parents, and their token white-picket fence house with fresh flower gardens in the nicer area of Royal Cross. My life was dramatically opposite with my high spiked fence, extreme security systems, constant fear of police coming around and to top it off, filled with lots and lots of all different types of weapons. Granted, I wasn't allowed to play with them, but I knew they were there.

Our compound, because let's face it, this place doesn't scream family home, a whole section of it is dedicated just to storing weapons, illegal parts, and pot, their other lucrative markets.

As I grew up, my brothers, one by one, and then eventually myself, were all taught the various types of weapons, what they were made of, how you use them, how to safely store them, where we get them from, how we sell them, how we move them, and the importance of secrecy and privacy. The most important step is secrecy because, in my family's line of work, you can't do anything effectively without it. My family wouldn't be here if the cartel made mistakes like that, even thinking about it still makes me sick to my stomach.

I vividly remember growing up, every time we would see a police officer or any person of the law near the compound or our vehicles, there was always this mad rush to make sure everything was well hidden if we were in the house or car. I became prematurely anxious and paranoid from a way too young age, constantly worrying about when they would come by and take us, what they were doing here, and if I would be left all alone. I would spend my entire childhood sitting on the edge of my seat just waiting for the other shoe to drop, and it was terrifying. I didn't understand why we were always hiding at first, but when I realized what my family did was illegal, it made it all so much worse. All of a sudden what we were doing and what we were supplying to people meant that I could never feel like I was able to sleep safely again. Every morning when I wake up after a restless night, even now as an adult, the first thing I think of is can I hear anything out of place? Is anything wrong with my loved ones? Because I am perpetually terrified of the day when the police will come and take everybody I love away.

It's honestly only one of the many reasons why I won't have anything to do with the cartel side of things, ever. The mechanic side of our family is a whole other story, though. The Hernandez Garage is technically the front for the Hernandez cartel. However, I take that side much more seriously because of my deep and forever love of cars. And when I say I love cars, I mean, I really love cars. I look at a well-made machine the same way a dying man looks at water in the desert. I love cars the same way other people love the smell of a newborn baby. Cars are my refuge, my peace. My one place where my mind can go without a care in the world as I work on a puzzle I know I can fix and nothing else in the world matters anymore, except for me and the sexy machine my hands work to make purr. The vibration and rumble of my own car as I drive down the driveway give me the courage to keep going toward my family. As the automatic gate slides open, I enter the main part of the property located between Royal Cross and Charmington Center, welcoming me back to the tight fold of my family's chaotic embrace.

I love my family more than words can say because I never missed out on a moment of love and support, but this family keeps my heart beating irregularly and with an anxiety-ridden race that doesn't suit me. For once, I'd just like to have normal parents, and basic problems other families face, issues that aren't life-and-death. But alas, here I am and when it comes to blood ties, you get what you're given.

"Hola, chiquita," Juan yells out to me as I pull my car into park, he makes his way over with a smile so wide and bright it makes me feel momentarily guilty about my earlier thoughts until I realize what he just called me. He knows I hate that fucking name.

"Cállate pendejo." I shake my head at him, getting out of the car.

Ignoring my pissed-off face, Juan pulls me into a massive hug that makes me feel way smaller than I am. My brothers aren't overly tall, with the tallest, Alonzo, being five foot eleven, but Juan and Mario are buff as fuck. All four of them, like my papi, spend a good chunk of time in the large home gym we have on the property, but Alonzo and Antonio focus more on the athletic build than the tank look of the others. Working out has always been deeply ingrained in all of us since we were super young, with our papi practically demanding that we stay fit, but it's never been an issue for any of us because we all love the pain and competition it brings out in us. We are a super competitive family in everything we do. Since living away from home, I've had to improvise without being able to afford a gym membership by running every morning and using my own body weight to do what I can, whenever I can. I'm not overly vain, but even I know my ass and curves are bomb.

I shove Juan off me half-heartedly, hiding how good it is to see the big fucker, and ask, "Where is everyone?"

"They're all still at the Garage, except Mami." He starts opening my trunk and grabbing out my two bags because that's all my life comes down to, apparently. "She's cooking up a feast. I know this isn't ideal for you, chiquita, but she is over the moon to have her niña home again. I think she's over the testosterone since you left her with all of us."

We walk to the large front door together, and I kick at a rogue stone that fell out of the garden. "I don't blame her; I'd hate to be stuck with the lot of you." I give an exaggerated shiver, and he shoulders me, almost tipping me over with a deep laugh. "Hey? Keep your boulder shoulders to yourself."

The door flies open before I get a chance to grab the knob and Mami comes flying out, wrapping her arms around me and squeezing tight, the wild curls that match my own all in my face.

Antonio and I are the only ones that took after our Brazilian mami, with our darker skin and unmanageable curls, while our brothers all look like our El Salvadorian papi. Our mami moved to El Salvador when she was very little and met Papi in her teens, where they apparently fell head over heels with each other. It wasn't always smooth sailing because my mami's skin was so much darker, but neither of them gave a shit about anyone else's opinions. My papi's family has always been in the 'business' and was happy to support him when he decided to come to the US for expansion, and it worked out really well, obviously. At least until recently because the new El Salvadorian president has really cracked down on crime and that's why Mario and Alonzo have to go back. Too many of their contacts have been arrested, and it's caused some supply issues. I just hope they don't get caught while they're over there, but personally, I think he's doing an incredible job and the country is better off because of it and as much as I don't want my brothers to be caught, it will serve them right.

One of my main reasons for agreeing to come back is a hope that I can use this issue to convince them to take a step back from the cartel and choose a life without crime. Yes, it's harder to have less money, but it feels so much better for the soul, and I don't want to lose any of my family because of their poor life choices.

"I'm so glad you're home." Mami's excited voice and tear-filled eyes make me smile despite myself. I've really missed her. "I'm making pupusas, yuca frita y gallo en chicha. You've lost weight, mija," she adds, stepping back and looking me up and down. "Come, and I'll give you some frijolitos to tide you over before dinner. Juan hacele un café."

Like the whirlwind that she is, Mami is gone as quickly as she came back to the kitchen. I swear, she is a never-ending battery.

Juan puts my bags down at the door, laughing quietly and shaking his head.

"Welcome home chiquita, still one sugar?" he asks as he follows Mami, walking backward and looking genuinely happy that I'm home again. I nod a yes, and he calls back as he turns to face forward, "Go put your stuff in your room, and I'll meet you in the kitchen."

I pick up my bags and walk up the stairs and left toward my old room that I just know will look exactly the same as it always does. Opening the door, I instantly know I'm right. The cleaner comes once a week, and dusts my room, but other than that nothing ever changes.

CHAPTER 3

FOXY

After having my coffee and Mami's mouth-watering frijoles that taste like home, I spend the afternoon unpacking my clothes and then help Mami finish up in the kitchen. I'm practically salivating over the food I've missed so freaking much. It's a definite plus for me coming back that not only do I not have to cook much, but I also get my favorite food again.

With the sound of cars pulling into the drive, I know my brothers and Papi are home for the day, and I brace myself for the shit I know I'm about to receive. Juan went back to work after making me a coffee earlier, so I'm sure they spent a good portion of the afternoon bitching about how it's my duty to be here in the first place.

Papi is the first to spot me and, with arms wide, pulls me into a hug. "How is my baby girl?" he asks in my hair. He has always treated me like the princess that I'm not, but he's the only one allowed to. My papi and I have always had a really great relationship and our deep love for cars, really helps. Pulling back he looks down at me, "I'm sorry for this Foxy, I know you are busy with your own life, but I really appreciate that you came to help. When our regulars found out that you're back for a while, they all booked some time in. I hope you're ready to get busy because your schedule is almost filled up."

"No joke, sis, I lost heaps of work because of you," Antonio grumbles as he slides past us, his big ass frame almost filling the hallway.

I smack the back of his head as he walks past. "Do a better job, and you won't lose any. It's not my fault you don't know the difference between an alternator and an exhaust pipe."

Antonio looks back at me with a scowl. "Ha ha, very funny."

"Oh, and what's this I hear about you getting into trouble?" I add, stepping up to him. "I'll be watching you like a hawk while I'm here, so you better watch yourself while I'm here. If I see you slacking off at work or hanging around any losers, you're going to get it. Understand?"

"I'm older than you," he reminds me with an angry tone as a warning.

I laugh loudly with my head back at the hilarity of his statement. "Then act like it."

"Enough you two," Mario states firmly as he enters but then smiles at me warmly, our oldest brother is tough as nails but has a great heart underneath his hard exterior. "How are you, chiquita? You look good."

I decide to ignore the stupid nickname because I know they're always trying to goad me with it. Instead, I bang knuckles with him and smile back. "Thanks, bro. I've been working out my frustrations extra lately, exercising. Bet I could give you a run for your money."

Putting his arm around my shoulder, he guides me to the dining room, while chatting happily. "We should spar sometime and test that theory. It's been ages since we had some fun in the ring. I'd like to make sure you haven't been slacking off."

"No doubt she's been kicking ass and taking names all around Sinhaven, haven't you?" Alonzo asks, stealing my seat before I can take it, poking his tongue out like a child. "Snooze you lose."

Mami comes in and finishes setting up the table with cutlery. "Watch your language, Alonzo. I won't say it again. I don't care how you speak at work, but you better watch your mouth in my house. That goes for all of you."

When she turns away, I flip Alonzo the finger with a shit-eating grin, and he flips one right back. It's our way of saying I love you, hi, or you're a dick. Depending on the mood.

We all take a seat and have a really nice family meal, and it's times like these that I like the best because it's just like everyone else's family. We laugh, we bicker, we share our day and the outside world doesn't matter so much during our dinner.

I find myself smiling down at my empty plate, my stomach way over full, and Alonzo pats my knee. "It's nice to have you home with us. I wish I could stay with you instead of leaving. Will you stay for a bit after we get back, or go back to Sinhaven?"

"What do you think?" Antonio grumbles and Mami smacks his arm with a heady warning in her gaze to not start a fight so quickly after me getting home.

Not wanting to upset her, I ignore the youngest of my big brothers and focus on Alonzo instead. "I'm not sure. I guess it depends on how long you're gone and how things go while I'm here." I pause for a second, choosing my words carefully to keep the peace. "Is there any way you and

Mario could choose to stay home instead and focus on the garage side of things?"

Silence fills the dining room, and Mami chooses that time to start clearing the table, knowing that this conversation might not end well. Once she leaves, Mario clears his throat and quietly says, so that Mami can't hear, "Let's not start this again, alright? You know where we stand already."

Frustrated and unable to hide it, I stand up, hard enough that my chair almost falls back, but Alonzo quickly catches it. "I can't even talk about it? Even though I'm a part of this family too? You know that everything that happens to you, affects me as well, right?"

Antonio gets up slowly, scowling at me from across the table and leaning his hands on it. "You lost the right to have a say when you put our family last. You think just because you came for a visit that you have any right to have an opinion on what goes on around here? Well, you're wrong."

"Sit. Down. The both of you," Papi commands in a low tone that is not to be messed with, and Antonio complies immediately. I turn and storm from the room, unable to keep my eyes from welling up and showing what I know they'll perceive as woman's weakness, and it just infuriates me even more.

I hear something slam on the table behind me, but I don't turn around to see what it is. I smile to myself when I hear a thud and Antonio grumble in pain and my mami's quiet scolding. Ha ha, sucker. Sometimes it really pays to be the little sister.

Leaving the house, I head directly to our garage to see my papi's real pride and joy, next to me of course. I open the door and step inside, switching on the light switch. Papi's black 69 Mustang GT500 is sitting in the center of the room with its own headlight shining on it. Dios mío, that is one sexy car.

My steps echo through the room, and the familiar smell of engine oil hits me as I walk up to it, a soft smile on my face. "One day papi is going to let me drive you, pretty girl," I tell the car as I softly run my fingers over the bonnet.

"You wish," my papi replies from just behind me, and I jump because his steps never made a sound when he approached me.

I turn to him and puff out a breath. "You're one scary man, papi. You and your ninja ways." He laughs at me, his eyes squinted tight with happiness.

Moving to one of his tool benches, he picks up a microfiber cloth and brings it back, wiping away the invisible fingerprints I apparently left on his car, and I roll my eyes at him. "Please. I didn't mark your precious; you're being ridiculous."

"Says the girl who was just drooling on it and praying for the keys. If she was yours, you wouldn't like other people's sticky hands on it, either," he remarks with a chuckle.

I huff at his over-exaggeration, "I'm not ten. I don't have sticky hands anymore." But I totally get it because he's right. I wouldn't. Changing the subject, I choose to get to the point. "I'm tired of being scared, Papi. You can't blame me for that. I know this is what you do, but can't you retire from it? It's not just you on the line if something goes wrong, it's Mami and those stupid brothers of mine. They're a pain in the ass, but the idea of Mario and Alonzo going back to El Salvador and getting caught or worse scares the shit out of me."

The whole time I look down at the car because I don't want to see the disappointment in his eyes at how I feel about their lifestyle. I know it upsets them, even though they've let me get away with staying out of it, which is honestly a feat in itself for any other cartel.

His heavy hands fall on my shoulders, squeezing reassuringly. "I know, baby girl. I know this is hard for you, and it scares you, even though you act as hard as stone most of the time. Your tough shell is built to hide how much you feel and help you bury any vulnerability that tries to sneak out, but when you're with me, you don't need it."

I let him pull me in for a hug and sigh. "I have a bad feeling about this. Just tell me that you'll consider it, Papi? That's all I need to hear."

"I can't do that, mariposa. You know I can't, and you're old enough now to know when to pick your battles with us and your brothers." He pauses before adding, "As for Antonio, you have my full support with kicking his ass, the little shit deserves it. He's been hanging around some bad news lately and if he keeps it up it's going to get him, or us, into big trouble. If you see or hear anything that's worrying, tell me, so I can take care of it before it gets out of control. Keep your other brothers out of it, though, I don't want them getting messed up with his damage."

I agree easily with that, because Antonio has always had a complex about being the youngest brother and makes some stupid fucking choices. I just hope he's not digging a hole that's too deep for him to get out of.

CHAPTER 4

FOXY

Not wanting to waste any time, I get straight into work the next morning after taking an easy five-mile run instead of my usual big workout, while Mario and Alonzo head out on an early flight. The day is busy, filled with appointments already lined up for me and a shit ton of locals just dropping by to say hi.

Despite my family being in charge of a cartel, our family is revered by all the local businesses and throughout a lot of Beastville because my family makes it a point to give back to the community whenever it can. Sure, it's mainly to keep everyone silent about the illegal comings and goings, but it works well. The respect and care both of my parents show to the community, especially when people are in dire need, has earned them an equal amount of respect in return.

My family does everything it can to keep crime out of the Royal Cross area, and it's noticed by all. We are known for being charitable, friendly, and honorable, but also for showing zero mercy to anyone who threatens those under our protection. The sheer brutality of my two oldest brothers and Papi is well-known and swiftly applied. The term fuck around and find out is definitely relevant to the Hernandez family tree, and I'm no exception. I may not be a part of the business, but I will fuck a bitch up if I need to.

My mind drifts to the bliss of a busy garage, while my hands play the tune of a mechanical melody. Some say it's genetic, some say it's talent, but I say it's good old-fashioned hard work with a massive dose of obsession. I couldn't be happier than when I'm at work, elbow-deep in grease and oil, listening to the roar of engines all day.

With a sigh of happiness, I pull the garage doors down at the end of the day and wipe my hands with a rag. "It's good to have you back, chiquita," Juan tells me as we walk out the back door. "You've always had the gift. It's a shame Antonio can't keep up."

Right on cue, Antonio, as predictable as ever, goes into defensive mode and starts talking shit as Juan and I ignore him, walking to our cars. "Fuck you guys," he grumbles after a big squeal and races out of the car park like a lunatic.

"That pendejo is gonna get someone hurt someday if he doesn't pull his head out of his ass. I'm glad Papi left earlier, so he doesn't have to feel embarrassed by that piece of shit today," Juan complains, shaking his head after our dickhead brother. Agreeing with him, we both head back home, closing the gate behind us before we go.

Even though we are all coming and going from the same place it's very rare that we share a car, none of us are willing to give up the driver's seat.

As soon as we make it back home, I head straight for the shower. Luckily, the house has great water pressure, so we can all shower at the same time without it being an issue because we are all gross at the end of the day. I get cleaned up and put on a pair of jeans and a tank top before heading back downstairs, in dire need of a cold beer.

I walk straight into the kitchen, past Mami making dinner, and open the fridge. At the same time, Antonio comes up right behind me, making a satisfied, "Aaahh" sound. I turn from the beerless fridge to him and find a shit-eating grin on his face before he takes a big gulp of the last fucking beer.

"You prick," I growl at him as he laughs and leans on the counter in Mami's way. She swats at him and gives me a warning glare at my choice of words, and I grumble. "What happened to ladies first?"

Antonio snickers, walking out with a swagger and calling back, "Shame you're no lady."

I swear I'm going to kick his dumb ass if he keeps this shit up.

"Here." Juan throws me a wad of cash, and I catch it just in time before it hits the floor. "Go grab some more from the shops. The one in Charmington has the best deals, you could get a couple of cartons for next to nothing and since you're home we're gonna need to stock up if you still drink like you used to."

Yeah, he has a point. I think to myself before I complain about being the one to go buy it. With a quick thanks, I head out with the full intention of keeping the change because I'm broke as fuck right now. I don't like getting something for nothing, but I'll just think of it as fuel money.

Before long, I'm on the road, driving toward Charmington Center with my windows down and music blaring loud. The newly cooling breeze from the typical fall weather caresses my cheeks and sends the rogue curls that have come loose from my bun whipping around my face in a chaotic rhythm. I love this time of year when it's no longer stinking hot, but it's not yet too cold to go out without a jumper on. It's not far from it though, I decide, from the notable extra nip in the air tonight.

I enjoy the cruisy drive and relax to my tunes until the town ahead comes into view. While Royal Cross has a nice neighborhood feel, Charmington Center is anything but charming, with high crime rates and an all around shitty appeal. It's pretty much the Dante's Circle of Beastville, and I never stay here longer than is absolutely necessary.

When I pull into the liquor store entrance, I make a note to double-check that I've locked my car properly before I head inside. I buy three cartons of beer at a ridiculously cheap price, scoring myself a decent stash with what's left over and pocketing it with glee.

The attendants follow me to my car, and I open the trunk so the three of us can fill it with my newly acquired beer. When they go back into the store, I open the driver's door, but pause when I hear what sounds like a pained whimper coming from the alleyway beside where I'm parked.

Now if I were anyone else I'd be terrified of going down there alone in this part of town, but I'm me, and I know how to shoot better than anyone I know bar my papi and Juan. Grabbing my Glock 17 from the glove department, I check that it's loaded then cautiously approach the entrance to the alleyway, all the while keeping a strong and ready stance in case someone tries to get the jump on me. While I don't necessarily like being armed in the street, I'm not stupid enough to not be ready because of instances like this.

The sad little noise happens again, and I look down the dark corridor, barely lit up from one small bare bulb halfway down. But it's enough for me to make out some kind of child-sized lump curled up not far down. After quickly surveying the rest of the space and deciding that there's no immediate threat, I carefully approach the mound that sometimes makes small movements and more whimpering.

To my horror, as I get closer it becomes clear that it's a severely wounded dog, left for dead, and barely conscious. I step in close and kneel beside the poor creature slowly, not wanting it to lash out at me in fear. Up close, it's clear that the pup is actually quite large with what seems to be a long white coat of fur, but it's so mangled with blood that it's not so easy to make out.

I put my gun into the back of my jeans and take another quick look around to make sure it's safe to do so, then carefully raise my hand to its face. "There, there, perrito. I'm not going to hurt you," I croon softly, making kissing noises, and my heart breaks as one beautiful brown eye stares up at me as the dog below me shakes uncontrollably with what must be a mixture of fear and pain.

To my absolute astonishment, the dog doesn't growl or nip at me, but instead lets me gently stroke the side of its face. I keep my voice soft and look around for something, I don't even know what, but I know that I can't leave it here like this.

I quickly survey the dog, which turns out to be a female, and decide that I'm going to have to back my car down here because she's too big to carry all the way to the car park. "I'll be back, pretty girl. Just give me a minute."

Not wanting to waste even a second, I run back to my vehicle and with careful precision back it down the alleyway until the dog is right beside my passenger door. Getting out, I scramble around to the other side, open the door and look at the limited space I have inside for this big ass injured dog.

"We're gonna have to make this work somehow. Just

bear with me; I'll get you help as quickly as I can," I tell her as I lift her with the greatest care. She yelps in pain as I touch her bloody side, and I wince in apology, carefully maneuvering her into the car and onto the seat. The sweetness of this dog while in so much pain breaks my heart even more. Her large brown eyes seem to plead quietly with me to help her, and not even once does she lash out at me in any way. *What kind of person would do this to such a special creature?*

Circling the car as quickly as I can, I jump into it and look over at the poor girl at the same time I grab my phone. When I get onto Google I find a twenty-four-hour no-kill animal shelter only one block away and instantly drive toward it being as gentle with the car as I can, as I take the corner to drive out and again as I pull into 'All Beasties Welcome.'

With impressive speed, I run to the door and fling it open, finding a shocked man in a white vet's jacket almost directly in front of me. "I need help," I cry out, pointing toward the parking lot. "I found a dog, and she's really hurt, but I didn't know where to go."

The surprisingly handsome man in front of me goes straight from shocked to action as the words leave my mouth, rushing out of the door I am still holding open and toward my car without a second thought.

I ran ahead of him and ripped the passenger's door open to the poor mutt. Tears fill my eyes at her poor state and for a second I wonder if she went and died on me, but she flinches as the vet lays his hands gently on her.

"What happened?" he asks me urgently as he sweeps her up in his arms as if she weighs nothing and starts racing back inside.

I follow him through the lobby and into a back room

with a large, cold bench, not wanting her out of my sight for a moment. The need for her to be okay rides me hard and makes me choke on emotion. "I don't know," I tell him, my voice is shakier than usual. "I found her in an alleyway and just brought her straight here."

Straight away, he starts to look her over from head to toe as an older woman walks in through a back door and stops, stunned by the sudden appearance of the two of us in the back room.

"Uta," the vet calls out. "Come watch this pup while I scrub up. I'm going to have to help her now, and I don't have time to take her back to the clinic if I want any chance of saving her."

The lady shoots into action, coming straight over and taking his place beside the injured dog, and then he looks up at me as if he'd forgotten I was there. "I'm sorry, Miss, but I'm going to need you to leave so that we can work on her. Thank you so much for bringing her here, you may have saved her life, or at least that's my hope," he says all of this as he ushers me back into the lobby, closing the door behind him before I can say anything in reply, and my heart drops a little more at the urgency in his voice.

Please be okay, pretty girl.

CHAPTER 5

THEODORE

Four hours it took me to save this Maremma. To be honest, I'm surprised she's even made it this far; this girl is a real fighter. The wounds all over her body were gnarly and brutal, and it's not the only time lately that I've seen something like this, but this is the first one I've seen that's survived.

Without a doubt, this bitch has been subjected to illegal dogfights and came out of it on the wrong end. I don't know why, but over the last few months, this has been happening more and more. It makes me sick to my stomach that anyone would do this to an animal for money. Sick bastards. If I get my hands on them, they'll be sorry.

I hope this girl pulls through, I think to myself after I call for the animal ambulance from my main location back in Royal Cross. It's just lucky I was popping in here to check on supplies before heading back home. Otherwise, tonight's story for this dog would have had a very different ending. The fast response of the lady that brought her in, made a huge difference. Unfortunately, it's not often that a bystander steps in when there's an injured animal on the side of the road, and I'm very grateful that she did.

"What do you want me to do with the girl asleep on the chair in the lobby, Dr. Bell?" Uta asks me suddenly, and I look over at her in confusion.

"What girl?"

I walk over and open the door to the lobby, shocked to see the lady that brought the dog in, fast asleep in one of the truly uncomfortable chairs lining the back wall. *She's still here.* I can't believe my eyes.

Turning to Uta, I let her know that I'll take care of it and tell her to go and have a coffee, thanking her for all the help she gave me. Tonight's endeavor certainly isn't a part of her normal work duties; I'll make sure to put a little bonus in her pay this week.

The girl on the chair turns her head to the side, giving me a better view of her profile as I approach. I take a good look at her, remembering her watery eyes last night as she stared down at the dog she brought in. This girl has got a kind heart, there's no doubt about it.

Hmm, girl is the wrong word because the thing before me is most definitely a woman. Her soft, beautiful features are just the icing on a very curvy and delicious cake. Holy shit, how did I not notice how hot she was last night? Even fast asleep, she's drop dead gorgeous, and I try my best not to be a creep and check out her straining t-shirt as she breathes deeply while sleeping.

Okay, time to be a gentleman and not the total sleazebag I feel like right now looking down at her. I lean forward and lightly tap her shoulder, which has her jumping to her feet and slamming her head into my chin, and we both yelp from the pain of it.

Ignoring my own sore face, I check on her first, hoping

she didn't get hurt too badly. "Are you alright?" I ask, feeling terrible that I scared her awake.

She looks around the room wildly for a second, rubbing the top of her head. "What the fuck happened?" I see the moment that recognition hits her and her features change instantly to one of concern, but not for herself but for the dog she brought in. I feel my heart warm significantly toward this stunning woman and know in that second I need to get to know her because she is someone that deserves to be known.

"I'm sorry for startling you," I say, trying to be cool and ignoring my suddenly racing heart. "You fell asleep waiting. You didn't need to stay here; it's been four hours, and it's two am. Don't you have someone at home waiting for you that might be worried about you?"

Smooth, dickhead. Real smooth.

Thankfully, she doesn't seem to notice my terrible segue into, 'Are you single' and replies automatically, "I told my parents that I would be out late and explained why. How is she? Please tell me she's alright."

Her dark brown eyes moisten with emotion, and it takes all of my strength not to pull her in for a hug. *Get a grip!* "Luckily, you brought her into me in time. It's still touch and go at the moment, but if all goes well, she'll pull through this. I can say without a word of a lie, she wouldn't have made it this far without you. Thank you from the bottom of my heart for taking the time to help her, it made all the difference. She doesn't have a microchip or collar, but I will do what I can to find her owners."

With obvious relief, she closes her eyes and exhales. When she opens her eyes, a new hardness is there that surprises me, and she stands up straighter like she means business and asks, "How much do I owe you?"

The change in demeanor sets me back for a second, and to back it up is her question. "This is an animal shelter, I'm not going to charge you for bringing in a stray dog, miss?" I forgot to ask her name earlier.

"I want to pay for her medical care so that she doesn't miss out on anything because of the cost. I don't have a lot on me, but my Papi will pay for whatever you need over the phone if that's alright?" she insists.

I smile warmly down at her charitable offer. "I promise you, I will give her only the best of care. If it makes you feel better, I can give you my card, and you can contact me later to check up on how she's doing. No payment necessary, it's why I opened this place. To make sure every animal has an opportunity to have a good, healthy life, regardless of money."

Not wanting her to turn down the offer of calling me, I go behind the front counter and grab one of my business cards that have the numbers of my three shelter locations and my vet clinic. I also jot down my own personal cell number on there as well.

"Here." I hand it to her as she stands when I approach. I can't help but notice her curves again and make sure to snap my wandering gaze back to her face again before I get caught gawking like a teenager. "Call me any time, and I'll answer. This is my cell number, and it's always on. I'd be happy to update you on her progress and if we find her owners."

The front door opens and Buzz walks in with his token big smile on, even at this ungodly hour. "What's up doc? I got the Scooby mobile out front and ready to go. Where is the lucky lady getting the VIP treatment tonight?"

"Just in the back, but you'll need my help carrying the crate, she's a hefty bitch," I answer with a light laugh. "She needs a little extra care, so we've got to take it slow, alright?" I turn back to the hot chick and tell her. "Buzz is our animal ambulance driver, he's going to take our girl to my clinic in Royal Cross. The address is on the card if you're ever in the area and want to check in on her."

She thanks me quickly, nods, and is out the door before I even realize that I never got her name, let alone her number. Dang it. I hope she calls in later.

CHAPTER 6

BEAU

I put a fresh pot of coffee on as I hear Theodore grumbling his way down the hallway of our two-bedroom apartment. Considering how late I was up last night before going to bed, Theodore must have come in pretty late.

"Coffee," he moans in a pretend zombie voice as he drags his feet into the kitchen, joining me, then leaning over the marble bench top.

With a small laugh, I put a fresh cup in front of him, knowing he's enjoying the life altering aroma as much as I do. "Rough night, huh?"

Theodore groans again and sits up, sipping from the mug with a satisfied smile. "Yes and no," he tells me, instantly perking up, his eyes widening suddenly with excitement. "I saved a dog last night, and I met a girl, not of the animal variety for a change. You should have seen this chick, she was sexy, empathetic, patient and so freaking sweet, but I also got the impression that she likes to keep a hard exterior by the way she closed off before she left. Oh, did I mention that she's smoking hot!"

It's not often that a woman captures Theodore's attention, so I don't bother hiding my shock at his words. Neither he nor I are easily swayed by the female persuasion because we want to find life partners and not just temporary distractions. Both of us for different reasons, he wants a close bonded relationship like the rare one his parents have always had, and I want one nothing like my parents had. Even thinking about my dad pisses me off, so I focus on the conversation at hand.

"Is she a client of yours? What's her name and when is the wedding?" I ask jokingly, and I only get an eye roll for my efforts. "Come on, don't leave me hanging. She must have been something spectacular to have you drooling this much so early in the morning. What time did you get home anyway?"

Theodore scoffs, but still indulges me. "I got in around three-ish I think; I had to transport the dog I mentioned to the clinic after performing emergency surgery out of the Charmington branch of All Beasties Welcome. Luckily, I keep it stocked up for these very reasons. As for the chick, she's not really a client, she found the Maremma dying in an alleyway and brought her straight in. If she'd waited any longer, there's no way the pooch would have made it," he tells me, face solemn thinking about it. "It was another dog fight; I'm sure of it."

My blood boils, hearing that. No animal asks for abuse, but yet humans seem to think they have the right to dish it out anyway. The girl he mentioned must have been really frightened finding a dog that way. "Was the lady alright? She wasn't too upset, was she? I bet she took off and cried in her car straight after she dropped her off."

"That's the thing," Theodore gulps down the last of his drink and turns to me. "She stayed for four hours in the lobby, eventually falling asleep there, and then was really attentive when I found her, super worried about the dog's wellbeing and even offering to pay for whatever she needs as long as I don't give up on saving her."

Now it all makes sense because there's nothing more attractive to Theodore than a lady who likes animals as much as he does. She could be an old hag, and he'd still see the most beautiful girl in the world if she behaved like that.

"Did you even get her number, dude?" I ask, going off a hunch that he forgot because he was too busy making heart eyes at the savior of innocent animals.

I can't help the pop of loud laughter that comes out of me watching his face deflate, and I know I hit a bullseye alright. I love my best friend like a brother, but he is absolutely clueless when it comes to women and has zero game.

"Maybe you'll see her around somewhere. Did you grab her name by any chance?" Perhaps I can ask around Miss Potts' to see if anyone has heard of her. Not that I would think she'd be at one of my women and children's shelters, but you never know, she could know someone through association.

"No, because I'm a total idiot, but I did find out that she lived with her parents, even though she looked like she was in her mid-twenties, and I also gave her my business card, with my number and told her she could call me for any updates at any time." He crosses his fingers with a hopeful grimace, and I laugh again. *Absolutely hopeless.*

Turning my wrist, I look at the time on my watch and decide I better get going if I want to make it to the mechanics on time. My usual guy, Earl, is taking some time off and traveling across the country to visit his daughter who just had a baby, and he and his wife want to help out a bit because her husband recently got deployed. Luckily, he gave me the name of another mechanic he swears by. In fact, he said he only gets her to work on his car when he needs a hand because he would not trust anyone else with it, and that's a massive compliment because he is as car crazy as I am.

My twin turbo E60 M5 is the love of my life, and I will only give her the best treatment available. I recently bought a new clutch for it that Earl has already sent to the Hernandez Garage ahead of time for me. It's a big place, and I've heard great things about them, but I've never heard anything about a female mechanic there before. Earl said that she's the owner's daughter and the best hands they've got. She's been living in Sinhaven recently, and it was a pain in the butt for him to drive over there whenever he had a two-person job on his own cars. Apparently, she's come back to work for the family business though, and if she's as good as he says she is then business will surely boom even more.

I head out after wishing Theodore luck at finding his mystery woman and drive to the Hernandez Garage with my princess, excited to give her a new upgrade. Not that she needs it because honestly she's already fitted with the best parts money can buy.

I may not look like I have much, but I'm easily in the top 1% of richest people in Beastville thanks to my dickhead father, may he not rest in peace. I get a real kick out of spending so much of his hard-earned cash helping all the women and children that I can. In the way he never looked after me and my mother when we were starving in the streets.

It wasn't until my precious mom died in my arms in a filthy gutter when I was only thirteen from an illness that could have been easily treated if he'd acknowledged our existence, that I'd even met the man. Mr. Money Bags, the owner of the world-famous financial institute, Cogsworth, just showed up, picked up his heir, and plonked me in a mansion of riches. The rest of my life before then was nothing more than a slight inconvenience. To say I have father issues is a massive understatement.

After he died suddenly from a heart attack alone in his cold office, I inherited everything because he doesn't have even one other relative. I used my top-tier education that he bought me and the years of accumulated knowledge of finance that he slammed into my head every day I lived with him and used it to build another empire through stock, new business ventures, trading, and many other avenues. Nothing makes me as proud as my true passion, other than my car, Miss Potts' Safehaven for Women and Children.

I wanted to create a safe place where no child or woman would be turned away, somewhere they could be safe and warm, with full bellies and access to free healthcare. I dedicate every second and every dollar to my mom, Rose Potts, and pray that she's proud of how I grew up because of her and in spite of him.

My car pulls into the garage drive, and I focus on the here and now. Parking my car in the designated area, I head toward the reception, where an older Latina lady sits behind the desk with a warm and inviting smile on her face.

"Hola, welcome to the Hernandez Garage. You must be Beau Dallas; it's not often we get a new face around here. I'm very glad Earl sent you to us," she greets me happily, and I'm already happy that I decided to come if the people here are so welcoming.

I extend my hand, and she happily takes it. "It's a pleasure to be here. I've heard incredible things, especially about someone called Foxy," I mention to her. "I don't know what Earl told you, but I don't often trust people with my princess, but he swears by her, and I swear by him, so it must mean great things."

"Sí, mi niña has a gift with cars, just like her Papi. She will take good care of your princess, I assure you. Would you like to meet her to put your mind at ease?" I'm surprised to hear that the mechanic is her daughter. I knew it was a family business, but I assumed for some reason that the receptionist would just be a hired worker. I kind of love it.

I agree happily and follow her into the open garage area with several vehicles filling the enormous space from expensive to cheap. They are propped up and carefully looked after by a few different male mechanics that are all Hispanic by the looks of it, and at the end of them where Mrs. Hernandez leads me, is a Dodge Charger with two small feet sticking out from underneath, as someone works on it.

"Mija, come and meet Mr. Dallas. He is your next appointment," the kind lady beside me says down to the feet before they start to slide out, and I almost choke on my own spit.

A freaking goddess rolls out from underneath the car; her hair a wild mass of curls atop her head, grease smeared on soft medium-brown cheeks. Overalls hugging a strong curvy frame with the top open to show a dirty white camisole, barely holding onto her sizable breasts, and two dark brown eyes staring up at me rimmed with luscious lashes. For a moment, I legitimately forget how to breathe as I stare down at the woman of my freaking dreams, and not all of those dreams are clean.

Her lips curve up to one side, and her eyes twinkle as

she sits up. "Take a picture, it'll last longer." *Oh fuck, I've been staring for way too long.*

"Sorry, um, hi," I stammer like an idiot. *Great job Casanova, it's not like first impressions are important.* I scold myself internally, wishing I could start again but with my tongue on the inside of my mouth.

CHAPTER 7

FOXY

Who does this gringo think he's staring at like that? Anyone would think I look like Jessica Rabbit the way this poor sap is ogling me, but I've got to say, he's definitely one of the best-looking guys I've seen in a while, minus the vet from last night.

Both guys had their own brand of sexy going for them. While this guy has an easy-going indie rocker vibe with his dark man bun, short neat beard, tattoos, and brand name ripped jeans. The good doctor from last night was more built, with dirty blond hair, a stubbled square jaw, and a good boy vibe that's just begging for me to taint. Either way, I'd be happy to donate a night or two of my time if they play their cards right. God knows I could use the pleasant distraction.

"You're the owner of the twin turbo E60 M5?" I ask, cutting to the chase instead of indulging my fantasy of just what that distraction would look like. I stand up, wiping my hands on the rag hanging out of my hip pocket. "Good choice of car, I hope you've been taking care of it. There's nothing worse than a boy with a toy that he treats as such."

A wide, bright smile lights up his face, and my pussy flutters a bit more than I'd like. "You'd be pleasantly surprised how good I am with my hands, and I'm happy to play with toys when the event arises, but my car is not one of them." He winks conspiratorially at me, obviously forgetting that my mami is standing right beside him.

"While that's very good news for many, I doubt it's the kind of information you'd want to share with her." I nod at my mami, who is now looking at him with disapproval, and he winces. "Anyway, I have the new clutch that you ordered, and I'll work on it today. It should be ready for you to pick up tomorrow morning, but if I come across any complications, I'll let you know."

Mami excuses herself, and I look closer at the now squirming man; I love how easily she can make a guy do that. Her glare is praiseworthy. Deciding to cut him some slack, I ask him to show me the car, and we walk in silence to the parking lot, where I see his meticulously cared-for vehicle.

With appreciation, I take in all the little details added to it and pop the bonnet to look inside. "You've really done this girl up, and she shines like a diamond. Did Earl do all of this?" I'm not going to lie, I swoon a little over it, and it also doesn't hurt the attraction I feel for the owner either. It's clear that he takes care of his car and takes a lot of pride in it, and I can really appreciate that.

"I do what I can myself, but I live in an apartment in the center of town and don't have access to a fully stocked garage. That's where Earl comes in, and it's great because half of the time he's happy to let me help out, and sometimes he even lets me do my own thing at his shop if he's busy." Fuck me, he even knows his way around the engine.

While leaning into the bonnet, I turn to ask him something and find his gaze firmly landing on my ass, and can't help the smirk that grows on my face. "See something you like, Mr. Dallas?" I ask, snapping his attention to my face, and I'm secretly delighted that instead of acting embarrassed or coy he smiles at me wickedly and replies with a purr, "Abso-fucking-lutely. Call me Beau."

With perfect timing, Juan strolls past, pats him on the shoulder, and says with a laugh, "You can't afford that kind of problem, gringo. Best to keep your hands to yourself if you plan on keeping them."

I scowl at my stupid brother and tell him to fuck off and not wreck my chance at getting some local dick in Spanish, making him cringe and pretend to dry heave, before walking away. Shaking my head, I turn back to my new customer. "Ignore him, he was dropped on his head as a baby."

Beau's eyes twinkle with humor, and he steps closer to me instead of being intimidated by my brother's gesture. I lean my ass against the car, and he bends forward putting a hand on each side of my hips, his face so close that his mouth almost touches mine and huskily whispers, "Don't worry, he didn't wreck anything."

Dios mío, he speaks Spanish, apparently. Unlike most girls, I love a little sexual aggression and hate beating around the bush when it comes to men, and decide to grab this bull by the horns. "Good, then tomorrow after work, how about you take me out for some drinks, and we'll see if you're worth my time?"

He licks his lips, tempting me to taste them, and steps back. "It's a date," Beau says as he walks backward toward the bus stop out the front of the garage wearing a smile filled with mischief, and I can't wait to see just how well he can give and take.

* * *

My day flies by as I have a blast playing around with Beau's car and installing his new clutch. He clearly didn't need a new one, but by the looks of the rest of the car, he just likes to have the newest and best of everything outfitted to it.

Looking at him, he doesn't scream money, but there's no way his car would look like this if he doesn't have a good stash of it. I wonder what he does for a living? I hope it's nothing illegal because I'm so over that shit in my life. Not that I want him in my life or anything, but I plan on at least taking him for a test drive soon, if tomorrow night goes well.

The hot vet from yesterday flashes in my mind, and I wonder if I should try my luck with him as well. He was pretty hot, and it's not like I plan on settling down with Beau or anything.

I've had the dog on my mind since I left anyway and have been really worried about her welfare. Deciding that it won't hurt to check up on her, I give Dr. Bell a quick text to the number he had scribbled on his business card.

Foxy: Hi, this is the girl who brought the injured dog in last night. I just wanted to see how she was doing today.

Almost instantly, I get a reply as I wash my hands thoroughly in the back sink. I dry them off and pick my phone up, reading the response.

Dr Bell: It's great to hear from you. She's doing really well today and has turned a big corner. I bet she'd love a pat from her savior if you're free.

Foxy: Have you found her owners yet? I'd love to see her if it's really ok.

I put my phone down and feel a smile form on my face at the thought of being able to see how she's doing with my own eyes, and I'm so relieved that she is doing better today. A part of me was freaking out that something would have happened, and she'd pass away.

Straight away I go to the locker room at the back, have a super quick shower so that I don't smell like motor oil, and get changed into my emergency clothes. I don't want to waste time going back home when I could go straight there.

My low-ride cargo pants and white camisole aren't anything to brag about, but it's better than my dirty overalls. Slipping my sneakers on, I think about the man as well as the dog. I should probably fix my hair a bit.

With expert movements, I retie my hair into a cute messy bun and put on a small amount of lip gloss. I may come across as boyish at work, but I have pride in my appearance when it comes to getting some dick and if he plays his cards right, the good doctor might just get to know me a little better.

I place my clothes in the washing hamper, making it tomorrow's problem, and pick my phone back up to see a message waiting for me.

DR. BELL: NO OWNERS YET, UNFORTUNATELY. WE ARE at my main clinic in Royal Cross, the address is on the card. Do you think you'll pop by tonight? I'm happy to wait for you because I'm pretty much done for the day.

SHIT. I SHOULD HAVE READ THIS EARLIER. I HOPE HE hasn't gone home yet. I type back as quickly as I can, walking out the door and calling back to Mami without waiting for a response. "I won't be home for dinner."

FOXY: ON MY WAY. I'M NOT FAR.

I CHECKED OUT THE ADDRESS THIS MORNING WHEN I got up and already know it's only about ten minutes down the road. For the dog, of course, but the guy is happily a nice bonus.

With a quick trip, I arrive at the clinic and hop out of my car to see a tasteful establishment that screams money, and I'm a bit taken aback. While I know that vets make decent cash, because of the less-than-stellar neighborhood the shelter was in and the rundown buildings all around, I was kind of expecting a similar type of venue. This place even has a brand-spanking new silver Jaguar XF out front.

Without meaning to, I pull the bottom of my white, short camisole down a little bit, unconsciously aware of how much of my midriff is showing. Maybe I'm not dressed appropriately to visit here, even though it is at the end of the day.

Before I get a chance to back out, Dr. Bell opens the large glass door at the entry and smiles over at me warmly. Holy crap, look at those dimples. How did I not notice them before? Is it getting moist out here, or is it just me? Fuck being dressed appropriately, I have a dog to check on. Yep. That's why I'm here. The dog!

With my head held high, I leisurely walk toward the fine man holding open the door for me, making sure to put a little extra sway into my hips as I do. Pride swells inside me as I see him visually take in his fill and look a little flustered. That's right, I'm a goddess, and you should know it from the get-go.

"Dr. Bell," I purr when I reach him. "Gracias for letting me come and visit."

With glittering eyes, he smiles wider and his dimples almost blind me. "Please, call me Theodore, and it's my pleasure. Anyone who truly cares about the welfare of animals as much as you seemed to is always welcome here."

Hmmm, Theodore. That's a super gringo name, and I hide a chuckle at it. Can't say I've ever fucked a Theodore before, at least not that I can remember.

He ushers me inside, placing a hand on the bare skin of my back, almost making me shiver from the unexpected but very welcome contact. This guy better not be married or something because I've got some serious tension I need to work out, and he looks like the perfect outlet. Either him or Beau. If I'm lucky, I might score one of them as a regular hook-up with no strings to keep me busy while I'm staying in Beastville.

The young, pretty brunette girl behind the receptionist counter looks up at us and takes in our body language. Her lips twist tightly and a good dose of green bursts out of her now squinting eyes; the envy she's giving off is almost palpable.

Ah, so the receptionist wants a taste of her boss. Well, tough shit because I'm planning on keeping him busy for now. She can have him when I'm done. We walk by her, and I can't help but give her a quick wink before we disappear into the backroom filled with sick or injured animals.

I smile wide at the exchange that no doubt pissed her off something terrible, and Theodore catches it. "Are you that excited to see how our girl is going?" he asks, and I feel instantly guilty because I am genuinely worried about her and hate that my pussy overrode my head for a second.

Focusing on why I'm really here, I listen as he tells me about her progress as we approach her sleeping form in a large crate at the back of the room. The tubes and shaved spots on her body make me feel sick to my stomach, and I feel my eyes burn at seeing her like this.

"Will she make a full recovery?" I ask, after he told me a bunch of things I really didn't understand.

Seeming to realize that his medical jargon went straight over my head, he squeezes my shoulder and smiles much more softly, putting my heart at ease. "I believe she will be fine. She made it out of the worst of it with flying colors, now it's all about her wounds healing and getting her strength back."

When I look down at her again, I come to a decision because somehow I've already bonded with this beautiful girl and if she doesn't have a family to love her the way she deserves, then I will be her family. Every day, I will give her so much love to make up for everything she's been through.

"If you can't find her family, can I adopt her?" I ask

looking up at him, knowing that's probably too soon to ask but also knowing that I want him to understand that I'm committed to this, and I take her recovery very seriously.

CHAPTER 8

THEODORE

When this queen of a woman looks up at me like that with her big brown eyes and her perfect words, it undoes me. Where have you been my whole life?

I'm momentarily rendered speechless and find myself lost in her emotion-filled gaze, that is until Millie practically throws open the door to the back room, giving away her discomfort that I'm back here with anyone other than her. The fact that this chick swayed in here like sex on a stick doesn't help.

I had to hold in a laugh at the wink I saw her flick to Millie when we came through, obviously in an effort to fuck with her. I didn't let on that I saw it, but it was so freaking funny. Knowing how much that would have riled Millie up, made my day more than it should have. That girl has been hitting on me relentlessly since I hired her two months ago. Her lack of any type of personality, other than when she stares at herself in her handheld mirror all day, did her no favors.

"We're closed up for the day, Theo," Millie tells me,

pointedly ignoring the chick by my side. I hate when she calls me that, if I wanted to be called Theo, I would introduce myself that way. "I'll wait for you, and we can walk to our cars together."

I try not to grind my teeth at her blatant disregard for addressing me properly in front of a client, let alone someone I'm interested in courting. "Thank you, but you can head out, we have more to talk about. Good work today, but in the future I'd like you to remember that I don't appreciate being called Theo. It's the tenth time I've told you, and next time I won't be as understanding. It's Dr. Bell, or Sir, during work hours, and Theodore otherwise. Theo is not my name."

Hopefully, I didn't come out too harsh because I actually hate having to correct my subordinates, but I've asked her nicely several times and feel quite disrespected at this point.

The chick beside me scoffs as Millie goes bright red, apologizes, and promptly leaves. I feel bad for embarrassing her, but enough is enough.

"Well, that was entertaining. Note to self, don't call you Theo." Her words lighten the mood, and we both laugh quietly.

I lean back on the silver bench and ask, "What exactly do I call you? You still haven't given me your name, and I'm very much hoping that we will continue talking after today." I'm taking a risk being so forward while at work, but the way she looks at me and her body language tells me that it's worth the risk.

She licks her lips and looks at me like she's trying to decipher something before saying, "Maybe I like being anonymous. Maybe what I want from you, apart from checking on the perrita, doesn't require a name."

Holy fuck. My brain short circuits and my dick twitches as she steps between my legs and very much into my personal space. "Oh yeah, and what's that?" My question comes out much huskier than intended, but it has the desired effect as she places her hands on each of my knees, leaning in even closer and slowly pushing them up my pants until they stop at the top of my thighs.

"Well, that depends. Are you married?" she asks, and I shake my head. "Is there any partner that I should be told about because I won't step on someone else's territory, no matter how sexy those dimples of yours are?"

The side of my mouth turns up, and I grab the top of her cargo pants, pulling her against my now very hard body and wrapping my arms around her small waist. "Well, there's my housemate, but he's not really my type. Other than that, I'm free as a bird. Give me a name, any name."

She wraps one hand around my neck, pulling my face so close that her words brush against my lips at the same time her other hand rubs against my dick through the straining fabric of my pants. "I'll give you a name if you earn it, but I've got to warn you, I have high expectations when it comes to sex and won't settle for anything less."

Challenge accepted. My mouth crashes with hers in a desperate need to be closer to her, our lips parting and tongues exploring with equal fervor. Our hunger for each other adds more fuel onto an already hot fire as she slides down my zipper and undoes my button.

I've never been with such a sexually enthusiastic woman before, and it's hot as fuck. I let her take control, pulling my rock-hard dick out of my pants, and I grab her messy bun, pulling her head back forcefully and biting down her neck, tasting her as I go.

Suddenly, she pushes me back and drops to her knees in

front of me, taking my entire dick into her warm mouth and swallowing around me. "Fuuck!" I cry out, my head flinging back at the intense feeling of her throat closing around me over and over again as she takes me in and out.

My hands grab the side of her head, and I look back down at her to find dark pits of desire staring up at me. Her heated gaze has me thrusting my hips wildly against her mouth, but it's too much, and I need her to catch up before I can be inside her.

Pulling her up by her shoulders, her full lips pop off my dick and smile seductively, letting me bring her to her feet. I spin us around so that her back is against the steel table and flip her so that she's facing it, whispering in her ear as I undo her cargo pants. "My turn."

I rip them down along with her barely there g-string, push the front of her body against the bench, and dive between her legs, pulling her perfect round ass cheeks apart. To get the best view of all she has to offer and practically growl at how hot and wet she looks, just for me.

My tongue glides up her slit, and she wiggles against the table with a small moan. "Keep still, I'm in charge now, and I'm going to taste you until I'm done," I tell her before my mouth lands on her again, using every trick I know with my tongue and fingers, making her cry out again and again, soaking my face with her ecstasy. I intermittently tongue her ass as I work my fingers inside her tight pussy. She's so responsive to everything I do, and I pay close attention to what she seems to like the most, and one of those things is ass play, which I'm very happy to find out.

As she comes on my hand again, my dick at this point so hard that it hurts, I tell her with a groan, "I don't have any condoms here." We are in a vet clinic after all, not exactly sex central.

"I'm clean and have an Implanon," she groans as she rides my finger.

I place another finger in her ass the way she liked before and rub my hardness along her clit with my other hand. "I'm clean too. Is that the go ahead?" I push against her hole slightly for emphasis, but don't push any further in case she wants me to stop. *Please say yes!*

"Fuck me right now, I need that big dick balls deep inside me," she moans, raising her hips back to encourage me.

Without warning, I slam my dick inside her, all the way, and she screams out at the intensity of it because I am not small by any means. I give her a second to get accustomed to my size, but she starts pushing back almost immediately, begging for more, which I happily give her. Her tight confines feel like home as I fuck her hard against the bench, possibly bruising the front of her thighs. But she keeps demanding I fuck her harder and deeper until we're no better than the animals all around us, getting a free show in human mating.

My hand pushes on her neck, keeping her face against the bench for leverage as I slam in even harder, and she cries out in a muffled voice, "I want you in my ass." I think I've died and gone to heaven, and she is my God.

What my goddess wants, my goddess gets. I pull out, dripping wet, from her pussy and gently slide inside her back hole, using my free hand to stroke and roll her clitoris the entire time. She mewls in satisfaction, telling me I'm doing a good job, and it takes all my effort not to instantly cum in her ass.

"Don't be shy, big boy, I can take it. Fuck me harder, like before, but make sure you cum in my pussy," she tells me, pushing her hips back again.

Doing what I'm told like a good boy, I go to town on her ass, while my fingers play a tune of orgasms from her clit until she's shaking. Her legs trembling so hard that she might not be able to walk properly for a few days. Unable to hold it in anymore, I pull out of her ass and slam back into her pussy, thrusting a couple of times while digging my fingers into the rounded flesh of her sexy hips. I climax so hard and deep that I fucking see stars, falling over her body in a sweaty, hot mess.

We just lie there like that for a few minutes, the both of us catching our breath and finding our sanity again after what was hands down the best sex I've ever had in my life. My own fantasies don't even come close to how hot and unforgettable that was.

I then realize that I'm still mostly dressed with my long white coat and button-up shirt firmly in place, if not soaking from the sweat we've both worked up. My pants are even still around my ankles, just like hers, our shoes keeping them from coming off. The realization has me suddenly laughing hard, and the goddess of my dreams turns to look up at me, her hair wild and her face flushed and moist.

"What's so funny?" A smile plays at her lips, and her eyes are hooded with a mixture of exhaustion and pure bliss.

I pull out of her and tenderly help her up, helping her lean against the table and help fixing up her clothes for her. Because she honestly looks like she doesn't have enough energy to stand, let alone move on her own.

"Us," I tell her as I go. "I just realized how we must have looked, mostly dressed and bent over in the middle of the clinic."

She chuckles lightly, and her features soften more than ever, and just when I thought she couldn't look more beautiful than she did before, now she takes my breath away.

I pull my pants up and watch with interest as she seems to come to her senses a bit more, looking around the room and fixing her hair as well as she can under the circumstances.

"Thanks for that," she tells me suddenly, and looks back at the dog she saved. "Let me know how she does and if I can adopt her." To my absolute shock, she pats me on the shoulder and walks toward the exit. Just when I think she's going to leave without even a backward glance, she stops and turns around with a big smile. "You can call me Ana-Lucia. Very well-earned, call me."

And as simple as that she's gone from the clinic, and I'm left with a bewildered smile, a name, and a feeling that I can never let her go now.

CHAPTER 9

FOXY

I can't believe I gave Theodore my real name. I can count on one hand how many people in my life, other than family, that know what my real name even is. My train of thought at the time was that he wouldn't be able to find me later when I get sick of him because I'm pretty well known as Foxy in these parts.

Foxy was a nickname I got when I was only a toddler because I was more like a little beast than a sweet little girl, and it stuck. I wouldn't have it any other way either because Ana-Lucia doesn't suit me at all, and I can't remember the last time I was called it. Except for when Mami is particularly pissed off at me, then I get the entire name spiel to nail home the disappointment.

My alarm sounds to 'get out of bed, bitch,' and I turn it off straight away because I've probably been awake for about half an hour staring into the darkness. Thinking about how hot last night was and trying to decipher how I feel about it. On one hand, I am pleasantly surprised by how talented Theodore is with every part of his body, and unbelievably impressed by how many times he made my body literally shake with ecstasy. On the other hand, I don't like how much I've been thinking about him since. It's like the orgasms he gave me rerouted my brain to not being able to get him out of my mind, and it makes me super uncomfortable.

I'm all about the 'Hit it and quit it' life, and usually by now last night would be so far in my rearview mirror that I can barely even see it. It's not like I love him or anything, I don't even know the guy, and I secretly have always wondered if I'm too broken to love anyone in that way. Maybe my body is just so thrilled over his skill that I just need to tap that a few more times before moving on. Yeah, that seems right, and I can get behind that idea. It's not a permanent thing, just a little fun, or more like a lot.

My body shudders involuntarily, and my pussy clenches at the memory. I can't believe I'm horny already, at least I'm meeting up with Beau tonight, but he's going to have to bring his A-game to top last night. Poor guy doesn't have a chance.

With a big stretch, I throw my legs over the bed and get up to put on the activewear I prepared last night. There's no better way to start off the morning than working my body into the ground with a hard workout. I love the burn and the challenge, it sets my mood for the day and pumps me up. Hopefully, the boys are still in bed and will give me the gym to myself today.

Navigating through the still pitch-black house is as easy as breathing because my parents hate change and never move anything, so I make it outside and into the gym building in no time without making a sound. I grab a towel and drink bottle from the front of the room and get straight into my stretches and warm up before moving to the weights to fuck myself up. Pushing my body to its absolute limit over and over again until I drop like a bag of potatoes onto the mat, breathing heavily with my eyes closed and reveling in the burn.

"Who pissed in your cereal?" I hear Juan ask and open my eyes to find my brother standing above me with his hands on his hips, looking at me with what could be mistaken for worried eyes. "Are you alright?"

I blow out a big breath and sit up, taking a big gulp of my water before answering in a monotone voice. "Sí. I like to work hard and play even harder, what can I say?"

He squats in front of me, his eyebrows knitting together. "Do you want to talk about it, or do you want to destroy yourself even more with a sparring session?" I love this pendejo.

"Let's do it," I announce, jumping to my feet with renewed vigor. "It's been a while since I flattened you; it'll be a good, humbling experience."

With a hearty laugh, Juan follows me to the ring we had put in years ago. "For you, maybe, chiquita."

We bounce around each other in a silent agreement to bare-knuckle it, the way I prefer it. Our dance comes across well practiced as we expertly dodge and jab, our footwork both fast and distracting. Juan has been my main sparring partner since we were kids, after all, second to Alonzo. Only a couple of jabs from each of us even get through, and our concentration gets broken up by Antonio's stupid voice.

"Why are you going easy on her? She's been asking for a fight since she got here."

Juan winks at me before turning to Antonio, both of us knowing he wasn't going easy at all. "Yeah, you're right. Do you want to take over hermano? I'm just not feeling it today because I had too many beers last night."

A smug smile grows on Antonio's face, and I make sure

that I don't let my confidence show, giving away the game. The two of them swap over and the estupido puto does a big show about the size of his muscles, and I wait patiently, knowing that he's trying to distract me, but I know he's always been a dirty fighter.

Right on cue, he tries to throw in a sudden unannounced punch that I'm ready for and easily dodge, much to his chagrin. I dance around him, letting him attempt a few more low blows, waiting for Juan to call it and the second he says, "He's had enough," I go on full attack, kicking and punching him in all the right spots so fast that he can't do anything other than groan and try his best to block. He failed.

After taking several shots of his head while straddling him on the ground, Juan gives one loud clap and I stop instantly, standing up and grinning with pride at the writhing ball of sweat and blood on the ground, my knuckles split and pulsing from the blows I delivered, and I couldn't be happier.

"Did you have to mess him up so bad?" Papi says from behind me, surprising me and making me jump. I spin, thinking I'm in deep trouble but relax at his shaking head and small smile. "I have to put him to work today, but perhaps it's for the best, and he will back off from thinking you're an easy target just because you're a girl."

He goes over and yanks Antonio to his feet, smacking him harder than necessary on the back of his shoulder. "Learn your lesson, boy, and stop underestimating your opponents."

"Lo siento, Papi. He asked for it, in my defense," I tell him but know he isn't mad at me. "I'm gonna go wash up for work, I'm a sweaty mess."

Juan takes my hands into his when I try to pass him.

"Make sure you treat your knuckles properly. How's your ribs from when I kicked them?"

I assure him that I'm fine and remind him to treat his own face from where I split his eyebrow. Sharing a laugh, we head back to the house together, leaving Papi to deal with Antonio and the mood swing that's no doubt about to hit.

With my mind now firmly back on track for the day and last night's sexcapades behind me, I go to work with a new skip in my step, feeling productive and ready to get dirty all over again.

* * *

GETTING CHANGED AFTER MY SHIFT TODAY, I'M MUCH better prepared because I already knew I was going to go out for drinks tonight. I put extra effort into my makeup and hair, going with dark red lips and a simple black wing for my eyes. I put on a little black dress and some simple stiletto heels to finish off my look as I wait for Beau to pick up his car and take me out for the night.

I managed to get all my work done quickly and Papi was fine with me finishing work earlier than normal, so I had time to get ready for my date. No doubt, my parents are hoping I'll find someone to settle down with to give me a reason to stay in town. Too bad their expectations don't align with mine.

"Chiquita, that gringo is back and asking for you?" Juan grumbles at me, coming into the locker room at the back and leaning on the doorjamb with a disapproving frown. "What the fuck are you wearing? You don't think that's too short?"

I shake my head at his predictable big brother routine; there's never been a time when my brothers have ever cut me any slack when it comes to going on dates. No one's good enough for their little sister, after all.

"It's exactly short enough, not that it's any of your business." I flip him the bird and tell him to fuck off, at the same time my phone dings, telling me there's a message waiting for me. I pick it up to see that it's from Theodore.

Theodore: Hey, I'm finishing up work and wanted to see if you'd like to meet up.

Foxy: Sorry boo, I'm already booked for tonight. Talk later.

I keep my reply simple because he needs to know right off the bat that I'm not girlfriend material, and I'm not going to be at his beck and call. It might seem mean, but I refuse to fuck people around or give a false impression that I'm going to give more than I will. Luckily his reply isn't needy, and it makes me like him even more, maybe I will keep him around a bit longer.

Theodore: No problem, have a good night. See you when I see you.

With one last quick look in the mirror, I dubbed myself hot as hell and strut out the door with a confidence I've never had trouble finding when it comes to men. I hope you're ready Beau because I'm in a good mood tonight and ready to hit the town.

Beau comes into view, leaning on his beautiful car, dressed in dark gray jeans and a collared shirt that hugs his body in an almost sinful way. His man bun lets loose a few hairs around his face, making him look way more sexy than it should.

He stands up tall and smiles widely at me, letting his gaze slowly travel up my body, pausing at all my best assets, and it just fuels me. I love a man that doesn't shy away from what he wants, one that knows how to devour me with his eyes before even laying a finger on me. Fingers crossed he'll devour me for real before the night is through.

"Hey there, beautiful," he greets me, putting his hand on my hip and leaning forward to kiss my cheek softly, his facial hair making it tingle. "I honestly don't know what's sexier, you in this dress, or you all dirtied up in overalls."

I laugh loudly, enjoying his honesty. Men these days are so busy keeping themselves in check, so they don't offend people, and it really wrecks the game for me, so he's a real breath of fresh air. I think we're going to get along just fine.

"Wait till you see me with nothing on, it'll definitely help you decide," I purr, smoothing my hands up his chest and leaning into his body. "So where are you taking me?"

He moves to the side and opens up the passenger side door of his car, flourishing his hand for me to enter. "There's a nice cocktail bar nearby that has a fantastic bartender if you're interested? There's also a delicious Korean restaurant right next door, but if you don't like Korean food, I can take you somewhere else." He puts his hand over the top of the door frame as I slide inside to protect my head, and I smile at the small but thoughtful gesture.

"It just so happens that I love Korean food." I smile up at him, pulling my feet inside seductively. "Shall we?"

In moments, he's sitting beside me and as we drive away from the Hernandez Garage, I notice both of my brothers scowling at Beau's car. I quickly put the window down to give them a one-finger salute, and both Beau and I laugh as we disappear down the road.

CHAPTER 10

FOXY

After absolutely pigging out on a hotpot, Beau and I lean back in our seats and joke around with each other as easily as if we've always known each other. His personality is easy going and carefree, and a part of me kind of hopes we can actually be friends later on. Hanging out with him is such a stress reliever and his reactions to everything around him are so genuine. At no point has he put on any unnecessary airs to impress me, which makes me feel like I can just be myself as well.

"Should we have another bottle of soju and stay here drinking, or do you want to go next door for fancy stuff?" Beau asks me with a smile, the four bottles we've already been through warm my insides nicely, and I tell him I'd rather stay here.

We order another two bottles, and somehow we end up talking about life details, which is something I don't normally do with a guy, preferring to keep things distant and physically focused. Before long, though, I'm telling him about what it's like to have four older brothers and how different they all are. I don't however mention what it is my family actually does, and as far as he's concerned, we are a family of successful mechanics.

"What about you? Do you have a bunch of annoying sisters getting all up in your business?" I ask, shooting another glass and pouring us both more.

Beau's smile slightly dims, but he tries to hide it, and I hope I haven't hit a sore subject, after all, people's families are either their pride or their shame.

"I'm an only child, but my flatmate is my brother from another mother," he tells me, looking into his glass. "My mom died when I was young and my dad was an asshole, but he and his parents really took me under their wing. He and his parents really changed my life when I was going through a tough time, and I'm grateful for it."

The atmosphere between us dims significantly, and I quickly decide to try to pick the mood back up again. "Funny you should say that, I have a sister from another mister, and my family is hers now. She's actually got a family of her own these days and lives over in Sinhaven. While I'm not into the whole relationship thing," I add to make it clear that I'm not leading him on in any way. "That girl has got her shit made."

I watch his face carefully as he registers my words, and only after a pause of thought he asks, "How's that? Did she marry rich or something?"

Ah, he might think I'm a gold digger. If only he knew I had an endless supply at my fingertips if I wasn't too proud to accept any. I laugh and tell him, "Ah, no. She just has a lot of dick at her disposal. The girl is hooked up with three brothers in one of those reverse harem type of deals that you read about in smutty novels."

His own laugh barks out then, "Can't say I've heard of that one before. Don't they get jealous of sharing her?"

That's a good question, one that I have had myself many times. "From what they've told me before, they all love her more than jealousy. Like her happiness trumps their selfishness and because of that they all share really well. They don't even fight, it's kind of weird, but it works for them, so who am I to judge when she gets treated like the queen that she is. She went through some really tough times and an evil ex-husband before she found them, so she deserves the life she has now."

Beau pours us both another drink, finishing off the new bottles, and we down them together. I love soju now, I'd never had it before today, but it's fast becoming a favorite.

"How about we get out of here?" Beau asks with a side smile. "I'd really like to see that other outfit you mentioned earlier, you know, for comparison purposes." He looks at his watch. "Tee should be in bed by now if you want to come over to my place, or if you'd feel more comfortable, I can rent out a room at a nice hotel and pamper you?"

I stand up, so ready to move the night onto the evening activities. "Your place is fine. I get up super early and will likely be up and out before either of you wake up anyway. Don't take it personally, but let me be clear that I'm a 'no strings' girl, and will want to keep it that way."

Beau joins me, pulling my hand as we head for the exit, paying as we go. He turns to me and says before hailing the nearby cab, "We'll see about that. I plan on challenging those words, just so you're clear where I stand. I'm happy to keep this a casual thing for now, but I'm determined to change your mind about those strings."

The taxi pulls in and Beau opens the door for me. We both slide in, and after he gives the driver an address, I tell him, "You're going to be disappointed and heart broken if you go in with that mindset with me. How exactly are you planning on changing my mind?" I'm genuinely curious if he has some kind of game plan.

Leaning in really close and putting one arm around me as he begins to stroke my upper thigh gently with his thumb, he whispers in my ear, "With my cunning linguistics." His voice and words send a shiver down my spine, and I shudder slightly.

"By all means, try changing my mind," I whisper back, with my lips moving gently across his and then nipping them softly.

He groans deep and pulls me in tighter, his mouth caressing mine in obvious hunger. I let him take control of the kiss and enjoy the way his lips and tongue move against me because this man can kiss. It makes me even more excited to experience those cunning linguistics he was talking about.

* * *

BEAU

We pull up to my apartment building, and I only know this because of the taxi driver clearing his throat uncomfortably at Foxy and my PDA. We pull apart, and I pay the man with an apology that I don't mean in the slightest.

This woman is like fire, she burns and consumes me with the barest of touches, and like a total sadist I crave more and more. Foxy was clear in warning me, more than once, that she doesn't do commitment, but God damn I want to keep her forever.

I barely know this woman, but I very much want to; I haven't felt this happy and alive in a long time. Just being around her is like a balm to the wounds that eat at my soul from the moment I open my eyes, to the moment sleep claims me. When I'm with her, my past is nowhere to be seen and my demons are silent. I don't even know what it is about her, but I don't even feel the need to lie to her or hold back. But with her personality, that might just be the thing that pushes her away, and I need to be super careful that I don't overwhelm her too early, or me. While my soul calls to her, I've never really been with anyone before with any kind of long-term endgame. I've had the odd girlfriend here and there, but no one I had any intention of keeping around for longer than temporary amusement, but somehow, inexplicably, Foxy is different.

We make it into my apartment between make-out sessions and make way too much noise as we bang into things. I make a shushing noise, but then follow it with laughter as I pick her up and throw her over my shoulder, carrying her laughing to my room and throwing her down on the bed with a big bounce.

I glance down at her wide smile as she flicks her feet, sending her stilettos flying randomly around the room, her short dress riding high up on her thick, strong thighs. I shake my head at just how perfect this woman is.

"Are you going to close the door or are you trying to wake up your friend?" she purrs, slowly opening her bent knees and giving me a clear view of her lacy black panties, and I thank God silently that I left my light on before I left the house.

Without taking my eyes off her sexy body, I back up to the door, closing it behind me and flicking the lock just in case. Not that Tee would ever just barge into my space, but I'm not leaving anything to chance tonight now that I have this girl alone in my grasp.

Foxy leans back on her elbows and nibbles on her

bottom lip seductively, and a moan of need escapes me. My feet carry me to her as if I'm in a dream because before I know it I'm on my knees at the end of the bed, knowing I'd happily worship her all night long.

I grab her ankles and pull, sliding her down the bed so that her dress rides up to her waist and her sheer lace-covered pussy is just inches away from my face. With slow deliberate movements, I trail my fingers from her ankles, up to her thighs, enjoying the warmth of her brown flesh as I go and loving the way it makes her shudder under my touch.

My fingers dance along the seam of her underwear, not close enough to where I know she really wants me to touch by the way she squirms, but I enjoy teasing her. I lean forward and blow a warm breath right up the center of her core, and she trembles beneath me.

"Please, Beau," she begs softly, looking down at me, her chest rising and falling heavily. "I want to feel your mouth on me."

I love a woman who can tell me what she wants, and it breaks some of my resolve to keep her on the edge. Instead, I keep my eye contact with hers and lean in lapping at her through the fabric, making it wetter than it already is with my tongue.

Foxy whooshes out a breath and her head falls back, but I pull back straight away and demand, "Look at me. Watch the way I want you."

Her head snaps back up, and she bites her lip hard, her eyes meeting mine again, thick with lust. I give her a satisfied smile before lowering my head to her pussy again, repeating the move again with my tongue, my eyes never leaving hers.

I nibble and lick along the fabric, making sure to bite her clit lightly. Her panties soak quickly with our combined wetness and I move up one of my fingers to tease along her entrance, tentatively pushing in and out slightly, letting the fabric restrict my movement and I love as Foxy moans and wiggles her hips below me. Her eyes burn hot with the need for me closer, for my skin against her and in her.

"Do you want more?" I ask her gravely. "Tell me what you want, and I'll give it to you. Anything you want is yours, all you have to do is ask."

Foxy shudders harder at my words, and I'm glad to see her react positively to my dirty talk. She pants out, "I want you to take them off and taste me properly. I want your fingers inside me and your tongue on my clit."

I lick my lips and say, "Good girl." My fingers pull the moist fabric to the side, and it takes all of my will power not to stare at what I know will be a glistening pussy just for me. But I don't want to lose eye contact yet because I'm enjoying both the intimacy and the power of it.

My finger slides along her opening, teasing it first and then slowly entering her as her eyes roll back in her head, and she moans, "Yes, like that."

Enjoying the game, I stop moving my finger, taking a quick second to look down at her tight hole while her head falls back. I suppress a curse because even her cunt is perfect.

Making my eyes go back up to her, I keep my digit still as I remind her deeply. "Look at me, or I stop."

I must contain a laugh at the frustrated gaze that meets mine again. I instantly lean in and suck on her little bud at the same time as I push my finger deep inside her, watching the anger immediately get replaced with lust.

All my senses focus on what her body and eyes respond to best, and I focus on doing those movements in a rotation that has her breath hitching and hips rolling against my face until she comes undone, desperately trying not to look away from me, and my dick is so hard for her at this point that it actually hurts.

Foxy moans my name almost silently as her mouth opens on a soundless scream, and I make a point not to stop until her hands grip at the side of my face, desperate to release me.

I let her pull me up to her as she sits her body tall, her soft mouth finding mine. She kisses me deeply, undoubtedly tasting herself on my lips, and fuck if that doesn't get my dick even harder.

Her hands grip the back of my hair, undoing my bun and letting my hair drop down the sides of my face in a messy tumble. She grips at my hair, and we devour each other like hungry animals until I pull back and look deep into her eyes again. "I'm not done with you yet."

Foxy lets me pull her dress above her head, and I'm pleased to find her braless underneath. Standing up, I undress myself in front of her, watching her every reaction because I want to learn everything she loves and dislikes. My new goal in life is to make this woman happy, and it's going to be a great ride figuring it all out along the way.

Her small hand reaches out to grab my cock, but I step back, tisking at her. "It's still my turn, sexy lady. You can have your way with me later. Right now, it's all about you."

She smiles widely at me and asks, "And what if I want you inside me, and I want to be on top? What then?"

I walk around the bed to the head of it and hop on, laying my body down the center and pat my hips. "Then I say, your throne awaits my queen."

Foxy's smile beams, and she hops on top of me eagerly, straddling my hips and taking my length into her grasp. My cock twitches in her palm, and my hips buck involuntarily, slightly lifting her up.

She gazes into my eyes the way I fucking love as she lifts her body up and back down again, spearing my hardness into her. Foxy's pussy is so wet that even though she feels so freaking tight, she manages to get me seated inside her as she sits down on me. Our sounds mirror each other at how good it feels.

I slide my hands up her legs, hips and waist, roaming them along her perfect breasts as she rides me slowly. The role of her body tightens my balls quicker than I'd like and reminds me how long it's been since I was inside a woman.

Foxy's hands cover my own as I pluck her nipples and mold my palms around her, loving the feeling of them in my hands. I make a point to keep my gaze locked on her, and something about the act makes everything we're doing feel more intimate, and it feels a lot more like we're making love than fucking. It surprises me that I want it like this more than any other way because it feels perfect just the way it is, and for once Foxy is letting me behind her giant walls.

My fingers and hers entwine, and she pushes them against each side of my head, leaning over me and grinding. She squeezes her hands tight around mine, in full control of both of us as she arches and twists her hips against me. She pants as my cock undoubtedly hits her g-spot in this position, and her clit grinds against me at the same time.

"Use me baby, I'm all yours," I moan out, loving it as much as she clearly is, and she does, increasing her movements and pushing herself further toward release.

I clench my teeth and core as I try desperately not to cum until she does. Her needs need to come first in this, and I can feel by the way her movements become more fierce and irregular that she's so close.

Her eyes get more hooded, and I can tell that Foxy is trying to keep them on me as the end nears. My balls tighten so hard and I growl out, "Cum for me. Cum on my dick, baby."

With a trembling whimper, her core grabs my cock like a vice as she lets go, riding herself through a ferocious orgasm, her body spasming around me, and I can't hold on anymore. My cock explodes inside her, and I growl her name, pull my hands free of hers, and grip the back of her head to crush my lips with hers. We kiss hard and deep, our bodies twitching together with our combined release still shattering the both of us.

Foxy's body becomes compliant in my arms, her weight settling on me, and we stop kissing to hold on tightly to each other. A wet glide of sweat between us, but neither of us care as we lie there, breathing heavily.

"You are something else, Miss Hernandez, you know that?" I ask with a chuckle. "If you're not careful, you might kill me with that pussy of yours."

She laughs, her head bobbing slightly on my chest, where she's now resting. "You haven't experienced my mouth yet. I still could."

I smile and let my fingers tangle into her beautiful dark curls, telling her that no matter where my dick is, if I'm inside her, it wouldn't be a bad way to go at all.

Her hips lift slightly, releasing my cock from her tight confines, and I pout. "Hey, that was mine, give it back." I wiggle my hips in protest because I was enjoying being in there and was half hoping I could fall asleep that way.

Foxy raises her head to look at me, and my eyes narrow at her cheeky smile. "It's my turn," she purrs softly, and I frown at what she can mean by that, but it doesn't take long to find out as she lowers her body down mine, her focus going completely to my no longer saluting member.

"Um, it might need a moment," I tell her shyly. I hate the idea of not being able to perform on will, but that's the life of a penis for you, and staring at it won't magically make it work on cue.

With a knowing wink, Foxy leans down while grabbing it and takes the whole, now kind of sad, cock in her mouth. The whole thing disappears, and she sucks on it, pussy juices and all. My body convulses at the sudden intense feeling, and I'm conflicted over moaning or pulling her off by the overwhelming sensitivity of it.

"Fuck," I swear between clenched teeth as she continues to work at it, her tongue doing some seriously good things, and in seconds it's risen from the dead and raring to go again. Apparently, this woman is magic because I've never seen it do that before.

My fingers slip through her hair, and I hold on hard, trying not to push or pull her in any way. She starts bobbing up and down, sucking me down and into her throat every time with ease, and I really start to wonder if I will actually die. The intense sensation of my already tender cock and her throat constantly swallowing me has my whole body shaking and my hips jerking uncontrollably. The noises coming from me are unrecognizable, and have me unloading down her throat in record time.

"Holy mother of God," I moan, collapsing my head back on the pillow as I try to catch my breath.

Foxy climbs up my body with a smug as fuck grin, and I can't help the laugh that escapes me. "You realize that I'm never going to let you go after that move."

She scoffs and says, "We'll see." As she rolls off the bed and heads toward my bathroom while fixing her hair up into a makeshift bun, her hips swaying sexily the entire time. My eyes are transfixed to the most beautiful sight I have ever seen, and I know without a doubt in my mind that what I said was true.

I follow her to the bathroom to find her already in the shower and lean against the door jamb as I watch her soap herself up and wash it off. My hunger for her only grows, and I step forward opening the shower door and hop inside with her, dropping to my knees and letting the water spray on me haphazardly.

"What are you doing?" Foxy laughs at me, trying to pull me up.

I resist and instead pull her closer, pulling one of her legs over my shoulder, making her grab the wall to steady herself and growl, "My turn again," before closing my mouth on her again and loving the way she moans my name.

Foxy better have good stamina because tonight's feast has only just begun.

CHAPTER 11

FOXY

With expert stealthy movements I extricate myself from Beau's apartment, not wanting to deal with the morning after chat or the housemate. I hop into the elevator with an old white lady giving me the Karen stare and looking my outfit up and down as if I'm wearing nothing but a garter and whip.

Unable to help myself, I give her a wink and say to her as we descend to the first floor, "I haven't clocked out yet if you're interested?"

The shade of red that she turns is a hilarious mixture of fury and embarrassment as her face twists in disgust. "You should be ashamed of yourself," she grumbles and practically runs out of the small space we were sharing, you know in case slut is contagious.

I laugh heartily at her departure, while I check my phone to find the taxi I ordered earlier is already out front. With a skip in my step from having such a great couple of nights, I greet the doorman and jump into the waiting vehicle, heading home for my much-needed workout. It took all of my self-control not to wake Beau up and ride him this morning. I'm feeling a little frustrated, and there's no better way to work that off than in the gym.

AFTER A WORKOUT THAT WAS NOWHERE NEAR AS LONG as I would have liked, I head to the garage and try to focus on the work at hand. Instead of the two new men in my life that both know how to fucking rock my world.

I get distracted in the middle of servicing a Honda Accord when my phone buzzes in my pocket. Pulling it out carefully, so as not to get it dirty, I smile to see a message from Theodore.

Knowing I can't properly look at it, I slide it back into my pocket and finish off the Accord as quickly as I can, but I'm still careful to do it right. I can't stand mechanics that half-ass their work and don't treat cars with the love and attention that they deserve. It's actually one of the reasons I don't charge much for services, because way too many people let their services go too long in between due to the price.

I hand the keys over to Finlay, one of our apprentices. I tell him to give it a quick wipe down and clean up before going into the locker room for my break, cleaning my hands, and checking my phone finally.

THEODORE: MORNING beautiful, thought you'd like to know that our girl is a lot more lively today and doing really well. Also, it appears that she has no current owners that we can find if you're still interested in adopting her?

Excitedly, I message him straight back, my mind already whizzing with possible names for her and how I'm going to tell Mami and Papi that I'm bringing home a dog when she's better.

Foxy: That's great news. Can I come by and see her? I'm not far away, and I'm just starting my lunch break.

Theodore: Absolutely. I'm about to go on mine too. After you check on her, I'll buy you some lunch.

I won't say no to a free meal, and if I'm being honest with myself, I'm kind of excited about seeing the man as well as the dog. With fast fingers, I send a quick reply saying I'll be there soon and look down at my attire. There isn't really time to shower, but I do have some clean overalls in my locker that should be alright for now.

Quickly changing and fixing my hair and face up enough to pass as decent, I head out to Theodore's workplace with my mind still on the perfect name for my new girl. I can't wait to see her.

Theodore is standing out the front with a big smile showing of his 'lick me' dimples and waving when I pull my car in. I let him open my door for me when he approaches, and he grabs my hand and pulls me into a tight hug that surprises me.

"Well, that's a nice hello," I tell him into his chest, then look up, wrapping my arms around his waist, enjoying the warmth of his body and musky scent of his cologne. "Did you miss me or something?"

A low sound of admittance comes from him before he kisses my forehead softly, "I did."

We look into each other's eyes, and for a second, I lose myself before my inner bitch reminds me that this is a little too intimate, and I step back, pushing him away at the same time. Getting too close to him will give Theodore the wrong impression, and I'm not ready to end this little tryst we have going on just yet.

I turn away and start heading for the entrance, asking how the pup is doing. I don't miss the quick show of disappointment that flitted across his face when I moved away, but I pretend like I didn't. He masks it just as quickly as it came, though, and I'm grateful that we get to skip any awkward questions or silence between us.

Theodore walks beside me, and I get instant satisfaction as I watch Milla's face drop at the sight of me, and I have to hold in a laugh. Call me a bitch, I don't care; that shit is funny because it's obvious when Theodore looks at her that he has no interest in her other than as a subordinate.

"Oh, you're back," she says to me with a monotone voice, in lieu of a proper greeting. "How nice."

Theodore clears his voice and places his hand on the lower part of my back, guiding me to the door to the back. "We'll be with her dog, if you need us, Milla. You can head off to lunch now and turn the sign over, I'll be taking my lunch with Ana-Lucia today."

Without waiting for any reply from her, we head to the back and my eyes fall instantly on my pretty girl, looking up at us with her tail wagging. Despite the pain she must be in, and I know straight away that she remembers me.

I stride down to her with a big smile. "Hola, mi perrita. How are you feeling, sweet girl?" Her big pink tongue lolls out of her mouth, and I fall in love with her all over again. How could anyone hurt such a tender thing? "I hear you're doing much better. How about when it's time you come home with me, and I take care of you? You'll be spoiled rotten, I swear."

In what I take as a yes, she licks my fingers as I put my hand inside her crate to pat her gently on the head, careful not to touch her anywhere else. So much of her looks sore, with large chunks of hair shaved off because of the operations she must have needed.

"Have you thought of a name for her yet?" Theodore asks, standing at my side and happily watching our reunion.

I nod, knowing exactly what to call her now that I see her again. "Freja. Like the goddess that she is." He agrees with me that it's the perfect name, and I spend a good ten minutes just petting and loving her, happy to see that she's doing so well, so soon. She's been through an incredible ordeal, but her spirit isn't broken in the slightest.

Reluctantly, I leave her to rest and let Theodore take me to lunch at a nice little café less than a block away. We order our food and coffees and sit down at a table in the back that has a modicum of privacy about it.

"What did the police say about what happened to Freja?" I ask Theodore while we wait, knowing that he'd contacted them after the incident.

He rubs at his stubbled cheeks with a weary look and says in a defeated tone, "They believe it's another illegal dog fight. Over the last few months, more and more dogs have been found dead and mutilated because some evil dickheads have decided that watching dogs attack each other to death is fun and profitable. It makes me sick to my stomach and so damn mad, but I don't know what to do about it. I'm so helpless to save them. In fact, Freja is the first victim I've managed to save."

My heart drops an instant before rage fills me. "Where is it happening, and who's doing it?" I ask, my voice louder and angrier than I meant to come out, but damned if I'm not going to find the pathetic pendejo who is doing this.

Theodore's face shows the shock he must be feeling at my sudden outburst, and he slowly replies, "They don't know. That's the biggest problem, there doesn't seem to be any leads other than the K9 corpses that are being found around Charmington Center, Ethic Park, and Morality Crossing. It seems to be somewhere near there, but no one can pinpoint exactly where and because those neighborhoods are such crime hubs, nobody is really talking to the cops."

They may not talk to the police, but they sure as fuck will talk to a Hernandez if they know what's good for them. I think this to myself because I don't have any intention of getting Theodore involved in what I have planned for these pendejos.

I make a plan in my head to take a drive around those neighborhoods tonight to see if I can find anything unusual. I'll ask around to some of our more unsavory contacts that are nearby to see if they've seen or heard anything. I can turn a blind eye to a lot, but never when it comes to hurting animals, children or anyone who can't protect themselves.

"Are you alright, Ana-Lucia? I know it's a terrible thing to find out going on so close to home. I know it keeps me up at night, so please know if you need to talk about it, I'm here." Theodore's concern for me is touching, and I try to tamper down some of the bubbling rage at what's going on and focus on him because tonight the hunt is on. They better know how to hide because once I have them, their life is null and void.

My fingers clasp between his across the table, and I thank him for his concern, promising that I'll be alright. I was going to see if he wanted to hook up tonight, but now I have different ideas about how I'll be spending the evening.

We eat our lunch together after that, and I silently marvel at how easy it is to just be in Theodore's company. I don't feel the overwhelming desire to run away, and he doesn't bore me when he speaks. Being with him feels motive free and comfortable, like I don't have to be anything other than myself. Which is funny considering the lengths I've been going to so that he doesn't know who I actually am, and the hypocrisy of that isn't lost on me.

CHAPTER 12

FOXY

"Mija, what's cooking in that head of yours?" Papi asks me as I walk to my car in the dead of night, and I jump at his words, not expecting to find him out here waiting for me.

"Ai, Papi. Don't do that. You scared the shit out of me," I cry out with my hand on my chest, feeling my heart trying to escape from my ribs with its pounding rhythm.

He steps up closer to me, so I can see him more clearly with his arms crossed over his chest. "You think I don't know my own daughter? You've been stewing on something since you got home and kept checking your watch. What's going on, and do you need my help because I'm here for you mi nina, you know that."

I should have known better than to think I could look into something like this here without Papi knowing that I was up to something.

With a sigh, I tell him. "Someone is doing dog fights not far away, and I want to get to the bottom of it. You know that dog I saved the other day, well she was hurt from it, and I can't just sit by and do nothing." Before he can cut me off with a lecture on minding my own business, I add. "It's important to me, and I want you to support me in this. I knew that you wouldn't like it, but just think of it as me looking after the family's territory and let me just do my thing. Por favor Papi."

He stands there for a minute silently, but then goes to my car, opening the driver's side door. "Be safe, my little fox, and if you need help, ask for it, and we'll be there."

"Gracias Papi." I give him a big hug and kiss on the cheek. "I won't do anything stupid, I promise. I just want to check around to see if anyone has heard anything, to see if I can find out where it's all going down, and I'll let Ardyn know, so he can forward it to the Beastville police and get it shut down."

"Sí, I know. I still can't get over Ardyn keeping everything we do on the down low, considering how much of a clean cop he is," he tells me as I sit in the driver's seat and turn the ignition on.

I spurt out a laugh. "After everything that happened with Allure and how the boys got her out of there in one piece, there's no way he'd put any of us in a bad situation. God knows what would have happened to her if they didn't get there on time."

Even the memory of how close we were to losing Allure and the awful things her ex-husband put her through makes me want to vomit. From the moment I met that piece of shit, I knew something was fundamentally wrong with him.

We say our goodbyes, and I head off toward Charmington Center first, where I originally found Freja, slowly driving up and down the surrounding streets while carefully looking down every alleyway and dark place. Nothing out of the normal crackheadville behavior can be seen, that is, until I see a familiar silver Jaguar XF parked in front of one of the many dive bars they have around here.

What on earth is Theodore doing here? I wonder to myself, pulling my car in beside his. He must be crazy to park this kind of car here. At least my car just looks like a run-of-the-mill shit box, but it sticks out like a sore thumb in this neighborhood.

I hop out of the car, quickly adjusting my black turtleneck, long sleeve crop top, and skinny black jeans, lock my car, and head inside. I walk hard, worrying about what shit he's gotten himself into, as my heavy black fuck off boots thud loudly with each step. Which are the complete opposite to fuck me boots, with their flat but thick heel, steel toe and military style laces. Let's not lie, I dressed for action tonight, and not the kind of action I've been getting lately.

As soon as I step inside, Theodore pops into view, with his nice dark blue jeans, shiny shoes, and polo shirt. Poor guy screams 'Beat me up and steal my money,' and I have to try hard not to roll my eyes at him.

A very large hand grabs my arm as I start striding through the room toward him as he talks to the bartender, and it stops me in my tracks. I look up at the big fucker, his face leering at me like a creep, and I don't have time for his brand of stupid tonight.

"Let go. I'll only tell you once," I tell the biker-looking Neanderthal, trying to be patient but falling very short.

Instead of heeding my warning, which they never do, he pulls me in closer and says, "How about you suck my cock instead? I promise you'll get a creamy surprise at the end." Disgusting pig.

His friends howl with laughter that gets cut off pretty quickly when I grab the dickhead's wrist and quickly snap it with a move I was taught as a kid. The big fuckwit squeals like the little piggy he is and tries to take a swing at me with the other hand, but I quickly duck it and promptly kick his kneecap in.

With an ungracious thud, he falls to the ground groaning in agony, and I yawn looking at his friends who get up. I just smile, get into a stance and say, "Alright ladies, who's next?"

To my disappointment, the owner of said establishment, which I've met several times before with my Papi comes over and stands in front of me with his arms wide and in a gruff voice growls, "Not a fucking chance. If you knew who she was, you'd be pissing yourselves by now. Thank your lucky stars you're alive and get Grant out of here."

They take a few seconds and look between them but with a "Get!" from the owner, they grab their friend and take off, some of them looking at me in confusion before heading out the door.

"I'm sorry about that, Foxy," he says now turning to me. "What can I say? They breed 'em stupid around here. Can I help you with something, or are ya just here for a drink?"

I turn and take a quick look behind me, seeing that I've drawn a bit of a crowd, and I see the moment Theodore recognizes me. He starts walking over to us, and I quickly whisper to the owner, whose name I cannot remember for the life of me. "I'm kind of undercover, don't tell this guy who I am." He looks behind me, seeing who I'm talking about, and nods just as Theodore reaches us.

"Ana-Lucia, what are you doing here?" Theodore looks behind me, and I catch the bar owner scoffing at my 'fake name,' little does he know it's actually my real one. "Are you alright?" Theodore continues looking me up and down and then at the door where the guys just left from.

I smile and place my hand on his chest softly. "I'm fine.

The stupid one grabbed me, so I kicked his ass," I tell him matter-of-factly, and his eyes go wide at my simple explanation.

"I saw that, I'm a bit shook, actually. Where did you learn to do that? You don't even seem rattled." Theodore, however, does look rattled.

Reaching down, I take his hand and start leading him back to the bar. "How about we get a drink, and we'll talk because I'd like to know why you're here as well." I turn to the bar owner. "Can we get a couple of light beers please, we have to drive after this." With laughing eyes, he nods and talks to the bartender on our behalf.

We take a seat at the bar, and I turn to him. "You know you stick out like a sore thumb here, right?" Our beers get set in front of us, and I keep going. "What are you doing here anyway?"

"You might think I'm an idiot if I tell you. Promise not to laugh." I nod. "Well, I was hoping I could ask people here if they knew where the dog fights were, so I could tell on them, but no one will talk to me. They just laugh in my face and turn around. How about you? And what's with the ninja skills?"

My promise apparently meant nothing because I laugh my ass off. "You seriously thought people would just tell you? Dressed like that? In a place like this?" I laugh even harder but take a sip and try to get a straight face as he goes bright red. "I'm here for the same reason, I guess, but it seems funnier when you do it. Oh, and my papi taught me and my brothers martial arts growing up for fitness. He's a real fitness freak, and he knew it might come in handy one day. He has his own gym at the house and everything."

I take another sip of my beer and look around the room. The two of us have garnered a few unwanted looks, and I make a point to stare right back. People are usually pretty good at knowing when to pick a fight and when to turn away. It seems like everyone else here tonight is happy to avoid instigating shit with me when they look back down into their drinks.

"That's pretty cool, maybe you can show me a thing or two? I do boxing at the fitness center, but it's just for a workout, not actual fighting," Theodore tells me cutely, and I can't believe how much I don't judge him for that. He's just too nice to pick on. I must have been staring because he suddenly leans in, taking my lips with his for a sweet kiss. "You seem distracted, beautiful."

"You're just so damn cute, and somehow it works for you. You're not exactly the normal type of guy I hang around." I decide to tell him honestly.

He kisses me again. "I don't mind. I just want to be the last guy. I know you have a commitment issue, but I'm willing to work on it."

I feel an unusual pang of guilt as I think about Beau and the night I spent with him yesterday and decide that I need to be extra honest with him. I realize that I don't owe him anything because we're only casual, but it just feels like the right thing to do. "You have some competition on that front then because you're not the only guy that keeps me company every now and then."

Predictably, his smile slowly drops off his face as he registers my words. I try to tell myself that it's for the best if he doesn't want to see me again because he'll only get hurt in the long run anyway. But my gut twists at the idea more than I'd like to admit. Both Theodore and Beau have gotten under my skin somehow, and I barely know them, maybe I should cut them both off before I get actual feelings.

"Okay." Theodore nods with sudden determination. "I

can handle a little competition; it'll be all the sweeter when you decide you can't live without me."

A chuckle pops out of me at his never ending good spirit, and I shake my head at him. "Good luck buddy, you're going to need it because I'm not a prized pig to be won; I'm the farmer feasting and don't forget it."

We talk for a bit, getting lost in his company and almost forgetting why I came here in the first place. I wave the bartender back over, and he asks me if I want a refill, but I tell him I'm after information instead.

"He doesn't know anything," Theodore adds. "I already asked, but I look back at the bartender and raise my eyebrows, waiting for a response.

The bartender looks at his boss across the room with a question in his eyes and nods at him, giving the okay to answer my questions. "What do you need to know?"

I smirk at how easy that was and ask, "Dog fighting. Who's doing it and where?"

He fidgets uncomfortably and rubs the back of his neck, answering me quietly while leaning closer. "I don't know much, but I've heard that the places the fights are at changes each time, with an invite only through text. I have no idea who's running it, though. I've heard two different stories, one is that it's a bunch of rich old white dudes that are doing it for malicious fun and the other," he stops, looking around him and lowering his voice again. "The other is another cartel is moving into town slowly, and it's not just dog fights that they're meddling with, but also people smuggling for the sex trade." He gives me a hard look that tells me he thinks it's the latter and knows what that will mean for my family, and I appreciate that he doesn't say it directly because of Theodore.

"Cartel?" Theodore asks with a scoff. "This isn't a

telenovela. Sure, there's some crime around in the bad parts of town, but that's a bit far-fetched, isn't it?"

Puta, if you only knew how wrong you were. I can't even imagine living in such a crime free lifestyle that you had no idea of the underbelly of the town you reside in.

The bartender laughs at him. "My man, are you living under a rock? I guess you don't know about the mafia or MC's either? How about the assassins in both Sinhaven and Beastville? That's cute." He turns to me, leaning on the bar and pointing his thumb at Theodore. "Where did you find this guy?"

He's not wrong, the amount of organized crime between those two places alone is shocking, and it genuinely surprises me when people don't have a clue it even exists. That right there is privilege, a privilege I wish I knew.

The bar around us starts to get more rowdy and unhinged as the night gets later, and I ask the bartender for a pen and paper, where I write down my phone number and give it to him. "You call me the second you hear about anything, and I mean anything to do with dog fights or possible second cartel, do you hear me?" I demand, and he agrees, knowing instantly that I'm not fucking around.

I grab Theodore's hand and lead him out of the dingy dive and back to his car. "Go home tonight, it's getting late and people are just messy past this point," I tell him, giving him a hug as I slide my hands around his neck, with my body flush against his. "Why don't you give me a call in a couple of days, and maybe we can meet up."

His dimples pop out, and his smile warms me while his hand slowly rubs my lower back. "Sounds like a plan. You sure you don't want to come over tonight?"

Reluctantly, I say no and kiss him goodnight before getting into my own car. I need some time to process everything I learned, and want to call Juan on the way home to see if he's heard anything about another possible cartel trying to lay claim to our territory. Because if that's the case, shit is about to get serious.

I wait until Theodore turns off toward what must be his place before I call my brother. Even though it's quite late now, I know he'll pick up almost straight away because he's the main one on call now that Mario is away.

Right on cue, only two rings in, Juan answers the phone, "Foxy, what's wrong? Do you need me to come and get you? Should I wake Antonio too?"

He's such a good big brother and the concern in his voice makes me smile but instead of letting on I say, "Are you trying to say I can't take care of myself, numbnuts?"

"Fuck off. Did you just call to piss me off, or is there a reason?" Juan replies, his tone more pissed off now.

I decide to get straight to the point and ask, "Have you heard of anything about a different cartel sniffing around town?" His silence speaks volumes and dread hits me and I ask, "Do Papi and Mario know?"

"Papi and I were talking about it yesterday, and we decided not to tell Mario until it's confirmed, but for now our sources are sketchy at best. How did you find out about it? You better be staying out of trouble, chiquita." Juan's voice rarely sounds as somber as he does now, his true concern is evident, and it kind of scares me.

"I've been looking into the dog fights because I wanted to stop it, but apparently there's speculation that it's either old, bored white guys with too much time and money or a new cartel. I also heard something about sex trafficking." I pause for emphasis. "You know how Papi feels about that. Not only is the crossing of territories an issue but if there's sex trafficking Papi is gonna blow a gasket."

Juan groans down the line, "Mierda, I didn't hear about that. It actually makes sense. I don't know if you've seen the news lately, but some kids and young girls have gone missing recently around town. This is worse than I thought. Right! Step back from this and let us look into it, especially if that shit is going on too. What better way to step on our shit than to take you? I'm serious, Foxy, stay away from that shit from now on and don't go off without telling us where you're going. That's an order."

Puta. I fucking hate when they lay down the law. I have to take it seriously, there's only a limited amount of times that the boys are allowed to say that to me, but this seems like a damn good reason. I still don't have to fucking like it, though.

CHAPTER 13
THEODORE

I scoop out another large spoon of ice cream as I watch 'The Fast and the Furious' again with Beau for the millionth time. Seriously, can he not find something else to watch?

A long sigh leaves me as I think about what Ana-Lucia said to me last week at that dive bar in Charmington and Beau pauses the movie, turning to look at me with eyebrows raised.

"What?" I ask, wondering what I missed.

He shakes his head at me. "Do you want me to braid your hair while you cry into the tub of ice cream like the girl you're acting like, or do you want to tell me what the fuck crawled up your ass and died? You've been moping around all week, and it's just getting worse. Did that lady dump you or something?"

I hadn't realized that I'd been that bad, but when I look down at myself, I can see what he sees. I let out a little chuckle, putting the ice cream on the coffee table in front of us. "Sorry, man, I've been sucking myself down a rabbit hole of self-pity. It's Ana-Lucia, I told her that I wanted to keep her pretty much, and she said that I'm not the only guy she's seeing, and it's fucked with my head a bit. I mean, I know it's casual and whatever, and it's not exactly like we were dating, but fuck, I don't want to share her."

"Fuck, dude, that sucks. I think I'd be upset too if Foxy told me that. Are you going to keep pursuing her?" Beau asks me, but I already know the answer.

"Absolutely. I can't describe it, she's sassy but kind, she's strong but sensitive too. There's just something about her that I can't put my finger on, and I truly feel like she's worth fighting for," I answer honestly. "Have you asked Foxy if she's seeing anyone else? I know you've been talking to her almost every night and you guys seem to get along well."

Beau frowns slightly. "Honestly, I've never thought about asking. I'm gonna ask her now." He pulls out his phone and fires off a text.

"You don't think it's rude to just ask in a text straight up like that?" I ask, surprised that he did that.

He just shrugs. "Nah, we talk openly and don't really beat around the bush when we talk; it's refreshing, to be honest. Most girls fuck around with wordplay and games, but Foxy never does that shit. It's one of the many reasons I like her. We should do a double date one night, that way we can get a chance to meet each other's girl without it being tense and shit."

Beau's phone dings, and he opens it up, but his mouth drops open like he's catching flies. "You've got to be fucking kidding me?" He passes his phone to me to read the reply, clearly unimpressed with what it says.

Foxy: Yeah, I've been seeing another guy too, that's not going to be an issue for you, is it?

"WELL, IT LOOKS LIKE WE BOTH NEED TO STEP UP OUR game." I give his phone back, feeling just as sorry for him as myself. "Maybe we should win them over before we set up something like that, they might bring their other 'special friend' at this rate."

Yes, I do sound bitter, but I'm feeling pretty bitter at the moment, and can you blame me? I haven't had serious intentions toward a girl, maybe ever and now that I found someone that I could actually see a future with, she doesn't seem to see me the same way. I don't want to be just another guy, I want to be *the guy*.

"I can't believe this?" Beau complains, staring at the message like he thinks the answer will magically change if he does it long enough. "We have really good chemistry. I mean *really* good. This can't be right. What could this guy give her that I haven't been giving her?"

I chuck a cushion at him and laugh. "Orgasms, dude, lots of orgasms."

"Fuck off, he is. I made that girl squirt more than once while riding my dick, there's no way he's able to top how good I made her feel. Maybe I should remind her soon exactly how good of a catch I am?" he grumbles and puts his phone on the table with an unhappy grunt

Beau picks up my ice cream and starts eating out of it, not caring that I was just using that spoon. He sits back, presses play, and pouts throughout the rest of the movie, but I do notice that he never texted her back. Perhaps he isn't as serious about Foxy as I am about Ana-Lucia.

* * *

I PULL UP TO THE LARGE GATES WITH SERIOUS 'FUCK off' security and call Ana-Lucia. She picks up straight away, and I ask, "Did you give me the right address? I think I'm at some kind of stronghold."

She laughs and tells me that I'm at the right place and that she'll buzz me in. What the fuck kind of money has her family got? I had no idea she was a rich kid like me and Beau were; it's not like she ever gave off that kind of vibe or anything.

The gates leisurely slide open, and I try not to acknowledge the pit of moths trying to escape my stomach as I edge my way slowly down the long drive surrounded by tall trees and bushes. A large bulky home comes into view with several other large concrete buildings behind it, some with their own security fences around them. What exactly does Ana-Lucia's family do? I never thought to ask before now. In fact, I don't even know what she does for a living.

I make a mental note to ask her later as I pull in front of the house, beside a home basketball set up. Three Hispanic men are shooting hoops together there, one an older but well-built one, an athletic one with a hard face, and a massive one. I realize this must be her family when all three stop playing and look over at me with obvious malice. Is it too late to leave?

With a big inhale, I turn the car off and step out, not at all surprised to see the three men headed my way, covered in sweat and not a friendly face to be found.

The oldest gentleman reaches out a hand to me in greeting as the other two stand behind him, the biggest one with the ball under one arm, making his bicep look even bigger. "You must be here for my daughter?" her father asks me, squeezing my hand painfully instead of shaking.

I use all my self-control not to show a grimace and answer, "Yes sir, Ana-Lucia is expecting me. I'm taking her out on a date. I'm Dr. Theodore Bell; we met at one of my animal shelters. It's a pleasure to make your acquaintance, sir." I'm babbling. Shit.

"Ai, mija. You never told me you knew such a handsome doctor." I hear from behind me, and her father's large hand lets go of me instantly, his face softening as he looks at the back. "Leo, you're not giving our daughter's friend a hard time, are you?"

My smile is wide as I spin and greet Ana-Lucia's mother, instantly grateful for her rescue. Her mom looks so much like Ana-Lucia that it takes me back for a minute, and her beautiful smile and kind eyes put me instantly at ease.

"Good morning miss?" I pause realizing I don't know their last name, but she saves me by saying, "Just call me Patricia, no need for formalities. Come inside and have something to eat, do you drink coffee?" Her accent is much more pronounced than her daughter's, but it's easy enough to understand, thankfully.

Ana-Lucia comes almost running outside, giving me an apologetic look before grabbing my arm and trying to pull me toward the car. "Lo siento, Mami, we have to go." I hold in a laugh that dies the instant I see what I assume are her brothers glaring at where her arm is entwined with mine.

I carefully extract myself and take a step back before I find one of Ana-Lucia's terrifying brothers' fists in my face and open the passenger car door, smiling back at her mom. "I'm so sorry Patricia, next time I'd love to catch up properly." I use my best manners because if I've learned anything in my life, it's that impressing a woman's mom is usually key to a happy future life. It certainly doesn't help that neither of her brothers or dad have said anything to me since I introduced myself. I was hoping dropping the doctor thing would help, but no dice.

"I might be late," Ana-Lucia calls out as she hops in the

car, but before I close the car door, she leans out and glares at her brothers. "You better change your face, or I'll definitely be late."

"You better not be," the smaller of the two says, still glaring at me and not giving his sister a glance.

My heart races at the threat that's clearly displayed, and I back around the car, unreasonably terrified to show them my back as if they were actual predators. When I'm safely at my car door, I smile at both of her parents once more and say goodbye, jumping into the car with a new line of sweat trickling down my back and whispering to Ana-Lucia. "They're fucking terrifying, you know that, right?"

She laughs loudly and flips them off. "Nah, they're just protective of their little sister, it's stupid."

The big one steps forward, next to his happily waving mom, and calls out as I turn my car around, "Bye *Ana-Lucia!*" he says it in a strange way, and I look at my date and find her scowling at me fiercely. I get the feeling those two aren't overly close.

CHAPTER 14

FOXY

"I'm sorry about them," I tell Theodore solemnly. I know they mean well, but it's such a pain in the ass bringing any guy home. It's probably one of the main reasons I gave up on any idea of a proper relationship years ago.

Theodore just chuckles and says it's fine, putting his large hand on my bare thigh, my cut-off shorts revealing more of my legs than my family would have been happy with when I left, but who cares. This is my body, and it's the twenty-first century. Long gone are the days when someone had the right to tell a woman what she can do with her body, and I'm damn proud of mine; if I want to show it off, I will.

I ask him where he's taking me for our date because he was determined to surprise me when he asked me out for the day.

His dimples deepen with his smile, his eyes never leaving the road. "I'm stealing you away for the day so that you can't escape me, but I promise you'll like it."

"Not at all a creepy thing to say to a girl," I say with a

laugh, not at all actually worried because there's not one bad bone in this man's body. My smile drops as I think about that, feeling bad for him falling for me because I know he is. I can tell by the way he looks at me and the way he touches me. It's as if I hang the moon for him and if I'm being honest, there's a part of me that wants to, but I can't let her through. Neither Theodore nor Beau deserve the life that someone like me would bring them.

My silence has Theodore quickly looking at my features before facing the road ahead again. "You don't have to look so freaked out. I was just kidding. If it'll make you feel safer, I'm happy to tell you my plans. I just thought it would be romantic to sweep you away and surprise you." His tone is apologetic, and I feel bad for ruining the mood.

"Surprise me. It's been a long time since I've been surprised in a good way, but I have to warn you," I make my voice high and cheeky, "I do bite if provoked."

"Promise?" Theodore answers my playfulness with his own, and we spend what turns out to be a long drive chatting about light-hearted things and the plans I have for Freja when I bring her home in a few days. Even if we didn't have a destination, this would have been enough. I let myself just enjoy his company today, choosing to pretend just for one day that I am his, and he is mine, and our lives are simple.

* * *

HE PULLS HIS CAR IN FRONT OF A LARGE PET SHOP AND turns to me with his dimples on full display. He leans in to give me a quick peck on the cheek. "First stop, Freja supplies. I thought it would be fun to go shopping together for all the things you'll need. I remember you telling me that you hadn't had a chance to get anything yet because you've been so busy with work, and I happen to know a few things about dogs and what they need."

Why is this guy so sweet? "Gracias Theodore. That's really thoughtful, but I have to say, you came a pretty long way for some dog food." I know there's more to the drive, obviously, but I've been enjoying our playful banter and don't want it to end today if I can help it. Today I am just Ana-Lucia, and I have no problems except what Freja needs. I smile wider than I have, maybe ever, at that thought and step out of the car feeling light and happy.

Theodore joins me, and we walk into the shop hand in hand like a normal couple, and he squeezes my digits. "Just so you know, I do have more planned than this." I ignore him and speed up my steps, excited about my perrita.

We get a big shopping cart and start filling it up with every dog need available, going with a red theme for everything. I most certainly go way overboard, but I have a blast doing it and Theodore encourages me all the while. I know I don't have much money, but I don't care because I'm having fun, plus I plan on putting most of it back anyway.

When we get to the counter, I happily turn back around, ready to unload it, but Theodore stops it with a quizzical glance at me, and I explain that I'm obviously not buying all that unnecessary stuff.

To my utmost shock, he pulls it into the counter and starts to unload it all at the check-out, telling the girl behind it that he's paying for everything.

It takes a moment for me to wrap my head around what he's doing before I tell her to stop. With my anger rising, I tell him strongly, "This is way too much. I can't let you buy all this stuff, do you have any idea how much money that will be? I know you have a good job and everything, but I'm not a charity."

"And here I thought I was taking my girl out on a date so that I could spoil her rotten and make her feel like the goddess she is?" he says simply, waving the cashier to keep going. "At no point did I think of you as a charity. I've seen your parent's house, and honestly I have more money than I ever know what to do with, but that's beside the point. If you don't want to accept it as a gift from a guy that worships the ground you walk on, how about you accept it as someone I'm eternally grateful to. You saving Freja when most people would have just driven away meant so much to someone like me. I'd buy this stuff for that person, even if he was a 350lbs truck driver with an impressive beard. So calm down your pride and accept my gratitude as a fellow animal lover."

Well, I don't know what I was expecting him to say, but it wasn't anything that came out of his mouth. Because I'm completely speechless, I just stand there watching the dollar sign get higher and know I can't refuse this without coming across as a total bitch. Swallowing and almost choking on my pride, I choose to be the better person for a change and let him buy the dog stuff.

I follow Theodore out to the car quietly and watch as he loads most of it into the trunk of the car, with the rest that didn't fit, going into the backseat. My parents are going to be pissed when they see all of that, I haven't even told them about bringing a dog home yet.

Theodore comes around and opens my door for me, and I sit inside it, doing my belt up and thinking of what to say to break the tension that's been building around us.

When he starts the car, he turns to me and asks, "Do you want to go home? Are you that upset with me for doing a nice thing because I never intended to make you uncomfortable, and I understand if you want to cut our date short." God, this guy is too good to be true. "Say something, please, anything."

I turn to him and say with a straight face before smiling at the end, showing him that I want to be playful again. "I never said I was your girl."

He breathes out a sigh of relief and turns back to focusing on driving, reversing the car out of the parking space. He flicks me a cheeky look and says way too confidently, "Not yet."

Feeling assured that we can get past the awkward moment I inadvertently made in the store, I let my shoulders relax a bit and say quietly, "Thank you."

Being as understanding as usual, Theodore puts his hand on my thigh again and squeezes softly. "Don't mention it, everything to do with you is my pleasure."

Feelings I refuse to name fill me, and I desperately try to mentally bat them away. The angry little Foxy inside me talking to them with a bat furiously, refusing to let them settle in.

I clear my throat and look out the window at the beautiful, large lake that is parallel to the road we're driving down. "It's a nice day," I remark to get my mind away from my uncomfortable feelings, instead focusing on the warmth of the sun on my knees and the bright sun glittering along the lake's surface.

Theodore hums in agreement and lowers both of our windows, letting in the unseasonably warm breeze. The fresh, encompassing scent of crisp water and birch trees fills the car, and I close my eyes, leaning my head back and soaking it all in.

I let the peace of it encompass me for the rest of the

drive, which isn't more than ten minutes. My body lulls from side to side as Theodore drives smoothly along the rest of the journey, and I feel when we come to a stop. For a moment I think about keeping my eyes closed and just letting the day slip away as I am now, but Theodore's soft close voice stirs me enough to open my eyes.

"You are so beautiful when you let yourself rest." I look up at his handsome face hovering over mine, the heat of his breath close to my lips. I close the distance, winding my hands behind his neck at the same time and pull him in, deepening our kiss, my eyes closing again.

We kiss long, slow and deep, a moan of need slipping out of me and I hear Theodore unclip my seatbelt, sliding it off between us, and then he pulls me in even tighter, his arms around my lower back. It should be awkward to sit in the front seat, but somehow it isn't, and we revel in each other's taste and touch without any desire to let go.

I happily get lost in him, and when I open my eyes and pull back enough to look up at him, his look of utter devotion takes my breath away.

He must sense that I'm not ready for that kind of look yet. He carefully pulls back from me, a soft smile in place of where my swollen lips used to be, and I take a moment to look at it. "Why are you so sexy?" I ask, smiling back at him.

"For you, my love. I'm pretty sure I was made just for you." Theodore winks and turns to face forward. I look at what he's looking at and sit up in excitement at the jetty in front of us. "How about we head to our next destination?" His voice sounds as excited as I feel.

In seconds, I'm out of the car and hurrying toward the jetty, I turn and run half backward along the grass. "Come on, I don't know where I'm going," I call out at the man slowly walking toward me, hands in the pockets of his cream slacks and white polo shirt bright in the midday sun.

Fuck, he's hot. Who knew a guy with a name like Theodore wearing cream slacks would be taking me on a boat date? I'm in a freaking twilight zone. There's no way Allure will believe this shit, I think to myself with a huff of laughter.

Theodore catches up to me and swings me up in his arms, swinging me around in a bridal hold and smiling down at me. "What's so funny, beautiful?"

"I'm just thinking about how opposite we are, and I found it funny," I tell him honestly, wrapping my arms around his neck, letting him carry me along the jetty. "Mi hermana is going to flip when I tell her about today."

He kisses me softly, strolling along as though I weigh nothing, and says in a semi-serious tone, "I don't think we're opposite, more like we were made to fit each other. Kind of like yin and yang."

Damn, he's got to stop saying shit like that. It's too much, too real. Plus, when I think about it, Theodore and Beau are the yin and yang in my head. One is loving, formal and proper, with the best manners ever, while the other is rough around the edges, cheeky as fuck, and a bit naughty. But both of them are great in the sack and always put my needs above their own. Why can't one of them be a dickhead or have a small, useless dick? It would make getting rid of one of them way easier. Not that I'm planning on keeping one, I tell myself as a reminder to not get too close.

Theodore sets me down on a nice little boat with a room built in below. I take off my sandals and carefully maneuver around to the front and take a seat on the edge, with my feet hanging down as Theodore gets the boat ready. I figure if he needs my help, he can ask for it, and it's not like I have any clue about boats anyway.

Before long, we are off, skimming along the calm lake surface with a playful little bounce. I lean back against the boat and enjoy the fresh spray of water on my skin and the warm kiss of the sun on all of my exposed flesh. And I'm glad I only wore small denim shorts and a white halter-neck tank top. My nipples are hard through the soft fabric, and I'm glad I didn't wear a bra today, knowing that Theodore would be getting a great view of my tits bouncing with the boat from this angle.

I almost drift off from the lulling movements when the engine suddenly switches off, but I don't open my eyes, wanting to see exactly what Theodore will do with me.

A few moments go by where I hear random noises behind me from Theodore doing stuff with the boat before I hear him approaching me.

Hot wet lips suck on my clothed left nipple and I arch my back, moaning at how good it feels. My eyes open, and I look down at Theodore looking up at me with ravenous eyes and a bare chest, glistening and golden in the sunshine.

I slide my fingers through his hair and pull him back down to my nipple when he lets go of it. His other hand slowly slides up my side, over my other breast and to the back of my neck, caressing me the whole way.

With expert moves, he undoes the halterneck and slides my shirt down, moving his mouth just long enough for the fabric to be pooled at my waist. He then takes my nipple between his teeth, nipping and sucking in a way that I love, and the motion pools moisture between my open thighs.

I want to rub them together, but they're parted by a pole in the middle of the boat, where my feet are still dangling. He takes advantage of my position and slides one hand down my stomach, unbuttoning my jeans, and slides his fingers below my barely there lace g-string to slip between my wet folds.

It doesn't miss my attention that we're out in the open in the middle of a usually busy lake. But the fucks I should have are nowhere to be found as he starts to finger me slowly, while still teasing my nipples. Let them watch for all the fuck I care.

"How does that feel?" he asks me, lifting his head to watch how I'm reacting to his touch, ever attentive.

I roll my hips up to slide his fingers in deeper and groan, "I want more."

The seductive smile I've grown to love pulls at his cheeks and he sits up, quickly pulling my body up with him so that my legs are inside the boat again. I watch in fascination as he stands up in front of me and removes his pants and underwear, flicking them further into the boat. His hard dick is on full display for all to see, and I revel in his little show of naughtiness.

"Why, doctor Bell, I should have known you had a freak hidden inside that proper exterior," I state, feigning shock. "Mind you, the day after we met, you were balls deep in my ass on your workbench. I guess that was a dead giveaway?"

I pull my shirt off and stand beside him, watching his dick twitch as I remove my own pants, turning around and bending over to make a good show out of it. My head turns back to look at him as I slowly stand back up, smoothing my hands up the back of my legs and ass seductively the whole time.

With more grace than I normally possess, I spin around and roll my fingers over my hardened nipples, pebbling them more with little squeezes. I let out a little moan,

Theodore's eyes never leaving me, his gaze like a hungry lion.

"Now that you have me here, all alone, what do you plan to do to me?" I purr, walking backward, then turning to sprint to the back of the boat around the side.

Theodore's footfalls pound behind me as he chases me, hot on my tail. Just before I reach the door to take me below the cabin, his strong arms wrap around my middle and lift me off the floor, slamming me against his body.

An uncharacteristic giggle squeals out of me as I pretend to fight him off, all the while loving every second of it. One of his arms lowers on my body and his fingers dive into my wet heat, almost pushing me up with the power of his thrusts, and I pant in need at how fucking good it feels.

"I'm going to make you cum for me over and over again until all you can remember is my name," he growls in my ear as he fingers me, expertly rubbing my g-spot with every thrust.

I completely give in to our animalistic natures as he divides his fingers, pushing one into my ass at the same time as my pussy, knowing how much I love it from last time. Opening my legs wide, I rest them on each side of the door frame, bending them as wide as I can, and his strong body holds me effortlessly against him the whole time.

My climax rushes toward me like a freight train and in minutes I'm screaming out with my head back. Theodore chooses that exact moment to slide his dick in my ass, using the wetness he'd already gathered to lubricate me just right, and I accept him happily, my pussy still clenching around his fingers.

"Fuck me hard," I cry out, and he does, hard and fast he pistons himself into my ass, using his digits to focus on my clit this time. My legs shook like crazy, trying to hold myself up while bouncing hard on his dick.

Theodore's movements start getting choppy with how close his own orgasm is, and he focuses even harder on my clit, working me to oblivion again and my legs start to give out.

Noticing my lack of energy, Theodore pulls out of me carefully and turns me in his arms, carrying me to the driver's chair at the top. He sits down, planting me on his lap and sliding himself into my hungry pussy.

I clench around his thick length and roll my hips, but he grabs them, pulling me down hard onto his lap, leaving no space between us. "If you do that, I'm going to blow my load too quickly," he moans into my shoulder.

A wicked smile plays at my lips and I roll my hips again. "Good, then you better fill me up really deep."

His hands shake, but he loosens his grip, letting me take control. Rolling and grinding against him, my full breasts bounce right in his face the whole time, and I get off on watching his vulnerable expression as I ride him.

"That's it, baby," I tell him as his mouth parts and his hip movement falters. He sucks one of my nipples in and bites down hard as he explodes inside me, and I clutch at his neck, pulling him in and loving the bite of pain with my pleasure.

Both our bodies relax into each other, and he releases my boob, kissing it softly all around where he bit me. The tenderness of his action soothing any ache it might have had, and he gazes into my eyes lovingly. "I don't care how long it takes Ana-Lucia, I want you to be mine. Every day and always."

The sincerity of his words breaks my heart as I picture Beau and with another first, I wonder if what Allure has going on is too much for me to dream of, and I know the answer is yes. These aren't brothers that have chosen to share, they're two separate men that want me in separate ways, but without a doubt, they are not counting on sharing me in the long run.

CHAPTER 15

FOXY

It's late at night by the time Theodore drops me home, and I get him to leave me at the gate, fearing that someone might make a scene if he came too close to the house. He readily agrees because like the smart man he is, he doesn't have a death wish.

With a kiss goodbye, I stroll down the driveway leisurely, refusing to let my stupid brothers ruin what was such a perfect day. We spent hours fucking, playing and eating a delicious picnic that he'd had a friend deliver to the boat before we embarked. I had so much fun and was filled with so much cum. An absolute winner of a day.

But like all good things, they must come to an end, I think as Juan and Antonio step out of the shadows when I approach the front door. *What now?*

"Your guy too chicken shit to face us, huh, Foxy?" Antonio jeers menacingly. "It's too bad, I was looking forward to getting to know him a little better." The threat is clear, and I bare my teeth at him, ready to let loose if he says one more stupid thing.

Juan holds his hand up to silence the idiot, thankfully,

and steps toward me. "What you did back in Sinhaven was none of our business, and we know that, but while you're living in the family home, working at our family business, and in our family's territory you will behave like a Hernandez daughter should."

"What's that supposed to mean?" I question, wondering what he's getting at.

Antonio scoffs and answers instead. "He's talking about you being a filthy slut."

Juan's punch comes out of nowhere and lands Antonio on his ass before he knows what's happening. Blood pools from his obviously broken nose as he swears and holds on to it.

"Talk to your sister like that again, and next time I'll break your fucking jaw," Juan growls down at him, somehow growing in size, and I realize I might be in real trouble here. It's not often Juan gets furious, but when he does, no one is safe.

His rage filled eyes turn back to me. "What's with the two separate guys?" Just like that, all the pieces are set in place in my mind. "You don't even look ashamed by your behavior, either. It's fucking disgusting the way you're going all around town with two different gringos. You think it doesn't get back to Papi? To Mario? Well it does, and I'm warning you right now, you'd better either pick one or none, but while you are home, you *will* be respectful to the family name."

As quickly as he came, he went with Antonio trailing behind him with a string of quiet curses, his nose still bleeding profusely.

Not for the first time in my life, I'm left standing alone in the dark feeling like shit but knowing that I did nothing wrong except be born into the wrong family.

* * *

Feeling grateful that it's Sunday, I don't have to go into work today and face my Papi's disapproving gaze. Instead, I use stealth mode to slink around the house for food and stuff.

I spend the morning texting back and forth with both Beau and Theodore, my sexting skills are really improving since I met the two of them. That's the downer about living with your parents, I can't exactly call them over for a booty call every time I'm horny, and it sucks big time.

More often than not, though, I try not to think about what will happen when my brothers come home, and it's time for me to move back to Sinhaven again. At least while I'm here, I can see them every now and then, but once I go back, they'll be too far away for any kind of booty call.

My stomach grumbles, telling me that it's lunchtime, and I slip down the hallway, tiptoeing down the stairs and toward the back of the house. Just as I reach the kitchen, the back door opens and the loud voices of the men of the house travel toward me.

I quickly run behind the wall as I hear them enter the kitchen and I freeze, hoping they won't take long to get something to eat because where I am, there's no escape.

"Are you sure it's just women and children?" Juan asks someone, and I'm instantly curious about what they're talking about.

My papi grunts loud and replies, "Sí, homeless, sheltered, or in need. Someone is targeting people that won't be missed if they go missing, but nothing gets by me."

"You don't think it's the Mexican cartel from down south trying to increase their territory, do you?" Juan's voice sounds worried, and I bite my lip at what this will mean.

Papi must have nodded because I hear Antonio curse loudly. The three of them eat slowly in the kitchen talking about where and who has gone missing, and I soak in every word. Our family may get into some shady business, but my parents have a strict policy on sex trafficking and child abuse. That's a whole different kind of monster.

When I hear them wash up and leave the kitchen, I run in to grab an apple and my car keys off the hook. My destination can't wait as I head straight out the door, starting my car up and heading toward town. There's no way I'm going to sit idly by when I could be out there helping find the missing people.

My trip doesn't take long before I'm in Charmington Center, one of the places Juan said that women and children were going missing. I pull in my car on one of the main drags and start going door to door asking if anyone has heard of anyone missing in the last few months.

Unfortunately, hardly anyone knows anything until I stop at the local bakery next to an alley with a few homeless people down it. I ask the owner, who's behind the register, if they've heard anything, and she instantly looks out the side window to an empty box down the alleyway.

"I'm not sure if this is what you mean, but it's been plaguing my mind, and I didn't know who to tell about it," she starts.

I encourage her to go on, "Anything you can tell me will help."

"Well, about six months ago, a young girl in her mid-teens started sleeping in the box out there. She was so young and looked so alone, so I sometimes threw her any leftover bread at the end of the day. Eventually, she told me her name was Desire. I highly doubt that's her real name, but I don't want to press her and make her feel like she needs to sleep somewhere else. At least if she was here, I knew she was alright. You see, I have a granddaughter her age and I felt somehow responsible for her."

She stops talking and presses her hand to her chest, grimacing before she goes on again. I didn't dare interrupt. "Last week, when I was packing up for the night, I happened to look out the window at the same time a black sedan pulled up to the alley. I didn't really see who got out of the car, but they approached Desire and in moments she was getting put into the car. I tell myself that she must have known them because she didn't put up a fight, but as they drove past the front, I saw her large eyes staring at me filled with fear and pleading. I ran out, but they were already gone, and I didn't know what to do. The cops won't care, and I don't even know her real name."

A tear tracks down the older woman's face, and she quickly wipes it away, looking over at me with hope. "Do you think your family can help find her? She's a sweet little thing and never caused me any problems. If you can get her back, I'll take her in like I should have to begin with. Guilt eats at me every day that I didn't give that girl a safe place to sleep and three healthy meals. Every child deserves to be cared for, no matter what her story is."

I really feel for this woman, and I vow to her that I'll do whatever I can to get her back. She gives me her physical details and tells me that someone had told her that a few people had also gone missing from the local Miss Potts' shelter around the corner.

She gives me the address, and I finish up my notes on everything she's told me so far, knowing exactly where I'm going to look next. The shelter is so close that I decide to leave my car and walk there on foot. It doesn't take me long before I'm standing in front of a four-story high refurbished old building with a large clear sign overhead that reads 'Miss Potts' Safehaven for Women and Children.'

I'm instantly impressed by the clean state of affairs, and the children's laughter ringing out from inside the open large double doors. It tells me a lot about how this place is run, and I'm glad there's somewhere like this around.

What impresses me even more is the security team installing cameras all along the front of the building facing in every direction. Clearly, the founder of this place has heard what's been happening, and is trying to make it safer for the people staying here.

A familiar voice carries out as two men exit the building, talking very animatedly about what they can do to further increase security not only to the building but also in the surrounding area.

When the man who seems to be in charge turns around, I'm shocked to find Beau, and he recognizes me instantly, his face going from being deep in thought to bright with happiness.

Waving to me, he calls me to come over, excusing himself from the man he was talking to early. With a skip in his step, he jogs to me, taking me in his arms and kissing the top of my head. "How did you know I was missing you today?"

CHAPTER 16

BEAU

The warmth of Foxy's skin instantly seeps into mine as I hold her tight. I've had such a terrible day with everything that's happened lately, and I really needed to see her, but why is she here? Did I tell her about this place?

I pull back and look down at her beautiful dark brown eyes and ask, "What are you doing here?"

My arms don't let her go, even when she tries to pull back. No way, she's all mine now that I have her in my arms. It's been too long since I felt her so close to me.

"Do you work here? I had no idea, I've actually come for a whole other reason," she tells me, looking past me at the security guys setting up the new system.

I explain to her that this is just one of my many women and children shelters in Beastville and that I named them after my incredible mother. Her facial features soften, and I know it touched her. Foxy always acts like she's some big bad guy, but her heart is pure gold, whether she admits it or not.

"I heard that a few people have gone missing from here,

and I came to see if that was true." I frown, why would she be looking into something like that.

"Yes, a mother and her two young daughters were taken right out front as they were about to go out," I tell her, still curious why she wants to know, as she doesn't come across as a gossiper. "Why are you trying to find out?"

Foxy chews on her lip for a second before saying, as she extricates herself from my arms, "A girl I know who was living in an alley nearby was also taken last week, and I really want to find her. Because she was homeless and no one knows her real name, the police can't do anything about it, but when I heard more people went missing from here, I thought I might be able to get a lead."

I wish she had come to stay here instead of sleeping on the streets, that's why I've made so many locations. Unfortunately, some of the younger girls don't because they think we're going to call their parents, which we only do under certain circumstances. But if it meant her being out in the cold, I would have kept her whereabouts private. Their safety is my number one priority always.

At least it now makes sense why Foxy is looking into the missing family. "I'll tell you what I can, if you don't mind doing the same for me, in case the two instances are related. It was just after dark, and the witness said that she had just stepped on the curb when a white van pulled up and someone reached out and pulled in her seven-year-old daughter. The mom screamed and grabbed for her but was also pulled in. However, the other daughter who was only four was so scared that she tried to run back inside, but a Hispanic looking man ran after her and took her back to the van. One of the other women saw what was happening, but she said it happened so fast that she didn't have time to react, but she came straight inside and told our guard on duty."

I take a moment to breathe, fury rising in me at the thought of how I failed to keep them safe. "It's not our fault." Foxy winds her arms around my waist and pulls me in tight. "What you've got here is fantastic, and you would be saving so many people, please don't let this one time bring you down. We'll find these people and bring those girls back."

The confidence in her voice gives me strength because even though we're just everyday people, we can make a change when we work together.

"Have I told you how much you mean to me lately?" I ask her, squeezing her even tighter, but I don't miss her body tensing at my words. Knowing if I don't want to scare her away, I need to change the subject. I ask her what she knows.

After clearing her throat, she steps back again, fixing a rogue curl. She tells me that in her case the girl was about fifteen and was taken on the side of the road as well but by a black sedan instead of a white van. I wonder if that means they're different people, or they just have different cars?

I invite her inside and show her the schoolrooms, large communal kitchen and entertainment room, the fitness room, the medical center and the elevator leading up to the many accommodations available. The whole time I explain that I wanted somewhere safe and free for people who need it, and that we supply all food and medical needs as well.

"The rules here are very strict though and once broken they have to move on and won't be accepted at any location. They are put in place for the safety of all occupants and keep this place running smoothly. Like, no violence, no drugs, no alcohol, all visitors must be signed in and approved by security, keep your space and the common space clean, no stealing and be kind to others." I tick them off with my fingers as I go.

Foxy nods in approval. "I love it. They must be very grateful to you." She looks around at the women that pass us by. "You realize that they're all scowling at me for taking up all of your time? I'm going to go out on a limb here and say you're very popular with the ladies?"

I laugh out loud because she's not wrong, but it doesn't affect me doing my job at all. I take looking after them very seriously and have not once ever looked at anyone here with even the slightest modicum of interest. That would be highly unprofessional, besides I haven't shown any genuine interest in a woman since school besides the one currently walking beside me.

"How about I finish up here and then take you back to my place for a home cooked dinner?" I propose quietly, so that the many curious ears nearby stay out of our conversation. "My housemate is away with his parents for the night. I was originally going to go too, but I wanted to fix everything up here first. Now I'm very glad I did."

She agrees easily, and I quickly run around letting everyone know what I need to get done before they go home tonight. The excitement about having her all to myself for the night is great fuel to get me moving.

I left my car at home having taken a taxi this morning instead in case I ended up staying in a motel close by if I worked too late, but luckily Foxy brought hers. On the way back to her car, we stop off at the supermarket nearby, and I pick up everything I need to make a romantic dinner.

We get to the car and drive back to Royal Cross, and I show her where she can park her car. Tee's space will be empty until tomorrow night, so it worked out well.

"I'm going to have to meet this housemate of yours one day," Foxy tells me, reigniting my hope that she might want to stick around after all.

I try not to let it show as we head up the elevator and say as flippantly as I can, "Yeah, he's cool. We've actually talked about doing a double date with you and his new girlfriend. Do you think that's something you'd be into?" *Say yes. Say yes.*

"Um, I guess so. Does he know we aren't actually dating?" she asks, and my hope deflates a little again. This girl is playing super hard to get, and I want to get her super hard.

We reach my floor and I walk her to our front door, saying truthfully, "I'm hoping that won't be the case for long." I haven't hidden my intentions with her, and I'm not about to start now. "Come on in and make yourself comfortable. I'm going to put dinner on."

I go straight to the kitchen, feeling my heart pounding in my chest. Nervousness fills me with how important tonight is because I really want to impress her and if everything goes well, I want to ask her to date me officially. Damn. I should have bought flowers too, but something tells me she's not really a flower and chocolates type of girl. I'm pretty sure she'll be happier with a new exhaust for her car instead.

The potato jackets go in, and I cut up the salad before putting on the steak. "How do you like your steak cooked?" I call out.

"Rare please," Foxy says from just behind me, and I jump, almost knocking the frying pan off the stove. "Holy shit. How long have you been there?" I clutch at my chest as she laughs at what was probably not a very manly squeal that came out of me.

She leans against the bench behind me. "Ages, you were just in your own world. It was impressive, actually; I love a man that can cook."

"I knew you'd fall in love with me eventually. Who knew that all I needed to do was cut up some simple ingredients?" I joke, turning back to the steak.

Foxy makes herself at home, finding two plates and the cutlery. She goes out and sets the table with place mats and napkins. She comes back in to grab two wine glasses and the bottle of pinot noir that I bought earlier and takes that to the table as well, only this time she stays out there.

I finish up with dinner and bring out both of our plates to find her standing out on the balcony that overlooks everything from our high vantage point.

Placing our plates down, I go outside and slide my arms around her waist from behind. Today she's wearing slip on shoes and a flowy gray wrap around dress that shows off the perfect amount of cleavage. She looks stunning as always.

"Dinner's ready," I whisper in her ear, nipping on the lobe and loving how it makes her shudder. "We better eat it while it's hot, and then we can sit out here and have some wine and maybe dessert," I growl the last word, nipping down her neck now, pulling her in tight enough that she can feel my growing erection.

Foxy turns in my arms and kisses me softly on the lips, and then moves past me and to the table, pouring us both a glass of wine. "This looks delicious. Gracias."

I sit across from her and hate every inch of distance between us. Picking up my fork, I wait until she has the first bite and smile when she moans around a piece of steak. *Nailed it.* I take my own bite and have to agree, this is one good steak.

Halfway through dinner, Foxy asks me as she looks

around the room, "Why don't you have any photos hanging around the place?"

Having never thought about it before now, I look around the way she was and guess she's right, we don't. "I guess it's because we're both guys and just don't think about that stuff."

She laughs and agrees that it must be the reason, but it makes me think. I don't have any pictures of my own mother because my father got rid of anything from my life before moving in with him, including everything related to her. And I don't want a picture of him because I hate that dickhead with every fiber of my being. Every woman's shelter I raise with the money he left me, I hope he's flipping in his grave.

Other than those two, I don't have anybody but Tee and his family in my life that means anything, at least until now. I look over at Foxy and decide that the first framed picture I'm going to put up on my behalf will be hers when she agrees to be mine. Because when I look in her eyes, I see my future, and it's never looked more beautiful.

When we finish our meals, I take the dishes to the kitchen and wash them, telling Foxy to go sit on the balcony and that I'll be there soon. I use my phone to put on some light music and finish washing up before joining her.

CHAPTER 17

FOXY

eau comes up behind me and slips his fingers through mine on each side of me as I lean against the balcony railing. I squeeze them tight and lean back into his warm body, looking out at all the glittering lights around us and hearing the bustling of the busy streets way below.

I close my eyes and let all of my other senses take in everything around me, but when Beau starts kissing the side of my neck, the town below all of a sudden holds very little interest to me anymore.

His hot lips trail along my jaw, earlobe, and neck as he intermittently whispers sweet nothings that shouldn't make me feel as good as they do. Against my better judgment, I find myself listening and feeling, but it's the feelings that I need to ignore. Theodore's face comes to my mind, and my eyes snap open.

What the fuck am I going to do? I ask myself mentally. How can I be falling for two completely different people when I didn't think I was capable of falling for anyone?

One of Beau's hands lets go of mine, and he brings it

around my waist, pulling me tight against his body. My ass rubs against his hardness, making my pussy flutter at the memory of how good it feels inside me.

Choosing to not focus on any feelings other than the physical ones that I'm very comfortable with, I grind myself against him, loving the groan he makes when I do.

His hand works under the wrap of my dress to my bare stomach and moves down to the top of my underwear before sliding underneath it and down to my core.

I open my legs more to give him better access and Beau wastes no time, gliding his fingers between my lips and slowly massaging them up and down, keeping his pressure featherlight and thoughtful. Rolling my hips forward, I silently ask for him to put his finger inside me, but he ignores the movement and continues his torturous petting.

My pussy clenches with need, and I feel myself getting wetter and wetter. Beau uses it against me, sliding it up and over me, increasing the sensation but not enough for me to get off on it, just enough for me to want more.

"What do you say?" Beau asks, nibbling on my earlobe, and I remember what he said last time about voicing my needs to him, and I feel a new flood of wetness at how much I love the way he does things.

Instead of complying though because I decide to play my own game, I let go of the railing with my free hand and undo the tie holding my dress closed, opening it wider and then placing my hand above his.

He stops his movements, but I slide my fingers in between his and use both of our hands to rub against my clit and lower. I breathe out a small moan as I dip my finger inside me and then guide him in as well on the second push.

Beau lets me take control as I use both of our hands to

fuck my dripping pussy while grinding my ass against his dick with every rocking motion.

I feel Beau's breathing pick up against my neck with my own, clearly enjoying what I'm doing with our combined hands. My hips rock harder as I also use his palm to rub against my clit at the same time, and my panting increases.

My release gets closer and closer with every movement and Beau starts to pick up most of the movement, now in charge of pushing our fingers in and out. I let him take control and focus on my legs not giving out as it gets closer.

"Make me cum," I plead. "I'm so close."

As soon as the words leave my mouth, Beau's tempo picks up, and he starts curling our fingers just right. In seconds, I let out a small scream into the crisp night air, with no fucks given if anyone can hear me.

Before I even begin to come down from my high, Beau spins me in his arms and drops to his knees, ripping my panties down with one swift movement. His lips are on me and his tongue is inside me before I know what's happening. Beau devours me expertly, and I'm torn between 'it's too much' and 'don't stop.'

Reaching up, Beau slides two fingers inside me and starts curling with my pussy still twitching from the orgasm I just had. The intensity and ferocity of his movements somehow rips out a more intense climax than before, and I cry out, my pussy pulsing wet cum all over Beau with each curl and stroke of his fingers.

My legs almost have me crumbling to the ground as I helplessly beg him to stop, the sensitivity too much to handle. Beau stops and stands, wrapping me up in his arms and carrying me through the apartment and carefully placing me on the bed.

His eyes follow every movement carefully as he

undresses me the rest of the way and then undresses himself. With our clothes discarded on the floor, he climbs up my body and between my legs until he's over the top of me.

"Tell me what you want?" he rasps, always making sure that I'm happy.

"You. Inside me."

With slow movements, he maneuvers himself at my opening and slides his rock-hard dick inside me. If I'm being completely honest with myself, I've missed him inside me ever since our first night together, and I wrap my legs around his waist, pulling him closer to me.

Beau holds me close in his arms and starts to rock inside me, grinding as he goes, causing his dick to hit me just right and my clit to get stimulation as well. He looks deep into my eyes in the most intense way, and we move together wordlessly.

With all the partners I've been with, and there's been a few, I've never experienced anything quite like this. Instead of taking from me and being reckless with his own wants and needs, this man turns every encounter I have with him into something sensual and caring, and not once has it been about his needs over my own. It's either all on me or what we can bring to each other.

My heart constricts as he starts kissing me tenderly, picking up the pace only slightly and holding the back of my head as if I'm special and fragile. For just a moment I let him into my heart and just feel what I want to, and it's long enough to bring an unwanted tear to my eye.

Beau must have noticed something different because he lifts his head and looks down at me again, his eyes tracking my tear as it slips down. He gently kisses down its path and holds me a little tighter, and I find my own arms and legs gripping him to me fiercely, not wanting to let go of this moment.

This might be the first time that I've ever appreciated having sex without searching for a happy ending. If anything I don't want it to end even if it means I don't climax because just this act of being together like this is a different kind of ecstasy. If only I was a different girl with a different path.

With that thought, I close off my heart again and try to get the upper hand, loosening my grip and slipping one hand between us to start rubbing my clit, needing to focus on an end game.

Luckily Beau isn't an idiot, and he takes the cue that I can't handle this kind of intimacy so soon, if ever, and uses his hand to knock mine away, lifting his body off me a bit and focusing on making my clit extra happy.

I focus on how good it feels, glad that he's so good at reading my pants and moans. My hips start to rock against him harder the closer he brings me to climax, and by the time I'm about to burst, his hips are slapping into me as hard as I can take. I explode seeing the stars I long for and happily let them distract me.

Beau cums right after me, and sensing I need some space slips, out of my body after we both come down to lie beside me, his head propped on his hand and a smile of satisfaction on his face.

"Now that's what I call a successful dinner date," he jokes, and I appreciate that he didn't call out my moment of weakness earlier and go along with his humor gratefully.

I scratch his scruffy stubble and smile wickedly. "I haven't had my dessert yet, though."

He crinkles his forehead in confusion. "Well, what did

you call that, then?" His voice comes out with fake shock and anger, pretending to be appalled and making me laugh.

"A palate cleanser, obviously."

My body rises, and I push his shoulder backward so that he lies back against the bed and kiss him teasingly on the tip of his nose. "I know just the thing I'm craving though and exactly how to get it."

With a look of mischief, I lower down his body and watch his eyes widen the moment he knows exactly what I'm doing. "Fuck, yes," is all he can say before I suck him inside my mouth, loving the salty taste of our combined satisfaction.

CHAPTER 18

Bed has never felt so good.

While my morning started well, waking up to Beau's head between my legs, making me climax three times until I practically had to beg him to stop, the rest of my day has not been so good.

Work was long and arduous, with both my brothers and Papi giving me dirty looks all day long. I made sure to get there before them and get changed into my backup clothes. Because I don't want to have to deal with twenty questions about why I didn't come home last night and where I stayed. I'm a grown-ass woman for Christ's sake, I don't need to report my every movement anymore, and I refuse to deal with that shit.

After work, it wasn't any better. Mami at least acted like everything was normal, but I thought I'd have a hole drilled into my face the way the men's eyes were all burning at me. Fuck them.

I got through the meal as quickly as I could and got the hell out of there, making sure to thank Mami on the way out. She gave me a sad smile that silently wished me good luck and distracted Papi when he went to follow me out. That woman is a saint sometimes.

My mind drifts to the two men I've somehow found in my life, and I really can't believe my luck. I didn't think there were any good men out there, and I feel kind of bad that I'm hogging the only good ones left. Not.

The last couple of weeks have been kind of amazing, and I even feel a bit different. I'm still a kick-ass bitch, but my heart doesn't feel so tight, my load doesn't feel so heavy, and my vagina has never been happier.

Maybe it isn't such a bad thing to let people close to me other than Allure, apart from the estupido men in my family, it hasn't caused me any issues. Yet, at least.

However, there is the little matter of the guys both wanting to make their relationship with me more official and, no doubt, exclusive. Theodore brought it up in the boat, but I managed to distract him with another blow job. When Beau brought up dating me properly this morning, I was conveniently late for work and ran out like my ass was on fire.

I know I won't be able to keep this up the way it is for much longer, and I'm either going to have to ditch them both, which is what I usually do. Or pick one and actually try this relationship thing everyone seems so crazy about.

For a second, I try to visualize them both agreeing to share me. I could introduce them and explain that it works for my friend to have more than one partner, and tell them how hot the sex will be.

This puts my mind straight in the gutter, and before I know it, I'm picturing Beau asking me how I want it, as Theodore fucks me in the ass, and my fingers are working my pussy furiously.

The image of Beau climbing up me and spearing my

front as they both fuck me hard and fast has me panting, my naughty release getting closer and closer.

Ding.

Ding. Ding.

Why God? Why?

I try to ignore my phone, focusing on my fantasy, but it goes off two more times.

Ding. Ding.

Frustrated, I grab the stupid thing and find messages from both Beau and Theodore waiting for me. My guilt is a fresh wave of cold water as I read them. Beau wants me to go on that double date with his housemate and Theodore asking if I'll meet his brother and his girlfriend.

My hand gives up, and I try to smother myself with my pillow, letting out a muffled scream at how unfair this all is, on them and me. Why can't I have my cake and eat it too, like Allure does?

If past me, saw present me, she would roll her eyes at me and tell me I'm being stupid and to fuck them each one more time and dump their asses off to become someone else's problem. Past me was a beast without mercy, and she loved it that way, but something has changed, and I don't feel like the same person anymore.

Somehow the beauty of the men that have entered my life is slowly taming the beast within me, and that admittedly terrifies me because what am I if not the beast in my own story? I have always been the strong one; scary, mean, and cold. The person that people instinctively know to stay away from because my bite *is* worse than my bark. Somehow, though, the warmth, patience, loving and charitable natures of Theodore and Beau are thawing me out one day at a time. They make me want to let go of some of the anger and fear I desperately hold on to. The draw to let them in gets harder to resist with every smile and touch, but even if I gave in, who would I choose? How could I choose? They're a perfect combination, and I honestly don't think I could pick one without the other.

Deciding not to answer either of their messages, even though it's a dick move because they can see that I read them. I dial Allure instead because if I've ever needed her to give me advice on something, it's now and that bitch owes me from years of my advice.

The phone rings a few times and a yawning Allure answers with a half-hearted, "Hello?"

"Are you seriously already asleep?" I ask way too harshly, my bad mood leaking through to my friend that doesn't deserve it. "Sorry, I didn't mean to be in full bitch mode."

She just laughs and yawns again. "I'm used to it. What's up? I've just been more tired these days with the pregnancy and all. Is everything alright?"

I pause, suck in a breath, and then blow out a long exhale, telling my pride to take a backseat and say, "Hermana, I need your help."

I hear a loud slap and one of the guys curses before Allure starts screaming for everyone to get up. "We've gotta go, don't ask questions, Foxy's in trouble. Get the car and the twins, Callum and Ardyn, grab some clothes for us and the kids. And Jamee, I need some snacks for the road and some lemonade."

My eyes roll into the back of my head at how over the freaking top she's being, and I shout into the phone to calm the fuck down. Ardyn's voice comes through the speaker, "Where are you? We're on our way. Do I need backup? Do we need our guns?"

"For the love of God. Está de verdad se pela, ni siquiera

se recordó de los gemelos... pasmada. Your girl is overreacting, I only called for advice, not a rescue. What the hell?" My frustration rises at my sister and her over-exaggeration of everything. Good thing I love this girl.

Ardyn laughs and calls for everyone to calm down because it's a false alarm, and passes back the phone to a confused-sounding Allure. "What's happening? Don't you need us?"

"No. Numbnuts," I moan, but secretly adore her worrying about me. "I wanted some advice about guys."

Silence reigns supreme on the other end of the line, and I look at my phone to see if it's still on and put it back to my ear. "Are you still there?"

"I'm sorry, can you repeat that?" she asks quietly. "Did you say you want guy advice from *me*? Holy shit, the world is coming to an end."

Grudgingly, I repeat myself and wait for her answer. After a beat, Allure excuses herself from the guys and asks me quietly in a no-nonsense tone, ready to take me seriously. "Okay, tell me everything, and I'll do what I can. I'm always here for you."

My stupid heart gets all soft again, and I have to hold back a sob, realizing just how much I've missed this bitch and how grateful I am to have someone like her in my life.

With a big breath, I start from the beginning of how I met Beau and my story with him. When she asks me what the problem is, I then tell her about meeting Theodore and all the stuff I've been through with him.

I pause and say, "I'm so confused because not only am I not prepared for any feelings toward a guy like this, but I'm having them for two different people at the same time and unlike your situation, I don't have the option to keep both," I huff out in exasperation. "Why do I even want to keep anyone? This isn't like me, and I don't know what to do anymore."

A traitorous sob leaks out of me, that leads to another and then another, and before I know it, I'm sobbing like a little girl, my breaths heaving uncontrollably. The last time I cried like this was when Allure was in trouble. Before that, I have no idea, but somehow these two men are breaking down what I thought were my impenetrable walls, and I don't know if I can build them back up again.

Allure lets me cry it out with low soothing words, telling me she is there for me and that everything is going to be alright. I cry to her more about how my family is behaving about the whole thing on top of it all, and now I'm walking around home tip-toeing on eggshells because I'm suddenly the shameful daughter.

While I know that no advice will be good enough because it's something I'm going to have to deal with head-on eventually. It feels good to finally say everything out loud and let it all out to the one person I trust the most in the world.

We spend hours crying and laughing together over the big and small stuff and by the end of it, I feel a lot more human but just as confused about what to do.

"You are going to have to be honest with them both. At least they both know about the other, so it's not exactly going to be a shock to either of them. But if you are having feelings, and they are wanting to take the next step in your relationship with them, then you need to lay it all out on the table and see where the pieces fall. Maybe one of them will make the decision for you and back out. If that's the case, then they aren't worth your time anyway," Allure tells me honestly before we hang up for the night, and I already kind of knew that this is what I was going to have to do, but it was nice hearing it come from her. "But no matter what happens, I want you to let me know what's going on and next time unload on me before shit gets this tense for you. I love you, bitch."

"Love you too." I hang up after agreeing to her terms and feel ten times lighter than I did before.

Even if it's hard, I'm going to have to step up soon and see where it all takes me.

CHAPTER 19

FOXY

"We need to talk," I say to Theodore after he asks what my plans are for the day. Last night made me realize that I can't just keep pushing these men away and when he called me, I decided to just go for it.

Silence answers me before he replies, "I feel like that's a sentence no guy wants to hear from his girl, especially with the serious tone you're using."

I say and hear a beeping down the phone and look at my screen, it's not my phone. "You can call me back if you want," I tell him, in case whoever is trying to call him has something important to say.

"Nah, it's fine. It's just my bro," Theodore answers, his voice quiet, and I know he's nervous, but I doubt he's as nervous as me right now. "How about we catch up for lunch in town? I've got an hour break and couldn't think of a better person to spend it with."

My day is pretty free at work today because my main job got canceled yesterday, so I can definitely work with that. "Sounds like a good plan, I'll come by, and we'll take it from there."

We say our goodbyes and just as I hang up, my phone vibrates in my hand. Wow. My morning is busy today. I haven't even had breakfast yet.

Beau's number lights up, and I answer it after a big breath, might as well get two birds with one stone. "Hola."

Before I can say more, his voice trembles down the line with a quick greeting, and I know instantly that something is seriously wrong and ask him what's going on.

"I'm sorry for calling but I," Beau takes a heavy breath. "I needed someone to talk to, and I couldn't get through to my housemate. One of the young girls that have been staying at the same Miss Potts' you were at the other day was taken this morning, and I'm devastated. What should I do? I'm meant to be keeping them safe, not providing a place to take vulnerable women from."

His words end with a very obvious sound of heavy emotion, and it wouldn't surprise me if his eyes were filled with unshed tears right now.

I try to focus on his words and not how his emotions are cutting me to the quick. If someone was taken, then it has to be caught on camera with his new security system. "Were your cameras working at the time?" I ask hopefully.

"Yeah. The cops have just left with a copy, but they didn't seem to be overly concerned, and it pissed me the fuck off." His voice hardens with every word.

My feet start pounding down the stairs as I head toward my family, who I hear talking together in the kitchen. I burst in and raise my hand to Juan with a shushing motion, and he and the rest of them go instantly silent. No doubt from my stern expression.

I put the phone on loudspeaker and say to it, with my

finger still to my lips, indicating that they listen quietly. "I'm going to stop by with my brothers to take a look at the footage of the woman that was taken this morning." Immediately, recognition of what I am talking about has my papi standing up and standing beside me, on full alert of what's being said.

"What? Why?" Beau asks, confused.

"Look, I have a very close family friend that works in the police force and my papi is very well-connected to people around the community. Between us, we will hopefully be able to find something from the footage you have," I explain, obviously avoiding the subject of what my family actually does.

Papi looks at me and silently shows his finger pointing at his watch and then making an eight number with his hands, indicating the time we'll arrive there.

I continue talking, "We'll be there around eight o'clock, if that's alright?" It's not really a question, though, more of a polite demand because I know the Hernandez men will be there at eight whether he likes it or not. Luckily, Beau is in agreement and I hang up, explaining to my still-quiet family about Miss Potts' and everything I know so far.

Mami quickly feeds us, and we're out of the door in no time, heading toward the venue, with the three men in Papi's car, no doubt talking shop as I trail behind in my own car. Even though I'm sure they're happy with the new information, I know that they're still pissed off about me hanging around Beau. When I'm also messing with Theodore, and I didn't want to risk another lecture by getting trapped in the confines of a car with them.

As we pull up in the cars, I remember the lunch I'd planned with Theodore later. While we won't be here that long, I also know that Papi has said that we're all taking the day off today. This means he has plans for us all to talk about everything afterward, and the likelihood of me getting away for lunch looks small.

I pull out my phone and flick Theodore a quick message, canceling our lunch date, saying that a family thing suddenly came up but promising to catch up with him again soon. Not waiting for a response, I stick it in the back pocket of my overalls and head inside after my family, who already barged their way in. The last thing I want to do is leave Beau alone with them for even a second.

Beau's relief is obvious as I step in behind my brothers, with my papi on the right of us. I push through Juan and Antonio, grabbing onto Beau and pulling him in for a hug, his face looks drawn and his eyes heavy with concern.

We greet each other, holding on tight without a word, but my papi clears his throat loudly, reminding us both that they're still standing there. Beau's face flushes slightly as he pulls back, sliding me under his arm and to his side, and I don't miss Papi's disapproving look he gives me, but I decide to ignore it.

"Can you show us what you have?" I ask Beau, and he glides us toward a door to the left of us, and we head into what must be his office and around the table.

He lets go of me and leans over the keyboard, typing a few things before a recording pops up on the computer screen. Papi instantly takes over and the second Beau steps back, I grab his hand, pulling him to the other side of the room, letting the Hernandez men do what they do best.

"Are you alright?" I ask him quietly, stroking his short beard, and lean in to give his cheek a quick kiss. "This morning can't have been easy for you."

I can see a myriad of questions in Beau's eyes as he watches Juan use his phone to explain the details of the video to someone while quietly making demands. The intensity my family is giving off screams that there's more going on than I originally told Beau about.

I just give him a 'not now' smile, and I'm grateful that he respects my wishes, not asking me any of the many questions and just letting it all pass. For now. If I've learned anything about Beau, it's that he's straightforward with what he wants, and he is definitely going to want answers after this, and I'm not sure what I'm going to tell him. It's hard enough knowing that I still have to have that *other* talk with him yet. Shit is just getting more complicated by the day with these two.

Papi comes over to us as my brothers talk quietly among themselves and asks Beau, not unkindly though, "Can you email Foxy a copy of that recording? As she said earlier, we have a police officer in the family, and he will be able to look into the vehicles and happily prioritize it, I'm sure."

"I can do that," Beau replies, standing tall and refusing to look intimidated by my papi's bulking form and dark eyes, and I really respect him for it.

With a grunt, Papi replies. "Gracias. And let her know if anything happens again, even if it's just suspicious. We can't be too careful when it comes to protecting the innocent people of this world."

Beau's eyes widen at my papi's thoughtful choice of words, even if his tone of voice doesn't match it. I see a newfound respect in Beau's eyes for the older man, and a small part of me wonders if maybe this relationship has some hope for it after all. It's clear that even though Papi doesn't approve of my promiscuous lifestyle, he does approve of the man before him, otherwise, he wouldn't have talked to him directly at all, instead getting my brothers to do it.

I write down my email address on a piece of paper on Beau's desk as the Hernandez men say a gruff thanks to Beau, leaving the building as fast as they entered it.

"I've got to say, Foxy." Beau winds his arms around my waist from behind when I stand up again. "Your family is kind of intense, and I have more than a few questions for you. I think it's about time we had a little talk, yes?"

A resigned sigh leaves me, and I let my head fall back against him for a moment. I close my eyes and enjoy the nice moment while wondering if it's one of the last ones I'm going to have with him after we do have that talk.

I turn my body in his embrace, cupping his cheeks in my palms and giving him a sweet, but deep, kiss before pulling back reluctantly and saying, "Give me a couple of days to sort out some family stuff, and then we'll have that talk, but Beau," I pause for effect, looking between his eyes, "You might not like what I'm going to say."

"I figured as much." He kisses me one more time, and we part ways for the day. My heart is heavy, and my mind is filled with words I don't know how to say as I head back to my car. Knowing I have to go home and get mixed up in the family business I've tried so hard to stay out of until now.

CHAPTER 20

BEAU

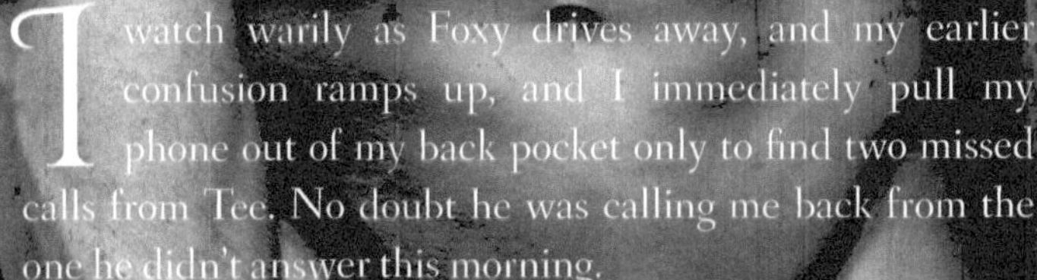

I watch warily as Foxy drives away, and my earlier confusion ramps up, and I immediately pull my phone out of my back pocket only to find two missed calls from Tee. No doubt he was calling me back from the one he didn't answer this morning.

Hitting the dial, I wait anxiously for Tee to answer, but thankfully he picks it up pretty quickly. "Man, you wouldn't believe the morning I've had," I start before he even has a chance to say hi.

I start off by explaining what happened with the young girl staying here and then tell him about how I tried to call him but when he didn't answer, I reached out to Foxy instead.

"She was adamant about bringing her family over and showing the recording of what happened. But man, they were hella intense and kind of scary," I explain and he listens quietly. "When they thought I wasn't listening, I overheard them saying something about going to the croc docks off Morality Crossing at Port Hook tonight. I think it has something to do with the women and kids that keep going missing. I mean, her dad said some stuff about keeping innocent people safe, but at the same time, I can't help but feel like her family might be into something bad. They just have a real criminal air about them, but I can't believe that Foxy would be like that. If I didn't already speak Spanish, I wouldn't have gotten even that much. I assume they just thought I was some stupid white boy or something."

"You didn't tell me Foxy was Spanish, so is Ana-Lucia. Hopefully, they get along when they meet," Tee says, completely missing the point of what I'm saying.

I roll my eyes at him. "Are you listening to me? Something is going down tonight, and I think we need to go there and see what it is." Excitement with a good dose of fear travels up my spine as I speak it out loud, but I need to know what's happening and as much as I really like Foxy, which I do, I'm not a hundred percent convinced that she's going to tell me the whole truth of what's going on. She seemed too tense and nervous every time she looked at me and then when she brushed my inquiry off, it just made me more suspicious.

"Nope," Tee answers straight away. "I'm not getting myself mixed up with someone else's illegal shit, bro. Just be patient, I'm sure there's a reasonable explanation. Maybe they work at the croc docks."

"The whole family works as mechanics, even Foxy. I told you that before. There's no reason for them to go there and why would they be all secretive about it, and I'm sure I heard them say something about a cartel." There's no way I can leave this alone. I'm way too curious for my own good, and I need to do whatever I can to get back those women and kids. I feel responsible for not being able to protect them while they were technically under my roof.

I hear Tee sigh deeply into the phone. "Please don't do

this. The whole thing sounds too dangerous, and how do you think your girlfriend's going to feel when she finds out you were tailing her family because you thought they might be criminals?"

He does have a good point there, but I add, "We won't get caught. I just want to have a quick look for myself and if you think about it, the missing people kind of also line up with the same timeline as the dog fights. What if we find an illegal dog fight at the same time and can actually do something about it? You were saying that no one has any leads on it so far."

"When I was out with Ana-Lucia, a bartender said something to us about a potential cartel moving into the area." Tee's voice comes out contemplative, and I know I've got him. "It does kind of make sense. What time did they say?"

"I didn't hear one, but if we go a bit early and hide out among the shipping containers, we should be able to see when they arrive and go from there. I'll deal with telling Foxy about it after I get some answers. One problem at a time, plus if she's in some trouble and stuck in an unhealthy family situation, I can help her get out of it." An idea comes to my mind and I ask, "If it comes down to it, would you mind if she came to stay with us for a bit until I can find her a safe new place?"

Tee agrees immediately, as I knew he would, he's the best man I know and would never turn away anyone or anything in need. He does bring up that I'm probably being paranoid though and reminds me to keep my wayward imagination under wraps until proven otherwise. But at least for now, he's agreed to come with me to figure out if anything is going on.

I really hope I'm wrong, though.

* * *

The darkness settles around us as we hunker down in the side of one of the large shipping containers. A cold chill shivers up and down my spine, even though I made a point to wear warm black clothes, ready for our sleuthing operation.

"This is a total waste of time, and I'm getting cold," Tee complains quietly, but by the way he's looking around us uneasily, it's more likely that fear is trickling in the later and darker it gets because it's spooky as hell out here at night.

Just as I'm about to answer, I freeze as a large group of heavily armed men slowly turn a corner in the distance, and I grab Tee's head, pointing his face in the direction, and he stills beside me. They're far enough off that they shouldn't be able to see us where we're hiding out, but because of a light shining above where they are, it's easy enough for us to see that they mean serious business. All of a sudden, I realize just how fucking stupid this idea was to begin with. What the fuck was I thinking? We don't even have a gun, let alone know how to shoot one.

"What do we do now?" Tee whispers shakily, obviously as freaked out as I am by the sheer size of the group and the intense-looking rifles and other terrifying-looking weapons that they're all carting around with them.

I look at the only other way out from where we are because of the water at our backs. Another group of heavily armed men slowly make their way through, guns drawn and pointing very professionally as they study their surroundings.

Pulling Tee down with me, we duck down behind the container, leaning our backs against it and breathing erratically with the sudden increase of adrenaline. "I have no fucking idea," I tell him honestly, regretting every decision I've ever made.

"You need to call your girl, dude," Tee tells me quietly. "Like now because if you don't, we very well could be shot."

I twist my head around the corner carefully while visualizing my head being blown off. I catch a glimpse of Foxy's bulky brother underneath the light at the back of the group, pointing for some of what appears to be his lackeys to span out more. *Yep. Foxy is somehow connected with this.*

My hands shake wildly as I pull my phone out and dial Foxy's number. She answers on the first ring, talking quietly, and I wonder if she's here too. "Hey, Beau, I can't talk right now."

"Don't hang up," I say quickly but quietly. "I need your help. I think I'm in big trouble."

Foxy's voice turns concerned straight away, rising in tone slightly. "What's wrong? Where are you?"

"Uh, I may have done something you're not going to like," I admit, now nervous about admitting where I am but knowing I may not have a choice. Turning my head to look around the corner again, I have to stifle a curse at how much closer the group of terrifying people are, and I swallow hard. "So, I speak Spanish."

She scoffs. "Oo-kay. That's a weird thing for me to get mad at." Her voice is clearly confused, as she should be because I'm admittedly beating around the bush because I don't know how to say, 'Your family looked like thugs, so I followed them like a stalker and now your brothers are literally going to kill me.'

"I heard your Dad and brothers talking about the docks, and I got curious, and now I think curiosity might kill this cat." I get out, squinting my face at the admission and waiting for the backlash.

For a moment Foxy doesn't say anything and then asks me slowly with a hard, angry tone. "Tell me you aren't where I think you are right now."

"I... can't do that." My voice lowers to an even quieter whisper as I hear the shuffle of feet getting closer. "I'm really going to need that help now. My housemate is with me too, and I'll feel really bad if he turns into Swiss cheese over my bad judgment."

"Me too, dude," Tee says behind me, whispering to the side of my phone. "Please hurry, Beau's girlfriend, I have someone I really need to see again, and I'm sorry."

I push him away with a fake scowl, and I hear the sound of heavy running coming from Foxy's side of the phone.

"Where are you exactly?" I ask her, and she says before hanging up, "Put your phone on silent and don't fucking move." I hear her cursing in Spanish quite harshly about how stupid I am before she hangs up, and I can't fault her for it because this is not my proudest moment. But holy hell does she have a lot to explain to me after this.

I tell Tee that she's on her way, and we hunker down, the sound of increasingly closer footfalls, like a constant reminder of our imminent death. I decide that I owe Tee big time for getting him into this situation in the first place.

CHAPTER 21

FOXY

I'm spying on what Papi and the boys are up to, way too curious not to, when I get the phone call from Beau. I go on an emotional roller coaster, from curious, to terrified for him, to fucking furious that he put himself in this kind of position.

My feet take me as fast as I can closer toward the docks where I spot Juan at the entrance of where they went in as Beau fills me in on the phone telling me where he is. Not only did he put himself in danger but also his housemate, apparently. What was he thinking?

Guilt overrides me as I hang up, and Juan sees me heading for him, a look of bafflement on his face at my being there. If I had a normal family, he would have never been in this position, to begin with.

"Chiquita, what are you doing here? Papi is gonna lose his hit if he sees you running around like this," Juan whisper-yells at me, as I get closer, his weapon loosely hanging at his side since he saw me approach. "If you wanted to be involved, you should have just asked."

"You need to let me in," I beg, grabbing his shirt, my

eyes no doubt wild. "Beau is in there with his friend, and I don't want them to get shot accidentally. Por favor, let me through."

Juan's eyes widen, and he looks toward the men spanning the docks behind us. "He's fucked if he's spotted. What the fuck is he doing here anyway?"

"It's a long story. He's on the right of the docks apparently, right on the edge of the water behind a storage container, and he has no way out. Can you get everyone to the left side long enough for me to get him out without Papi getting involved?"

My eyes plead with him, and my breath comes out ragged because of the adrenaline and fear pumping through my veins at the idea of losing Beau to my own people.

Juan shakes his head angrily, giving me a look that says this conversation isn't over, and calls Antonio, "Move everyone to the left side, Foxy's about to come through and rescue one of her fuck buddies who's hiding behind one of the containers. Make sure the guys near there know not to shoot her or the guys she's with."

I hear a string of angry curses coming through his phone before he shuts it off, giving me a look that could kill. "Well, hurry the fuck-up then before I change my mind."

Without a second to waste, I bolt down toward the area where Beau said he was, being careful all the while not to get any unnecessary attention in case an idiot gets an itchy finger.

I text Beau to give me a drop location through Google Maps and almost collapse with relief when it comes through, and I see he's not far from me.

Antonio comes into view, standing next to a few other close guys, and he shakes his head at me as he ushers me forward. I flip him the bird and keep running toward the drop location.

My heart beats hard as I round the container I believe they're behind and stop in shock at what I find. Why the fuck is Beau with Theodore? I thought his housemate was with him.

Ideas that can't possibly be true filter through my head as I stare down at both of them in shock, and Beau jumps up, hugging me close as I continue to stare down at an equally stunned Theodore. He stands up slowly as Beau says something about getting the fuck out of here, but I'm absolutely frozen to the spot until Theodore speaks, snapping me out of my shock and into reality.

"Ana-Lucia? What are you doing here?" Theodore looks at how Beau is clinging to me with his eyebrows crinkling together. "I don't understand."

Beau lets go of me, still holding my arm, and looks between us curiously before settling on Theodore. "What did you call her? This is Foxy man. Did you hit your head?"

Antonio comes around the corner and looks at both men before snorting. "Ha. Looks like you've got some explaining to do, chiquita. Hate to be you right now, but in the meantime, fuck off the lot of you before Papi finds you here because I guarantee the only greeting you'll get from him is a bullet between the eyes. He's in a hell of a mood today, and it's only going to get worse if he finds you back here with both of these bozos."

Knowing he's absolutely right, I grab one of each of their hands, insisting we move now and talk later because this connection between the three of us is the least of our problems right now.

They let me lead them along as we run out of there as

quietly as we can, Antonio agreeing to distract Papi and the group away until we're out of sight.

When we make it to Juan, he's taking a swig out of his drink bottle. When he sees me holding on to both of the guys' hands that he knows I've been messing around with, he chokes on the water in his mouth, bending over as he coughs and splutters.

"Dios mío, chiquita. What the fuck is going on?" he manages to get out, and I drop both hands, feeling suddenly self-conscious now that we are out of immediate danger. I watch him take in the two guys staring at each other with eyes full of questions, and he gets this pretty quickly, changing his face from one of anger to one of humor. "This is better than a telenovela. All we need now is someone with amnesia." He laughs loudly, then makes a shooing motion with his free hand not holding the rifle. "Now get the fuck out of here and take your problems with you." He points to the guys at my side.

Too anxious to fight with him about being a dick, I ask them where their car is, and we jog around the corner together to where Beau's car is hiding. We stop there, the silence thick enough to cut with a knife.

"You guys should go home and don't tell anyone about what you've seen today. It won't end well, and there's only so much I can do to protect you," I tell them, unable to look either of them in the eyes and backing away in the direction of my own car. "I've got to do some damage control."

I turn and start jogging away when I hear Beau call out, "Call me when you're done."

Unable to turn around and face them, I just wave my hand above my head and run all the way back to my own vehicle, my mind racing with how the fuck something like this could happen. I knew it was going to be hard to have the 'I have feelings for two guys' conversation. But never in a million years did I think they were going to know each other, let alone be the 'Foxy and Allure' of the guy world.

My mind races a million miles a minute as I drive home, unable to comprehend the situation I've found myself in. I've never been a coward in my life, but fuck if this doesn't want to make me run away with my tail in between my legs. I seriously consider changing my number and disappearing back to Sinhaven, then having to admit to either Theodore or Beau how much I feel for the other. Both of their looks of betrayal when they realized what I did, keeps slamming into my mind like a punch in the chest.

I try not to think about the fact that right now they've got to be talking to each other and asking questions about who I am to them. But I can't help it, and it makes me sick to my stomach.

Holy shit. I fucked Beau in the room right beside Theodore and didn't have a fucking clue. How could I have known? Beau called his housemate Tee, and Theodore called his friend Bro whenever he talked about him. It certainly doesn't help that they both knew me by different names. Why the fuck didn't I just give Theodore my real name? Then this would have come to a head way earlier when things weren't so fucking complicated.

How is this my life right now?

How could I fuck up so badly?

I pull into my driveway and look up to see my mami waiting for me, her face somber and I just know that one of my brothers, probably Juan, filled her in.

She comes around to the driver's door and opens it, widening her arms for me without a word, and I'm in her embrace in seconds crying on her shoulder as if I'm not the kick-ass bitch I've always claimed to be, but I am human after all and right now I need my mami.

As I let out all the disappointment at myself and the inevitable fear growing inside me of losing something I never knew I needed before I even had a chance to really admit how much I needed it, my mami holds me tight without an ounce of judgment or condemnation.

When I start calming down, I let her guide me into the house and toward the kitchen, where she sits me on the bench and starts making me a cup of tea quietly. Not one word has come out of her mouth because what could she say?

"Gracias Mami," I snivel when she passes me the warm cup and I take a sip of the delicious brew before I finally raise my eyes up to look into hers, and to my relief, I only find love and understanding staring back at me.

My mami has always had strong views about things and to my own shame I never thought she would react this way or support me the way she has tonight over such a controversial issue.

She smiles at me warmly and sits at my side, sipping at her own tea and just keeping me company while I mentally try to build up enough courage to come to terms with what I have to do. I need to come clean and then let them both go because I will never come between a friendship built on years of love and support. When I know exactly what it feels like to have that kind of person in my own life, no matter how much I've grown to feel for them both.

CHAPTER 22

THEODORE

What in the actual hell is going on? First I'm dragged into finding missing people and animals, then I'm surrounded by some scary ass motherfuckers with guns that are apparently connected to Beau's girlfriend Foxy. All of a sudden Ana-Lucia is standing in front of me, and he's calling her Foxy. This can not be happening right now!

I stare at her, completely stunned and speechless as Beau prattles on holding onto the girl I'm pretty sure I've fallen in love with like he has some kind of claim on her. Ana-Lucia's eyes meet mine with the same level of confusion and horror that I'm sure is mirrored in mine, but she doesn't correct him, and I can't seem to move.

Coming to my senses, I ask her what she's doing here, using the name I know her as, and Beau seems as perplexed as I am. Ana-Lucia's brother fucking laughs at us before reminding us to get the hell out of there, and I get the distinct feeling that we really are in as much danger as my gut told me we were. Who even is this girl?

A mixture of feelings encompasses me as we quietly

escape the dockyard from anger to sadness, with a good dose of impending doom to go along with the scary situation I can't believe I'm even in.

With her other brother behind us and back at our car unscathed, I let out a small breath of relief, only to be reminded that we have a new issue right in front of us as Ana-Lucia tells us to go home and not tell anyone about what happened. She finishes with a quip about talking later and disappearing into the night. All the while looking everywhere but at us.

We get into the car and Beau drives us away from the surreal scene. At first, we don't speak, just stare out into the night before us, falling down our own rabbit holes of whom the fuck is this person we're inadvertently connected to.

Beau exhales forcefully and asks me outright, not taking his eyes off the road. "Is she the Ana-Lucia you've been seeing?" His voice comes out rough, as if he hadn't used it for a while.

"Yep," I reply simply, not needing to ask the same question in return when it was more than obvious that she is the same girl.

"Well, this is fucked," he states, and I nod in agreement. "Why do you think her name is Ana-Lucia?"

That's what I'd like to know, too. "That's what she told me her name was." Did she lie to me or to him? Maybe her name isn't either of those and she's been lying to us both.

A whistle comes out of my friend's mouth and he shakes his head. "I wonder why she lied to you about it. Her name is definitely Foxy, Dude, my mechanic recommended her by name, and it's what her family calls her at work too."

Well, there you go. I guess I'm the only chump in this situation after all. "Guess I was just some kind of side piece she wasn't planning on keeping around. Sorry to get in your guys' way, dude." My tone comes out as bitter as I feel, and I try to mentally remind myself that it's not Beau's fault, as he clearly had no idea. But how the hell am I meant to be happy for them after everything I've been through with her? After everything I pictured building with her.

"Bro, don't be like that. I'm sure there's a good explanation for it," he says trying to comfort me, which is crazy because there's no doubt he's hurt by this too. "We'll give her a call when we get home and see what the fuck is going on. I mean, she seemed as surprised as us, right? Foxy's probably feeling super overwhelmed after being faced with the two of us being friends and in such an intense situation. Which is a whole other thing, what on earth is her family into? I legit thought we were going to die, man."

He's not wrong. Never in a million years did I think that she was from a crime family. I mean her dad and brothers were frightening for sure and way intense but in some kind of criminal organization, no. It kind of feels like I'm in some kind of action film that I didn't sign up for, and the only thing it's missing is Liam Neeson.

"I don't know about you dude, but I need some answers, and soon because my head is a mess, and I think I might throw up." I press my head against the cold glass window, trying to keep my breathing slow and not think about the fact that I almost died, and my best friend has been fucking my woman. And that I can't even get mad at him about it. Talk about a shitty night filled with shitty revelations.

With a grunt of agreement from Beau, we sit quietly the rest of the way, probably both thinking about what we're going to say and how tonight can end in any way other than in misery for everyone involved.

A loud bang has me sitting up in bed, startled and confused. Looking around wildly with my heart pounding hard inside my chest, my papi comes into view, his hand gripping my door handle hard and his face as cold as steel.

The fury radiating from him immediately informs me that my brothers told him about last night. I look at the window, where the light of early morning shines through, and I realize he's been out all night.

"I don't even know where to begin," Papi booms at me in a terrifying voice that I don't think I've ever heard directed at me before. "First you whore yourself around making a fool out of me and your family, and now you are letting these two gringo's get involved in our business. Do you have any fucking idea how much trouble you're in? You're lucky your brothers helped hide them from me because I would have put a bullet through their brains without a second thought. Do you have any idea the kind of pressure I have on me right now? I'm trying to run a cartel and keep my people and family safe from dying in an all-out war that seems inevitable right now, and you are making a mockery out of us all. Everything is on the line. Everything and everyone," he shouts.

My stomach tightens at the idea and the fact that I know he's telling the truth. "Papi," my voice betrays my fear as it trembles. "They didn't know what they were doing, and they won't talk about what they saw. I promise. Please, don't hurt them. It's all my fault, and I'm sorry."

"Shut the fuck up," he roars with rage and Mami comes running into the room, standing between us with her hands on his chest, pleading for him to calm down, but he doesn't even look down at her with all of his attention and fury aimed at me. "Give me one good reason why I should let either of them live."

Without even thinking, my mouth blurts out, "I love them, Papi."

Straight away, I realize that was the wrong thing to say, as his face turns a molten red and he moves Mami to the side. He storms into my room and leans over me with a shaking hand, pointing to the door of my bedroom. "Get out of my house."

Mami wails loudly, coming behind him and dropping to her knees, gripping onto his legs. "Don't do this."

Juan and Antonio crowd the doorway, looking on in shock. Juan's face drips with guilt, telling me it was him who told our Papi about Theodore and Beau being at the docks. Neither of them moves, indecision on whether to intervene playing out in their expressions.

"You have done enough damage to our name," Papi continues, ignoring Mami's pleas. "Get your things and get out of my house, you clearly don't belong here anymore. Allure living that way is one thing, but my daughter, no! I won't have it. If I ever see either of them again, I will kill them on the spot, do you hear me?"

Papi brushes Mami's hands off him and storms out, stopping at the doorway as my brothers swiftly disperse, not wanting to get caught in the crossfire. He turns back to me and coldly says, "I don't have a daughter. You have one day to be off my property."

He leaves me feeling cold and dejected, Mami screaming tears for the both of us on the floor, and all I can do is stare at the empty door frame. Unable to come to terms with how fucked I really am and that my papi, my hero, just told me to get out of his life and that I don't exist to him anymore.

"I'll fix this," Mami sobs out, getting up and stumbling out of the door after him, crying all the while.

I hear her wailing down the other end of the house and outside, before Papi's car roars to life and takes off down the driveway, leaving Mami sounding as broken as I feel.

"Lo siento." Juan's voice comes out smaller than usual, and I look up to find him at the end of my bed. I must have spaced out because I don't remember him coming into my room. "I couldn't keep it from him, and I tried to downplay it, but he... Well, he didn't take it well. He's stressed, chiquita; he'll come around when he calms down, and I'll try to talk to him."

I look back at the door without a word because what is there left to say? We both know that Papi won't change his mind, no matter how much Juan tries to convince me otherwise, which is why his voice was so soft without an ounce of conviction. I'm out and that's all there is to it.

Juan comes around to the side of the bed and pulls my blankets off my legs. "Get changed, and I'll meet you in the gym. You've got to get it out, one way or another, and I'm not going to let you just sit here."

He's right. I need to focus on getting this build-up of emotions out of me before I break down completely, and regardless of what Papi wants me to do, I'm not leaving Beastville until I've found these motherfuckers.

I flip my legs out of the bed and stand up as Juan disappears, closing the door behind him. I do everything I can to focus my energy on the idea that I still have things to do and not my papi's face when he looks at me.

My head shakes violently, dropping curls all around me from the loose bun I was sleeping with. I need to get the image out of my head. I pop my eyes open and get changed as quickly as I can, a mantra of 'I have shit to do' on repeat in my mind.

I'm changed and ready in record time, my feet flying down the stairs and out of the house with a renewed energy set on feeling and giving pain. I hope Juan is ready because I have a fire burning bright that only keeps building with every passing second.

Thankfully, Mami isn't anywhere to be seen, and I enter the gym without having to interact with anyone. I notice Antonio on the side of the ring boxing on a bag, while Juan holds on to it, but the moment I walk into the ring, Juan lets go and jumps in with me all ready to spar.

He comes over and wraps up my hands, which is probably for the best when I'm feeling like this, for the both of us. Antonio keeps quiet, thankfully, purposely keeping his focus on the bag in front of him, giving me a semblance of privacy. Sometimes he's not a douchebag.

We tap gloves and instantly start to dance around each other, Juan deciding on a more defensive style than usual, giving me the out to be as aggressive as I need to be. I get a few good hits in, but mostly Juan manages to block and swerve the majority of my attack.

I push my body harder and faster letting out all of my anger, all of my fear, and all of my regrets, but when I get to unlocking the sadness, I find myself momentarily faltering. A strangled sound slips out of me and I almost trip over my own foot, the sweat pouring off my body, also drips into my eyes.

Tears which I try to tell myself are just sweat start to drip off my chin and I use my arm to wipe at it with no avail. Juan steps back, letting his hands drop a bit as he watches me. "I'm fine," I rasp, completely unconvincing even to my own ears. "Hit me," I demand.

Juan licks his lips, uncertainty in his gaze as my tears continue to fall despite me trying in vain to ignore them. His arms lower completely, and he steps into my space. "It's alright." His voice is barely audible, but I shake my head at him.

"I said, hit me." I need the pain, I need anything that will make me feel something different from this overwhelming ache in my heart and Papi's words come back to me, "I don't have a daughter".

A harsh sob rips out, and I shake my head. No. I'm not doing this. I try to focus on Juan, but my eyes are filled with what I refuse to admit is anything other than sweat, and both of my forearms wipe at them wildly. "I don't have a daughter."

Juan's hands grab at me suddenly, and he pulls me in close, holding me tightly to his chest. We're both covered in sweat and any other time I'd deck him because it's gross, and he stinks, but instead my stupid body starts to shake violently, as more and more sobs flow out of me, completely unchecked.

My knees give out, and I collapse on the floor, with Juan following me down, never letting me go as I give in to the pain I desperately want to deny but can't.

"It's alright, chiquita. I'm here for you, and you can cry as long as you want." Juan soothes the hair away from my face, his tone soothing and without even a hint of judgment at my uncharacteristic emotional outburst.

I decide that for once in my life, it's okay to let my big brother come to my aid. But what surprises me, even more, is how Antonio joins us there, silently rubbing my back in a show of support that I didn't know he was capable of.

I may not have a Papi anymore, but at least my mami and brothers have my back.

CHAPTER 24

FOXY

Fuck my life.

I hold on to my phone tightly, looking down at Beau's name on the screen, knowing I have to call them. By the look on Theodore's face the last time I called, Beau will be the best person to break the silence with.

Without a doubt, I know what I have to do, even if it hurts me to do it. I will not be responsible for coming in between the two of them, and the way they talk about each other has always been with great respect and affection. I just hope the damage hasn't already been done.

I press my finger down on the screen and bring it to my ear, my nerves wreaking havoc in my stomach. The phone rings several times before Beau picks up and says hello, his voice coming across as unsure, and I know I'm doing the right thing.

"Is Theodore with you?" I ask, wanting to cut to the chase and get this over with as quickly as possible. "I think it would be best if you put me on loudspeaker, so we can all talk together."

"Did you want to come over? It might be the better

option," Beau tells me slowly, but I refuse, telling him I'd rather not. My inner coward that I've only recently become familiar with knows I can only do this over the phone, or I'll chicken out completely.

"Hey, I'm here," Theodore says, hearing both of them makes my heart squeeze at how real this is and how stupid I am for not realizing sooner.

I pull my big girl panties on, suck in a breath to give me strength, and go for it. "Good. I want to start by saying that I'm sorry for asking this of you, but I need what happened with my family at the docks to remain quiet, if anything comes back to you, you will both be in very serious danger, from both the people we're after and my family. My papi has made it very clear that he has no issue making a permanent decision that you won't live to regret. Do you understand?"

I'm more than aware that my words are coming out harsh, but I need to be unapproachable and cold if I have any chance of getting through this. And I don't want either of them left with any regret about letting me go. If they think I'm a bitch, then it will help them heal and forget all about me.

They don't answer me straight away, so I take the opportunity to keep going. "I really do regret either of you getting involved in that, and I had no intention of revealing that part of my life to you. Let me also make it clear that I have no physical involvement in that area of my family's business normally and the only reason I was anywhere near it at that time was because I couldn't just sit by and not help when women, children, and animals were being mistreated and in so much danger."

"Did they find anything?" Beau asks when I take another big breath.

"No, but when they do, and they will, it will come to an end straight away. I don't have a perfect family, but they have a strict moral code which they make sure anyone in their territory sticks to."

Theodore's voice comes next, slower and more cautious than Beau's has been. "What do you mean by territory?"

"The less you know, the better, but I can say that you are in no danger as long as you keep out of it and stay quiet. They're just trying to rescue those taken and stop it from happening in the future." I try to reassure them, but without giving them more than is necessary. "As for the 'us' situation," I pause again, closing my eyes and gaining all the courage I have. "I'm also sorry about that. I had absolutely no idea that you two knew each other, let alone were as close as you are. I'm so very sorry if it has caused friction between the two of you, which is why I'm taking myself out of the equation."

I stop talking, giving them a chance to say something, but only silence greets me on the other end of the phone, but I take it as confirmation that they understood exactly what I'm saying.

"I never lied to either of you saying that we were exclusive because I may be a lot of things, but I'm not a liar. However, it doesn't change the fact that somehow I missed the connection that you both shared with each other. I have enjoyed getting to know you both and maybe under different circumstances I could have seen myself taking a risk with one of you when I hadn't dared to do that in the past, but it just happened to work out this way."

"Foxy," Beau says quietly, and the longing in his voice makes me bite the inside of my cheek, needing to stay focused and not give in to how much this is hurting to say.

I go on, "Thank you for everything. You are both great

guys and I wish you all the best. When my family clears up the whole situation I will let you know, so you have peace of mind, and I will be over to pick up Freja tomorrow to bring her home, but apart from that I think it's best to limit communication going forward to help all of us move on from this."

Beau asks me, "Is this what you truly want?" As Theodore remains deadly quiet in the background.

"Please don't make this harder for me than it already is?" I beg quietly. "None of us wanted this, that much I know, so let's respect each other until the end. I am sorry for everything, I'll see you in the morning, Theodore. Don't worry, I'll be in and out of your hair as quickly as I can. Is it alright if I come in before you open, so I don't have to see anyone?"

"That's fine. Is seven an alright time for you?" Theodore asks in a professional tone, and I agree before saying goodbye and hanging up on them both and cradling my head in my hands.

I rock back and forth slightly replaying the conversation I just had and tell myself that it's good that they didn't try to fight for me because it would have just made it more complicated but my heart rips apart anyway, wondering if they ever cared about me as much as I grew to care about them.

My mind goes back to when I told Papi that I loved them, and I wonder if that was true or if I just blurted it out on instinct. I can't possibly love them both after only such a small amount of time, could I? Both of them? Fuck I hope not because I can't handle feeling this kind of pain for much longer. It tears me apart, and I literally don't know what to do as I keep rocking back and forth, completely overwhelmed and shaking.

A light tapping sounds on my door, and I look up to find Mami's head leaning into my room. "Dinner's ready. I let you miss lunch, but you need to eat, so come downstairs. I talked to Papi, and he's agreed that you can stay the week to get your affairs in order."

After Papi got back this morning, Mami went completely loca on him, and I could hear them yelling back and forth for about an hour before the house became quiet again. I decided not to go down to lunch because I wasn't hungry from feeling so sick to my stomach about everything, and also because I didn't want to have to face everyone, especially my papi. His disappointed face is already tattooed in my mind forever, I don't need a replay of it.

I know there's no way that Mami is going to let me get away with not coming down for a second meal, so I decide to make an effort and eat a few bites before I disappear upstairs again.

My feet carry me downstairs automatically as if I'm in a daze because sadness is steering my ship at the moment. I take a seat in my usual spot, my brothers already at the table as Mami flutters around, setting the table for dinner.

Papi comes in and gruffly sits down, refusing to even look at me. When Mami dishes up our dinner, she puts a plate in front of everyone except for Papi.

Juan and Antonio start eating quietly and Mami makes a point of banging things around the table as loudly as she can, clearly making a point that she's not happy. Papi looks at her expectantly, but she just starts eating, asking Juan how his new girlfriend has been going. He's the only one of my brothers currently seeing anyone, but it's really new and not at all serious.

Papi clears his throat and asks, "Am I not eating?"

Mami purposefully ignores him, and my brothers look at each other and then at me nervously, and I just shrug. Antonio gets up to grab a plate for our Papi, but Mami slams her hand down on the table hard, looking square at Antonio. "Sit down until you have finished your meal." He sits straight back down and whispers a quick apology to Papi.

Even though Papi may be the head of the family, when Mami is mad, we all know whose side to take because if you piss her off all hell will break loose.

"So, I'm meant to just sit here and starve, then," Papi grumbles, leaning back against the chair with his arms crossed tightly.

Mami looks at me when she talks, but clearly for his ears. "It's a shame your Papi doesn't know how to get off his own ass and get himself food. It's also a shame that he thinks he can tell my babies to get out of my house without my permission. Pass me the salt, please."

I lean over and give her the salt, not replying as we all notice Papi getting more and more tense by the second, before he gets up harshly, his chair scratching along the hardwood floor. He stomps into the kitchen, getting himself a plate and filling it with food from the kitchen. Papi comes back to the table and sits down hard, eating this food with a faked ravenous hunger.

My brothers and I are completely silent, barely eating a thing, and then Mami says, "Seems his feet and arms work, even if his sense doesn't."

"I don't have to sit here and listen to this." Papi drops his fork to the table with a clatter.

I pray that this will stop, feeling completely responsible but also knowing if I say one word they will both jump down my throat instead. And of course, Mami has to push it even further, throwing in a, "Then leave," which has Papi promptly storming out the door.

She keeps eating as if nothing happened and continues to ask Juan random light questions about the girl he's seeing. When we leave the table for the night, she tells us that she wants to clean up and reminds us that our oldest brothers will be back in the morning. Fingers crossed they manage to calm our parents down a bit, but knowing Alonzo, he might add fuel to the fire for fun.

CHAPTER 25

THEODORE

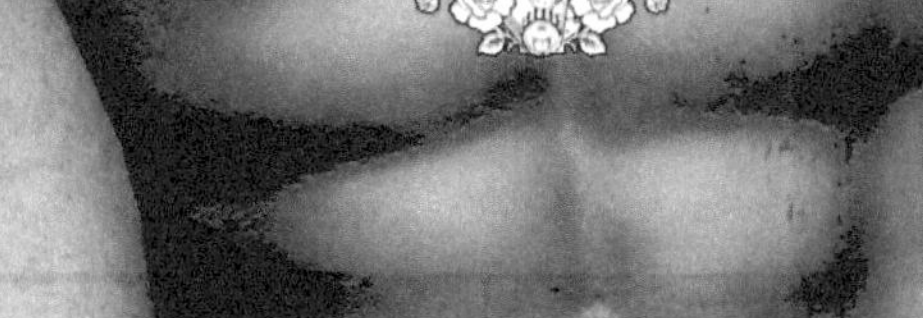

y eyes keep glancing at the time as seven draws nearer. I came into work at the ungodly hour of five o'clock just because I couldn't sleep last night knowing that Ana-Lucia, or should I say Foxy, is going to see me today. It could possibly also be the fact that I can't get the phone call from her yesterday out of my head.

I don't know what I was expecting from her when everything came to light, but I wasn't prepared for a five-minute phone call, with a sorry, thanks, and see ya later. Maybe the feelings that I thought had grown between us had all been one-sided, but I truly doubt that because like she said, she doesn't lie, and her feelings were always pretty clear. But then again she told me her name was Ana-Lucia and that was clearly a lie. Perhaps everything was a lie, I don't even know anymore. All I know is that my heart fucking hurts all the time and I stupidly miss her already.

The revving of a familiar car pulls into the lot out the front, and I quickly check my clothes and sniff my underarms, like I've somehow started smelling in the last few minutes. *Get a hold of yourself; she's just here to pick up Freja.*

I try to make myself look busy as I go behind the register, checking the calendar on the computer, even though I'm not really noticing a thing it says.

The door opens, and I look up as if I'm surprised she's here and not like I've been waiting for hours like a complete idiot. I smile professionally and wave her inside, refusing to notice how good she looks in her figure-hugging jeans or how tired she looks. "Freja is ready to go, you just need to collect her."

Without taking off her huge sunglasses, she strolls in and thanks me, holding onto the familiar red collar and leash that we bought together when we were at Storytime Lakes. My stomach drops at the picture-perfect memory we made together, and I can't help but wonder if she will remember it whenever she looks at Freja's new things like I would have.

"Has she had breakfast?" Foxy asks me in a rougher than usual voice, making me think that she didn't sleep very well either last night. I nod and she thanks me.

We walk out back together, and Freja's tail happily waves in the air at the sight of her new owner, and I'm glad they found each other. If nothing else good came out of this, at least there's that. I watch as she crouches down and lets Freja out of her crate and from the side I can see her eyes are swollen under her glasses, and I realize why she hasn't taken them off. I guess we aren't the only ones hurting after all.

Beau and I have barely said two words to each other since the night at the docks, other than the initial discussion over the fact that we were practically dating the same person. It's been really tense around the home, but not because either of us is mad at the other; it's more due to us both needing time to process what it all means and where we can go from here. I mean, seriously, what can I possibly say to make this an easier process to go through? It's the first time we've experienced any kind of strain on our friendship since we first became friends, but our relationship has always been so close that I know we'll get through this together.

I have no idea if Beau and Foxy have been messaging each other or talking when I'm not around because I wanted to give her the space she's made clear that she wants. I'm definitely curious, but I also don't really want to know. I don't think I could handle it if my best friend and the person I have feelings for chose each other instead of me.

"Hola, perrita, are you ready to come to your new home?" Foxy strokes Freja's hair and carefully does up her collar behind the cone that she still has to wear for a while longer. "Mama's gonna take good care of you."

It brings me back into the present, and I hold the door to the lobby open for them as they pass through together. Freja is doing incredibly well and has already made an almost full recovery. I have no doubt that she will be running around happily and playing before too long.

Foxy looks completely closed off as she passes me by, not even looking directly at me, or at least not that I can tell through her thick glasses. It doesn't change the fact that I can see how defeated she looks just by how she's holding her body. Foxy's usually confident and powerful presence is reduced to a mere shadow of her former glory with her head down, her strides slow, and her shoulders hunched over.

It takes everything I have not to pull her into my arms

and tell her that everything's going to be alright, and that I'm here for her whether she likes it or not. But something inside me refuses to let me move or speak. The fear holds me back from taking a leap of faith and throwing caution to the wind because what if she pushes me away? What kind of friend would I be to Beau if I did to him the very thing I am scared of him doing to me?

I follow them out to the parking lot and watch quietly as she puts Freja into the backseat of her car. Foxy goes to her door but pauses before opening it, her head down and back to me.

"I'm so sorry, Theodore. I never meant for this to happen." I watch as she lifts her arm up to quickly wipe away a rogue tear that escaped from under her glasses before she turns to face me. "Everything I had with you was real, I need you to know that. Take care of yourself, and I'll let you know when the dog fighting ring has been caught."

She gets in the car quickly before I can reply, but a question I desperately need the answer to has me striding to her car door and knocking on the window as she starts up the car.

After a second I breathe out in relief as she lowers the window looking up at me with those wide glasses showing my reflection and I ask, "Why did you lie to me about your name?"

"I didn't," she replies, confusing me, but adds, "My full name is Ana-Lucia Patricia Veronica Hernandez, but I've always been called Foxy for short since I was little. I told you, I've never lied to you about anything. Goodbye, Theodore, be happy."

I stare in a kind of shock as she drives away and guilt eats away at me for doubting her, for letting her go, for my friendship, and for not demanding she stay with me.

Despair fills me, and I stare off into the distance where she disappeared for much too long, only snapping out of it when Millie pulls in and asks what I'm doing, and I answer honestly, "I have no idea."

CHAPTER 26
FOXY

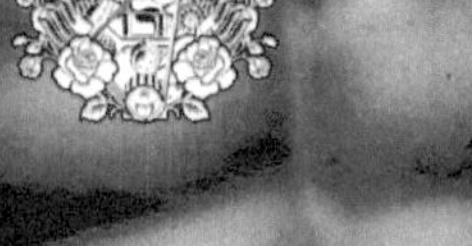

During my drive home, I feel numb, and I get there on autopilot replaying my interaction with Theodore in my mind over and over again, picking apart everything I did wrong.

Freja sits like a good girl in the backseat for the whole journey, content just looking out the window. I put the window down halfway, so she had some fresh air, and she seems to be loving it. The downside however is that the air is circulating a good amount of white fur throughout my car, but it's worth it.

I pull up in front of my house, happy to know Papi and my brothers are at work. At least I don't have to deal with them right now. Mario and Alonzo got home this morning about the same time I went to pick up Freja, missing them by probably minutes.

When I go around and clip Freja's leash to her collar, I'm surprised to find Alonzo coming out of the front door with his usual swagger in full force. His half smile greets me, and he pulls me into a massive hug, and I find myself sagging in relief that at least he isn't mad at me too. I wasn't a hundred percent sure how he and Mario were going to feel about everything.

"Missed you, chiquita," he says, holding me tight, then he leans back and looks down at Freja with a huge grin. "And who's this pretty girl?" He kneels down before her, giving her love and scratches while telling her she's a good girl.

Alonzo and I have always had the most in common; he's just like me in the way that he feels way more comfortable around animals than people. We are in agreement that most humans suck, while no animal can do wrong. I have a feeling that Freja is going to get more spoiled by him than me.

"She's mine, so don't get any ideas," I fake grumble. "How come you're not at the garage? I assumed you'd both go straight there, the workaholics that you are."

Alonzo laughs and stands up, putting his arm around my shoulder and leading me inside. "Normally I would, but I missed my little sister, and I have it on good authority that you won't be hanging around much longer." We walk inside, and I look around nervously, not expecting the same kind of greeting from Mario, who's the spitting image of our Papi, in looks and temperament. "Don't worry, it's just me here, the others are at work. I thought it might be the only opportunity that we'd have to catch up properly without getting interrupted. Go and set up what your pup needs, and then we'll have a chat. I'll be in the den."

He walks off, and I lead Freja out back, where I'd set up a special fenced area that is all for her. It is filled with toys, a fancy-ass dog house and dog bed, and a watering station I got built into the outside wall.

I let her off the lead and watch as she walks around slowly, sniffing every corner and checking out everything I got for her. I use that time to fill her dog bowl and make sure the water is topped up and fresh.

"How do you like it, pretty girl?" She won't be able to get into the dog house until after her cone has been taken off, and I want her to take it easy while she recuperates. I watch as she relieves herself and then carefully lies down on the grass, lying in the sun and closing her eyes.

Deciding it's best to leave her there if she's feeling comfortable, I go back inside, leaving the back door open for her, if she wants to come in. I head to the den, picking up two Pepsis on the way through for us to drink.

I hand Alonzo his drink and sit across from him in a matching gargantuan brown leather armchair. My body leans back, and I take a big sip of the refreshing drink, waiting for the third degree I'm no doubt about to get.

"What happened?" he asks outright, and I just fill him in on everything, leaving nothing out and not bothering with any kind of sugar-coating. To his credit, Alonzo just sits back patiently, listening to everything without any reaction whatsoever until I get to the end.

"So what you're telling me is that you bewitched some poor fuckers, they stumbled on shit they shouldn't have, Papi thinks he has some kind of right to decide who you fuck, Mami is a sneeze away from punching him, and you have to move out in a few days?" Alonzo ticks off his finger as he goes. "Oh, and you're a fucking idiot for pushing away two decent guys that seem to like you the way you are even though you're a cunt most of the time? Is that everything?"

"Fuck you. I'm not a cunt," I growl out, and he laughs heartily, shaking his head. "Okay, fine, but I haven't been a cunt to them."

Alonzo raises an eyebrow and says, "Really? You don't

think dumping them like a sack of potatoes at the first hurdle is a bit cunty? Alright, if you insist."

He may have a point, but I refuse to admit that, instead

I answer, "Well, what should I have done then Mr. know-it-all? Since you have such an extensive dating history." Alonzo never dates anyone, ever. He says it's because he has too many demons, so there's no space left for a woman, but I call bullshit. One day he's going to meet someone that will tame his stupid ass, and I want a front-row seat to that shit.

"If you want my honest opinion," he pauses, giving me an opportunity to tell him to fuck off again, but I actually really respect Alonzo's advice, I always have. "You should have told Papi to get over it because you're a grown-ass woman and can fuck whoever you want. There's no way he's going to enforce you leaving this house unless he plans on getting rid of Mami too because she might actually kill him if he tries. And as for the guys, if they're worth their weight, then they will get over the idea of you being something they can possess and share you. They already live together, so what does it matter if they also share the person they love, if they love you enough."

I'm not sure if he's wise, stupid, or just good at making difficult stuff sound easy, but I love him all the same. "I never said they love me," I correct him, and he shrugs noncommittally, downing the last of his Pepsi. "I'm serious, I don't think they feel the same as I do, and I can't expect them to do that for someone they don't love."

"We'll see about that. I mean, if they don't fight for you then you're right, they don't love you. If that's the case, they don't deserve you. If you want I can take a finger from each of them you can have as a keepsake, it'll teach them a lesson they won't soon forget about breaking my sister's heart because you just admitted that you love them and as a big brother it's my duty to grant you souvenirs when cockheads fuck with you." I love the way Alonzo can say such intense shit and look bored at the same time because he is one hundred percent serious. He does like his souvenirs.

I rub my face in exasperation. "I'm going to go with a no, but thanks anyway," I mumble into my hands loud enough for him to hear. I look up to find him with his trademark side smile and add, "I just want them to move on and be happy and as soon as this cartel shit is sorted, I'm out of here. I messaged Allure, and she said Freja and I can stay with them until I can get my own place since I lost the last one when I moved. It should be easy enough to find a garage to work at in Sinhaven. They don't exactly have the best mechanics down there except for Mike's Garage. I've only heard great things about that place, but they don't have much staff turnover because they're so good to work for."

"Whatever you want, you know I've got your back, if the others want to walk around ball-less then let them. Who gives a shit what their opinions are, but I do have to warn you," Alonzo scratches at his jaw in thought. "You'd better keep your boy toys away from Mario. He's of the opinion that Juan should have shot them the second he heard they were in the docks, and is mad as fuck that they're still walking around."

My sigh is long and drawn out because I kind of had a feeling that he'd be like that. It's probably a good thing I did break it off with Theodore and Beau for that reason alone. I wouldn't be able to trust Mario or Papi not popping them off when I wasn't around, even if I'd only been with one of them.

Alonzo stands up and comes around the table to stand beside me, with his hand out for me to take. I grab it, and he pulls me up and out of the chair and into his arms, he's always been a big hugger with me. It's a shame he doesn't date because someone out there would love this kind of attention, and a man that would literally remove the body parts of her enemies. I smile at the thought. Yep, that's the kind of sister-in-law that I could get behind.

"No matter what, I love you, little sis, and I will always be on your side." He ruffles my hair, fucking up my hairdo and instantly pissing me off, regardless of how sweet his words were. I pull back and scowl at him, trying to fix my now stray curls, and he looks down at me with a soft smile and adds, like it's a sweet gesture and not psychotic, "Let me know if you change your mind about their fingers?"

"You're a real freak, you know that, right?" I ask, a laugh escaping despite myself.

With a wide grin, he nods, "And you love me for it. Now go check on your pup before I steal her love and make her my bitch."

"Hey, hey. Don't talk about her like that. She's not some piece of meat," I growl out, squinting my eyes. "You know she doesn't swing that way."

"All bitches love me, human or dog." Alonzo laughs loudly, and I walk off, flipping him the finger over my shoulder, making him laugh harder.

I stop at the door and look back at him, standing there with his arms crossed and genuine humor in his eyes, "I love you dickhead, and thanks for not being like everyone else."

Turning, I get the fuck out of there before I let feelings take over again. I only just got through this morning without breaking down, I'm not starting now.

CHAPTER 27

BEAU

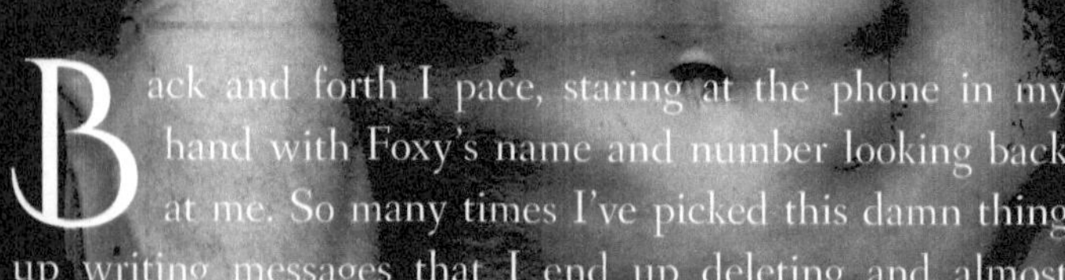

Back and forth I pace, staring at the phone in my hand with Foxy's name and number looking back at me. So many times I've picked this damn thing up writing messages that I end up deleting and almost calling repeatedly.

This whole thing is driving me crazy, and I'm not the only one. I've noticed the way Tee keeps staring at his own phone, which he purposefully puts on the other end of any room he's in, no doubt to keep from behaving the way I am right now.

One call can't hurt. I can use the excuse that I need to check up on the whole cartel issue and if she's heard any news about the people taken. Which is also something that is weighing heavy on my mind.

I've increased security at all of my shelters, going so far as to have a team of bodyguards at each location for the women to use when they need to leave for any reason. So far it's working because no one has been taken and everyone is feeling a lot safer having them around. It costs a pretty penny, but it's undoubtedly worth it if it means the safety of the people in my care.

I press Foxy's number and bring it to my ear, only to be told by a robotic voice that I can't get through to that number. Did she fucking block me? No way! She wouldn't, would she?

Trying again I only get the same response, so I opt for sending a message which, once again, doesn't get through. This whole time, I've been freaking out about contacting Foxy, and she's just up and blocked me.

It's for the best. I tell myself, trying to remain calm as I sit on the edge of the couch, squeezing my phone way too tightly in my palm. I think about how much she meant to Tee and how off he's been, and my heart drops. What if she blocked him too? It's been a couple of days since she picked up Freja, and he hasn't mentioned her since, so maybe he hasn't even tried to contact her.

Curiosity gets the better of me and the second Tee walks in the door from work, less than half an hour later, I practically pounce on the poor guy.

"Have you tried to call Foxy?" We've had a silent agreement between us not to mention her name but fuck that. I need to know. "She's blocked me, and I can't get through to her, and she hasn't been to work all week."

Tee put his briefcase down on the coffee table and raises his eyebrows at me. "You've been to her work? What are you stalking her now?"

Maybe a little bit, but that's not the point. "Answer me, can you get a hold of her or not? Is she alright?"

With my last question, his facial features tighten, telling me he still gives as much of a shit as I do. "Do you think something might have happened to her?" Tee asks, his brow deeply furrowed. "Wouldn't her family have contacted one of us if she was missing?"

"Why the fuck would they do that? What if they're the ones that have hurt her or sent her away or something? Give me your phone?" I demand with my hand out, freaking out a little more now that I've seen my worry mirrored in my best friend.

"No," Tee says simply. My mouth opens in protest at his flat refusal, but he continues effectively, shutting me up. "I haven't been able to contact her since she left with Freja. I called to see if they got home alright because she didn't look very good when she left, but I figured she just wanted a clean break and didn't want me to call her."

I go silent, coming to terms that my friend has been holding on to this for days and never said anything to me. A part of me was hoping that he didn't have the same depth of feeling for her that I did, but he gave in and called her straight after he saw her last.

If it meant the two people that meant the most to me in the world could find true happiness if they stayed together, I would have stepped back and supported their relationship. Yes, I would have died a bit inside every time I saw them together with me on the outs, but it would also be worth it to see them smile and laugh. They both deserve to be happy, and I could just love her quietly. It's not ideal, but it could be enough. Maybe.

"What do you mean, she didn't look well?" I latch on to the words that didn't sink in until now. "Was she hurt or has the flu or something?"

Tee walks past me and sits on the couch I abandoned when he walked through the door. With a heavy sigh, he explains, "No, it just seemed like she'd been crying a lot, and it was like all the light and joy were missing. I don't think walking out on us was as easy for her as we originally thought it was. Perhaps she had real feelings after all and it wasn't so one-sided." He leans forward, placing his elbows on his knees, and roughly rubs his face up and down in his palms. "I felt like shit for being so formal with her at work when she told me her real name was Ana-Lucia, she just uses her nickname Foxy instead. This whole time I'd been hanging on that she'd lied to me because she didn't care about me, but now... now it feels like I've been punched in the guts all over again." He looks up at me with wide eyes, as if he just realized who he was talking to about this. "I'm sorry, dude, that's selfish of me. Pretend I didn't say anything."

I really look at my friend and take in how haggard he looks, and it's like looking at my own reflection. This is the worst situation because at the same time as I've come to the realization that I want to fight for Foxy regardless of how fucking terrifying her family is. Because I love her just the way she is, even if she loves both me and Tee. I also know I can't do anything that would complicate or ruin my friendship with Tee. Just because I would happily live that way and share my world with them both, even if it meant they were together as well. I'm more than aware of the fact that Tee is way too tame for that kind of thing, and he's got his own family to worry about while I only really have him and her.

Could I really let him have her and give up any claim? I'd like to think I could, but the more I freak out wondering if Foxy's okay, the more I need to feel her in my arms to make sure that nothing ever hurts her. One thing is for sure, one way or another, no matter how it turns out in the end, we need to find her, and we need to have a proper talk. One where she can't run away because it's hard, and we get to have our say too.

"I need to know, Tee," I start sitting on the coffee table right in front of him, my eyes pleading for the truth, "Without any lies or holding back, do you love her?" He stares me down for a moment before giving a slight nod of affirmation and I continue, "If it wasn't for finding out that the other guy she was seeing was me, would you have fought for her? Did you see yourself with her in the future? Be honest."

Tee leans back, chewing on his bottom lip before answering. "Yep. I would have fought tooth and nail to keep that chick, but I'm not going to do that to you, dude, it changes things."

I nod slightly but say, "Then fight for her. Take away the fact that it's me and fight for her." He squints in confusion. "Don't get me wrong man, I love her too and would have fought just as hard, but I think she's worth fighting for. Why can't we have a little friendly competition between us and refuse to let the results ruin our relationship? Can't we agree between us that we will support her choice in the end and just be happy for the other? I love you both too much to not fight for both of you, but if she chooses you over me, then I will step back and will learn to love her as family instead. I'm not saying that will be easy, but at least we'll both know that the other will be there for her if she's ever in trouble."

My idea is radical as fuck, but I believe in our bromance to overcome everything, even a girl. I couldn't think of anyone that I'd rather see to make her happy if it isn't me.

I watch as Tee thinks it over, pursing his mouth comically. "It would make me happy to see you both happy, but I don't know if I'm capable of seeing it in front of me every single day without being jealous as fuck," he admits and I laugh.

"No shit. I'll be green as fuck but let's be honest with my cunning linguistics, I'm bound to be the winner." I smile, showing him that it's a joke because what better way to deal with such an important choice than some inappropriate humor?

Matching my wit just as I knew he would, Tee scoffs, "Fuck off. There's no way you can trump my dick skills, dude. Get ready to lose by a large margin because I won't be pulling my punches."

"Bring it on, motherfucker." We both laugh, easing some of the tension away. "Guess the next step is to show up at her house, hope we survive the guards, aka her scary fucking family, and then convince her to be the prize in our battle of dicks."

"Yeah because getting past her dad and brothers will be a piece of cake." Tee shakes his head. "Perhaps it's just who survives the boss stage gets the girl because there's a good chance we may not get to her at all in one piece."

He's not fucking wrong. I decide not to tell him about the two new but equally scary brothers I've seen at the Hernandez Garage the last few days. It'll be worth it when I see his face. I hold in the wicked laugh bubbling inside me at the thought as we head out of the apartment, with operation 'Win Foxy Back' in full swing.

CHAPTER 28

FOXY

The last couple of days, all I've been doing is trying to come up with a plan to make a difference before I have to head back to Sinhaven again. I've come up with an equally terrible and awesome idea. I refuse to acknowledge that it's a very Allure type of idea and just go with it instead as I hand Freja's favorite soft toy to Alonzo.

"Gracias hermano," I tell him with a smile, my gut twisting at the thought of just how badly tonight could go. Giving him a quick hug, I turn around with a quick goodbye.

"Chiquita," he calls out, and I turn around to his squinting, suspicious gaze. "I don't know what you're planning, but double-check that the SOS system we set up for you is working before you do it." My eyes widen at being caught out. "Don't look so surprised, I trained you but don't do anything too stupid and the second you even *think* you're in any danger, you press that button and stash the phone in your shoe. Promise me, or you don't leave this house."

I can't believe that Alonzo's going to let me go off, even knowing that I have an idiot plan brewing. Then again, if anyone's going to encourage stupid shit, it's this pendejo. I promise and tell him honestly that I've already checked, but I have high doubts that Papi will even give a shit. It's been set up so that Papi and all four of my brothers get an SOS message and a location tracker of my phone. We all have it set up that way for an emergency, but we've never had to use it before. Fingers crossed that tonight isn't the first time.

He waves his hand for me to leave with a quick "be safe" and I stride to my car, getting in and driving off before he changes his mind or tells somebody. There's no guarantee that he's going to keep it to himself, but I'd like to hope that he will, at least long enough for me to get a head start.

I'd already told Mami that I was going to have a girl's night with Allure in Beastville City, knowing I wasn't going to be home tonight and needing everyone off my back for the evening.

With a clear plan of what I need to do, I pull into a public restroom and get changed into my 'homeless' attire. I bought old cargo pants, an old band shirt, and some cheap canvas shoes from a thrift shop and then took them out the back and played tug of war with Freja using them as the toy. Once they were ripped, muddy and old looking, I gave them a wash to get rid of the dog smell, then dirtied them up again to make it more authentic. For an extra touch, I put them under the guys' dirty gym clothes after a workout because nothing says disgusting more than that.

Once I'm dressed and ready I pull my hair out, matting it up as best as I can, and then with some leaves and stuff I took from the ground earlier I ruffle them into my hair. It almost hurts me to do this because I know when I need to fix it, it's going to be a real bitch to deal with. Using a cheap contour pallet, I smear different shades of brown all over my face, arms, and neck. When I am happy with the look I'm going for, I put my things in the trunk of my car and drive it to a secure parking area in Morality Crossing. As night falls, I start walking to an area known for having a lot of homeless people, taking only my phone, a bottle of water, and some snacks with me that I stash in one of my many pockets.

It didn't take me long to get where I was going. Straight away, I notice a young girl no older than nine and head to where she's sitting near a broken-down box that offers her no reprieve from the cool night breeze. The way a few of the homeless men are looking at her made me instantly protective of her, and I glare at each and every one of them, silently daring them to try something.

The small, emaciated girl looks up at me with wide eyes, flinching as I lower myself beside her, distrust all over her features. I silently reach in and pull a small bag of chips out of one of my pockets.

I whisper quietly as I pass it to her, "I'll be your bodyguard tonight, eat this and rest. God knows this world is hard enough without having someone to keep the bad men away. Don't worry, I don't want anything, I just need a place to rest for a while. Have you had any water lately?"

Her little blue eyes squint at the food I'm offering her, and I realize she's not going to take it, so I decide to go with some honesty, "Have you heard of the bad men that have been taking women and children?" She scoots her bum back, fear making her look around wildly. "I'm here to catch them," I whisper conspiratorially hoping to calm her down, it grabs her attention and she looks back at me. "I'm undercover to make sure they don't take anyone ever again. I promise, I won't let anybody hurt you, so stay by me and be safe. You don't have to sit too close if you're not comfortable, but please take something to eat and some water. I only want to keep you safe."

She seems to mull over what I've told her, still not saying anything in response, so I place the chips on the ground beside her and put the unopened bottle of water beside it. "I'm Foxy, by the way," I offer, hoping that will help ease some of her tension.

I close my eyes and lean back against the brick wall behind us, letting her see me let down my guard. I stay like that for a little while, paying close attention to the noises around us the whole time. Holding back a smile, I listen as the sound of the chips being picked up crinkles, and not long after I hear the crunching little bites.

"Thank you," a small voice says, and I open my eyes, turning to look at her as she warily picks up the water bottle and gives me a tired-looking smile.

"I have more snacks if you want some," I tell her while pulling out an apple, and her eyes widen with hunger. With a smile, I give her the fresh fruit, and watching her devour it like it's the best thing she's ever eaten when most kids balk at fruit these days really pulls at my heartstrings. *Where the fuck are her parents?*

Examples like this are exactly why I think some people should be sterilized and not be allowed to breed. Fuck human rights. This girl had the right to have decent human beings bring her up in a safe and nurturing environment, not to be on the streets like this.

The night lingers on, getting darker and more ominous by the hour, and with time the little girl gets closer until she falls asleep with her head in my lap and me stroking her hair. I guess kids aren't so bad when they aren't hyped up on sugar, I tell myself as I look down at her soft white face covered in layers of filth. Her hair is so dirty and matted that it's almost hard to make out that it is supposed to be blonde.

The shuffling of feet as some of the other homeless people around us start to make their way further down the alleyway makes me turn my head to see what they're escaping from when I spot a familiar black sedan. Well, that was way easier than I was counting on. I pull the little girl in closer to me, suddenly feeling possessive over her and my promise to keep her safe.

Deciding that it's best to have my hands free, I carefully lift her head, but her eyes pop open with fear at the movement, way more hyper-vigilant than any young girl should have to be. I put my finger over my lips in a shushing movement and point to the car as three men exit the vehicle, slowly heading down toward us and looking down in every makeshift box house for someone worthwhile.

The size and shapes of these men indicate that they're not going to be so easy to subdue if they try to take one of us. But I was hoping that I would glimpse them and follow them back to their hideout, that there wouldn't actually be a chance of them taking me. As they get closer, my unease rises, and I try to tuck the little girl behind me, picking up the broken box and trying to use it as a shield in the hopes that they'll just walk on by.

My luck however was not going to let that happen, as the cardboard gets ripped from my fingers and two Hispanic men look down at me and the girl with lascivious scowls. *Mierde.*

"Hola, señorita," the closest one says, crouching down to squat in front of me. "We have a safe house nearby and thought you might want something to eat. What do you say?"

The little girl grips my side tightly as I feel her body get as close to me as she can, hoping I really can save her from the bad men. "No, thank you. We've already eaten." I try for a subtle refusal, not wanting to get into a fight with this tiny thing attached to me and in harm's way.

"I'm not asking." He stands up, grabbing my arm and effortlessly pulling me to my feet, the little girl still holding on but whimpering at my back.

I pull her fingers off my side and tell her to run, and to my relief she listens, booking it down the alleyway with the third man on her tail. Turning to chase him down, I'm momentarily caught off guard by the second guy's arm gripping me around my throat, but I quickly regain my composure and swiftly flip him over my shoulder.

With a quick movement, I pull my phone out and press the family SOS, knowing full well that I can't handle this situation on my own when I also have to keep this little girl safe. As soon as the message is sent, I punch out at the man who lunges for me and then tuck my phone into the sole of my shoe the way I've done a million times in training. Popping back up, I start running for the car, where the third man is pushing the little girl into the back seat. Just as I reach it, gripping the door handle ready to yank her right back out, a hand comes up behind me and smothers my mouth with a sweet-smelling cloth. I instantly know what it is, but before I can do anything about it, my world starts to shift, and I stupidly suck in a hard breath. My last thought is a silent prayer that they don't check inside my shoes.

CHAPTER 29

ALONZO

A smile turns up the side of my mouth as my inner demon laughs at the sight of two lost-looking gringos pressing the gate buzzer at the front of the yard. I look at them through the TV screen and know exactly who they are and have a pretty good idea who they came for. This ought to be good.

I let them in and stroll out the door, waiting for them as I lean against the front door, biting into my apple. The poor boys don't know how much trouble they're in coming into our lair in the dead of night. I've got to hand it to them, they have balls of steel to show up unannounced like this. What a shame that they get our beasts tonight instead of Foxy's.

Antonio comes up beside me, crossing his massive arms across his way too overgrown chest, and I scoff at his show of bravado. Overcompensating much? "I'll go get Papi," he growls, but I smack his chest hard, stopping him in his tracks.

"No. Don't move or speak," I demand quietly, wanting to see for myself what these two are made of.

My youngest brother knows better than to defy a word I

say and remains frozen on the spot, looking unsure. Probably wondering if I'm going to rip out their spines and use them for decoration for fun. To be honest, I haven't ruled it out. We'll see.

The men that captured Foxy's attention leave their car and start striding toward me. I'm instantly disappointed by their appearance because any men that look that pretty don't really deserve to be called men, and it doesn't help that I can smell the stench of their fear from here.

I smile darkly and meet them halfway, openly sizing them up. "What are girls like you doing in a place like this?" I ask, testing their responses.

The smaller one in the front with girly hair in a bun stands up taller and reaches out his hand, which I just look at with a raised eyebrow. "Hey, I'm Beau. You must be one of Foxy's brothers, I was wondering if she was around. I know it's late, but we can't seem to get a hold of her."

Sensing I had no intention of returning his need for a handshake, he lets his hand fall, and I look behind him at the other guy, who is fidgeting from foot to foot nervously. I look back at the first princess and ask, "So she blocked you?"

Ding. Ding. By the look on their faces, I'm right on the money. Good for her, she can do way better than these ladies. "I'm going to go out on a limb here and say she doesn't want to talk to you then. Off you fuck."

I turn around and start walking back to the house when lady number two speaks up, finding his balls. "It's really important, and we're not leaving until we see her. I need to know if she's alright and that you guys haven't hurt her." *Interesting.*

Antonio squints his eyes at the two of them behind me, clearly holding his tongue because of me, and I turn around to look back at them, my curiosity peaked. "And what exactly are you going to do about it if we have?" They look at each other and back at me like a deer in headlights, and I chuckle darkly. "Haven't thought that far yet, have you?"

"Look, we don't want any trouble. We just want to know if Ana-Lucia's alright, and then we'll be on our way." *Hmm, even more interesting.* "Please, she doesn't even need to talk to us if she doesn't want to, but we're just concerned."

My phone and Antonio's both buzz at the same time, and the tune is one that I've been dreading hearing tonight. "Puta." I spin to Antonio and demand without even looking at the screen, knowing exactly what it means. "Tell the others it's not a drill, and we've got to go now."

I storm toward my own car, a black 66 Pontiac GTO. Beau comes running beside me, his eyes wild, and stands in between me and helping my sister. It takes all of my effort to not shoot him between the eyes, but I'm pretty sure Foxy would castrate me if I did.

"What's going on? Is it Foxy?" he asks, and I hear his friend join us.

Deciding this is a great opportunity to see if these two have the ability to be worthy of her in any way, I tell them, "Foxy is in big trouble and if you want to help save her from possible death, I suggest you follow us and make yourself useful." I walk past them and lean in my car, pulling out two 1911's chambered in 45ACP and throwing them their way.

They awkwardly catch them and look up at me with eyes bugging out of their heads. Well, they've never held guns before. Tonight's going to be great fun, thankfully the safety is on, or they might end up accidentally shooting themselves, or others. I laugh out loud, and they look confused at my outburst. "Just picturing a good time. Good luck ladies."

I jump in my car as the rest of the Hernandez men come around the corner in Papi's Mustang and Mario's RAM TRX. They drive past and pull up in front of me.

Papi leans out the front window, his eyes burning a hole in the two guys standing next to my car, taking in the guns in their hands and judging their level of threat. "What are they doing here? Shoot them, and let's get moving."

I wave them off and reply, "Nah, I told them to come along. I thought it would be fun." Papi shakes his head and drives off, letting me have my entertainment for the evening. I turn back to them as I start my car. "Keep up, and remember, point it at the bad guys."

With a squeal of my tires, I blast forward, laughing into the wind and more than a little excited about the bloodshed that is no doubt about to go down. Foxy is going to be so mad when she realizes I brought her boy toys to play with the men for the night, and it only makes me laugh harder.

* * *

WE PULL UP IN FRONT OF A MASSIVE ABANDONED warehouse, and to my surprise were followed closely by Foxy's boys. I will give props to them, that Beau guy sure can drive, and his car is badass. I'd bet good money that it's a main factor of him getting into Foxy's pants. There's nothing that girl likes more than a good car, except dick, apparently.

In seconds, we're surrounded by our men in a massive display of just how powerful our cartel really is. With Mario already organized, the local police to block off every street heading out that these fuckers might be wanting to take when they're running for their fucking lives, if they can get past me. It really pays to be good to the locals and the community, it keeps us in good with the authority around here, who are more than happy to help out when shit like this goes down.

Lock and loading my favorite guns and storing them in my holster, I grin as Juan joins me, already weaponized and ready. "What were you thinking, bringing them along?" He nudges his head at the two guys looking around nervously next to their car.

They fumble with their guns, with the one whose name I didn't get drops his gun and I lose it, pointing at them. "Come on, it'll be great. Plus, then we don't have to worry about getting rid of them later."

Juan shakes his head and whistles out in exasperation. "Foxy's gonna lose her shit when she sees them, you know that, right?"

"I'm counting on it." My dark, twisted soul gets off on the anger of others, even the little sister I adore. She and Mami are the only ones I'm willing to kneel for, and I wouldn't have it any other way.

"Your funeral, pelado."

Mario makes the sign to move out, and we all close in as a group, and I wish I could see the faces of the pendejos inside as we do. I bet they weren't thinking they would be dealing with us tonight, and not in this big of a number.

The gunshots start the moment the first wave hits the door, and my heartbeat increases with my serotonin levels. I never get enough of this, my insatiable appetite for blood unrivaled as I run inside the large door, taking aim and decimating any poor fucker that has the misfortune of getting my attention.

I run harder and faster, breaking into a smaller room

just as my first gun runs out of ammo, but instead of grabbing another, I reach for my favorite knife and start hacking away.

Blood sprays and pours from my enemies, with a cheery tune of "Break Stuff" by Limp Bizkit playing in my head as I go. Face after face stares at me in terror as I grin down at them with a thirst that won't be denied, loving every time their lights go out, and the deep empty nothing is all that's left behind.

I shove another limp body away from me as Foxy's familiar voice yells from the next room, and I plow into the door, shoving it open to find a good two dozen women and children. They are wild eyes and terrified, with Foxy at the side tied up to a pipe connected to the wall. Four bogies turn to me, but at lightning speed, I take out three of them while another gets shot by someone behind me.

Turning, I see Mario at my back, drenched with almost as much blood as me, but without the crazy grin I have plastered on my face. "You're a sick son of a bitch, you know that," he growls at me and I wink.

"I'll let Mami know you called her that." I laugh, moving out of his reach when he tries to punch me.

"Seriously, take your fucking time," Foxy swears at us loudly, and Mario goes over to her, cutting off her ropes with a scowl. "Don't even start, I found them, didn't I?" she grumbles at him before he gets a chance to chew her out.

Gunfire still grounds off in rapid blasts from rooms all around us, as Foxy stands up and reaches for a little girl's hand. "She's with me. How are we doing out there? Give me a gun."

I throw her one of my spares, and she instantly does a quick check that makes me proud. "Good. It won't be long before it's all over," I tell her, walking back toward the door, needing to get back into the fray. There's no way those fuckers are having all the fun without me.

Beau and whatever his name is come running into the room, slamming the door behind them with their chests heaving erratically. Foxy's eyes widen, and then she turns to me with a scowl. "You did this, didn't you? **Cabrón, ¿cómo se te ocurre traerlos aquí?** " Mario and I watch in fascination as she goes up to them and starts patting them both down all over. "Are you hurt? Have you been shot anywhere?"

Beau practically jumps on her, wrapping his arms around her tightly, with the other one copying his lead. I don't know how she can breathe between them like that, and I also don't care.

"Move," I order them all. "I have a party to attend."

Foxy pushes them both off looking all cute and embarrassed and I scoff. I didn't know she was even capable of that. I fling the door open and stray bullets come flying past. Foxy and her boys move to a safer place, and Mario and I push into the busy room, laying out dozens almost instantly.

Foxy stands at the door, taking her place behind the door jamb and popping off well-placed shots. I watch as Beau tries to take one, but his gun doesn't fire because the safety is on, and I laugh loudly at the show, cutting some guy's neck open at the same time.

She grabs his gun, shaking her head, takes the safety off, and gives it back, and when he manages to shoot it, hitting no one the recoil smacks him in the face. You can't buy this kind of entertainment. This is the best night ever. I stomp on someone's face, smashing in their skull with my heavy combat boots, while I laugh some more.

Maybe I'll help convince Papi to let her keep them. We

don't laugh enough in this family as it is, it'll be good to have some humor around the house. They can be like funny pets.

My humor dies fast as Foxy's body recoils, and she falls back onto the ground, at the same time, four motherfuckers with a death wish barge into the room we just left. Fury bubbles inside me as I race back to the room, making it inside quick enough to see the four of them shooting down a good chunk of the women and children that were hiding inside.

Beau tackles one of them, knocking his gun off him, and starts smashing into his face over and over again with a rage I didn't think a guy like that was capable of. His friend gets off a lucky shot, shooting one of the men gunning down the women.

I shoot one of the others, but don't make it in time to get the other one. I watch in horror as he shoots an already bloody Foxy, who is using herself as a shield for the little girl she was with earlier. Her body jerks twice with both shots that make it before I take him down with one fatal, well-placed one.

"Foxy," Beau cries, jumping off the guy he's on, and running to where her body now lies still over top. I momentarily freeze, Mario doing the same right beside me, watching as he cradles her in his arms crying loudly and calling her name. The other guy slides across the room, shoving Beau aside and putting pressure on two of her wounds.

"She's not going to make it," he cries out, doing what he can to stop the bleeding by ripping off his shirt and using that. "We need to get her to a hospital." He looks up at me, and it snaps me out of whatever the fuck that was.

I look at Mario, who's white as a sheet, and growl. "Let's make a path. "You two carry her and get her there before she bleeds out, or I will be the last thing you see," I growl to the two guys as they pick her up and my brother and I take point, pushing out of the room and laying waste to everyone in our path until Foxy is in Beau's car being driven away at a dangerously fast speed.

She better fucking make it, or I will burn this world to the fucking ground!

CHAPTER 30

THEODORE

The car screeches to a jarring halt in front of the hospital emergency door after the longest ride of my life. It wasn't that far technically, but as I fought to control the profuse bleeding coming from Foxy in the backseat, every minute felt like an hour.

Beau runs around the front of the car and rips open the back door as I hold Foxy tightly to my body, jumping around and racing her inside the large glass doors. Hospital staff see us immediately and two men come rushing at me with a stretcher as Beau screams for them to hurry and tell them her name and that she's been shot.

"Please save her," I rasp out, tears rolling freely down my cheeks as they wheel her away and behind a set of doors we can't follow through.

Beau collapses to his knees on the ground right outside of it, holding his head in his hands and gripping his now loose hair tightly. "I can't go through this again." I hear him mumbling over and over again, no doubt remembering the pain of losing his mother, the only other woman he's ever loved.

I try to keep my shit together and help pull him to his feet, bringing Beau in for a constricting hug that we both desperately need. "She's going to be okay. She has to be." My words, meant to console him, come out shakier than I meant them to, betraying how frightened I actually am that she might not come out alive.

We stand like that for a bit and I pull back, going to sit on nearby plastic chairs. Beau follows me, but before he sits down his eyes travel over my body, and I look down at myself for the first time, and I'm covered in Foxy's blood. My hands begin to shake as I turn them over and over. As a vet, I'm not a stranger to blood, but this is different, this is the blood of the woman I love, and all I can see when I stare down at my hands, is how pale and limp her body was in my arms before they took her away.

"Let's go clean up a bit," Beau recommends, pointing to the bathroom nearby. His voice trembles slightly, and I know he's trying his best to keep it together and not break down again. "Her family will be here soon and her mum shouldn't have to see this. You go in first, I have my gym bag in the car that has some clothes in it. I'll go and get it and meet you in there."

His words center me a little bit as I realize that he's right. I watch as he walks out of the hospital, and I make my way to the men's room, going straight to the mirror and staring in horror at how covered I am. My arms violently rip my shirt off and then my pants, my hands shaking uncontrollably the whole time. I turn the water on full and start dowsing myself with it, splashing it all over myself. My face, hair, body, and underwear are saturated by the time Beau joins me.

Silently, he takes a change of folded clothes and a towel

out of his gym bag, handing it to me. I go into the stall, pull my underwear off and put on the loose white shirt and navy track pants. My shoes are still alright, even if they're a little bit wet.

By the time I make it back out of the stall, Beau is wearing gym shorts and a wife beater. All the discarded clothes I took off earlier and his own must be in the bag because I can no longer see them anywhere. It seems like Beau has cleaned up around the sinks too, for my benefit I'm sure. His face seems pale and his body heavy as he takes the towel and underwear from me, adding it to the bag without a word.

We exit the toilet, but just before we sit down, Foxy's mother comes running into the hospital waiting room looking wild, her face drenched with tears. I wave her over when she sees me and practically sprints to me.

"Where is she? Please? Where is she?" her mother wails and it breaks my heart.

I pull her in for a tight hug and tell her, "She was taken into emergency. I think they're working on her now, they didn't really tell us anything, just took her and ran, but she was alive and that's the main thing."

Her knees buckle from under her, and I hold her up as she sobs openly and loudly in my arms. Beau comes up behind her and rubs her back saying soothing words but looks at me with watery eyes and a trembling bottom lip. I let tears slip down my face, not giving a shit what I look like to others because this wailing woman is screaming a fear and grief that feels way too familiar right now.

Loud shouts call out from across the room, and I look up to see Foxy's father and brothers stampeding through the room toward us. Her mum turns in my arms and moves into the waiting ones of her husband, not seeming to care that he's covered with almost as much blood as I was earlier.

The scary motherfucker that we met earlier squares up in front of Beau and demands to know where his sister is, and Beau tells him the same thing I told his mother only minutes before. It seems to stop his boiling rage as he stomps to the reception, scaring the shit out of the nurses who promise to tell him everything they know as soon as they hear something. The men in this family are not used to waiting for answers, as they pace almost violently around the room, glaring at everyone in their vicinity until all the other people in the waiting room move to the farthest corner. Talking only in hushed voices, as if they're scared to surprise the beasts roaming around the room.

The brother we've gotten to know as Antonio comes over to us with a deep scowl, "Why are you still here? Get the fuck out before I end you." His voice is a deep guttural growl, and I have no doubt that he means it, and being in a hospital won't deter him in the slightest.

I look to Beau, unsure of what to do because it's clear that neither of us wants to leave, but we don't necessarily want to die either. We look around the room nervously, but with a nod to each other, we make an unspoken agreement and go to take a seat by the doors that Foxy was whisked away through.

Antonio takes a step toward us, and the one that the others have been calling Alonzo grabs him by the bicep and growls at him, "Leave them alone. They're under my protection from now on." He makes a point to look at each of his brothers and then his father. "From everyone."

Well, that's an unexpected development. Beau looks at me, and I shrug, I have no idea why he said that, but I'm sure as fuck not going to complain about it.

"What gives you the right?" Foxy's dad asks, standing up and glaring at his son as if he'd just made a huge mistake. Her mum grabs his arm to try to pull him back down, but he ignores her and continues. "Are these gringos worth the fight you're asking for?"

I don't want to be the reason Foxy's family is fighting, and I stand prepared to leave because they have too much on their plate right now to be having a disagreement just because of us. But Juan's head whips around and demands, "Sit down now. You want to stay, then grow some huevos and fight for that right, or you're just proving Papi right." My bum hits the seat again, and he turns his attention to their father, standing beside Alonzo. "I'm with him. If anyone should tell them to leave, it's Foxy. I think she's earned the right to make her own choices at this point in her life, Papi. Besides, if it weren't for them, she might not have made it here on time. We owe them."

Foxy's father doesn't look impressed and glares at the two of us before sitting back down next to his wife with a huff of disapproval, but it's enough to know we can stay. At least for now.

A doctor in scrubs comes into the waiting room, his eyes landing on the Hernandez family. "Are you here for Ana-Lucia Hernandez?" he asks simply, and in seconds he's crowded by the lot of them and Beau and I stand far enough back to give them space but not far enough that we can't hear what's going on. "Ana-Lucia had three gunshot wounds. Two went straight through her shoulder and thigh without too much damage, but the third ruptured her lung, causing significant damage and bleeding. Because she got here so fast, we managed to successfully stop the bleeding and repair the damage. She will have a long recovery, but she will pull through. Luckily, so far at least, the pregnancy is still viable. It's early days and anything can happen, especially after such a traumatic experience, but if all goes well there shouldn't be any issues."

The next few moments are surreal as fuck, as three of Foxy's brothers spin to stare at us with what only can be described as death. Meanwhile, Alonzo literally folds over into a fit of loud obnoxious laughter, even slapping his knee. Foxy's mum starts to beat down her dad, ranting in Spanish something about kicking out her pregnant baby, and Beau drops like a bag of potatoes, his ass on the ground and his mouth wide open. And here I am having some kind of mental breakdown as my brain decides if it's ecstatic that Foxy's going to be alright, terrified by her brother's glares, or processing the word pregnancy.

Before I can decide what to do, Foxy's mother turns her anger to her sons as she steps in between us and them, facing the three angry faces still staring daggers at me and Beau. "Don't even think about it." She points her chancla to the other end of the room. "Go sit over there and stay away from those two until Foxy has had a chance to talk to them. Apurense pues!" she demands, and the three of them don't even attempt fighting back as they lower their heads and go where she told them to. Then she faces her husband, and whatever must have been on her face had him joining them. And I thought the men were the scary people in this family. Boy was I wrong.

"Good job, Mami," Alonzo says, putting his arm around her shoulders, a massive grin on his face. Beau gets up beside me, looking dazed at the same time. "I'll stay with them and make sure no one bothers them until Foxy has a chance to kill them herself."

She squints at him, pursing her lips. "Why aren't you mad?"

Alonzo laughs loudly again. "Why would I be mad? You can't buy this kind of entertainment. Foxy is going to be okay, the guys are about to explode, Papi's in the dog house and these two are as good as dead when Foxy finds out that she's preñada. You know how much she hates kids?"

"Until Foxy is out of this place and safe at home, you'd better wipe that smile off your face, niño!" she warns him, and his face straightens immediately. It's actually creepy how quickly his features change, he's got to be an actual psychopath. "Better." Foxy's mum turns to us, with a somber look in her swollen eyes. "May God keep you safe and bless you with the patience and understanding you will need. Which one of you is the father?"

Beau and I look at each other, the realization that it could be either one of us dawning on us for the first time. Mrs. Hernandez must see it in our eyes, and she crosses herself muttering "Dios mío," and walks over to join the others on the opposite side of the room, leaving the two of us disjointed and overwhelmed, with our only company her psychopath son. *We're totally fucked.*

I sit back down, with Beau and Alonzo taking a seat at each of my sides. I find myself lost in thought, trying to figure out how on earth my life path took me here and what the hell I'm going to do about it all. To my surprise, when I think about the idea of a baby with Foxy, it doesn't give me any feelings other than good news, and I subconsciously smile at the thought of a tiny little Foxy with cute curls atop her head. I process how I would feel if the baby is Beau's and not mine, and I'm not even mad about it. I've always pictured him in my life and assumed when we had kids one day that we would just be like secondary dads to each other's anyway.

Turning my head, I take in his face as he stares off into

the distance with a similar smile playing on his own lips. It wouldn't surprise me if he was thinking of the same thing as me. My mind turns to the possibility of sharing her with Beau in a throuple type of situation, and it doesn't turn me off in the slightest. If anyone in this world can do it, it's us. We're both very straight, so it's nothing like that, but we are already a family of sorts, so why not just add another level to it by adding Foxy and her baby into the mix? We wouldn't even need to find out who the father is, and could just love them and her the way they deserve to be loved.

A flurry of movement comes flying through the door as a stunning blonde chick with three guys and two little, very tired-looking kids come barreling into the waiting room, the light behind them showing signs of morning. Foxy's mum goes to the chick, and they start holding each other tightly, crying openly as she explains to the new girl what happened. When she tells her that Foxy's pregnant, she points at us. The girl who I have now assumed is Allure, Foxy's best friend, spins her head in our direction with clear shock written all over her face. The three guys at her side mirroring her actions.

"This might be the longest day I've had in a very long time," Beau comments as he watches the same thing I am. Alonzo snorts in amusement, and I agree with him, sucking in a breath as the newcomers come over to join us. "Here we go again," he says under his breath, and we brace ourselves for another onslaught of judgment and hostility.

To our absolute surprise, the teary-eyed Allure smiles at us. A big guy to her left with his arm around her waist. A younger-looking guy to her right holding her hand and the third one following closely behind with a little girl on one hip and a little boy holding his free hand. The surprising part wasn't only that they clearly have a group relationship, but also that they all seem genuinely happy to meet us when they approach.

"You must be Beau and Theodore," the one with his arm around Allure says, and he reaches out his free hand to shake. We stand up and both accept it, happy that there's no new animosity to deal with right now. "I'm Callum, these are my brothers Jamee and Ardyn. Starling and Wren are our kids, and this is our lovely wife, Allure." We greet each of them, taking in the dynamic with wide eyes.

"It's really nice to finally meet you," Allure says softly, sniffing and still visibly upset. Her lip quivers and she starts to cry again, turning her face into Jamee's shoulder and muttering unnecessary apologies to us about being upset.

Ardyn takes a seat next to Beau, putting both kids on his knees, and they start talking quietly about random nothings and both focus on keeping Starling and Wren entertained to keep their notice off their mum. I watch Jamee and Callum with no small amount of fascination, as they equally seem to share and love her between them. The adoration shared in the group is more than a little enviable, and it only reaffirms my earlier thoughts.

Allure gathers herself together a bit and excuses herself to go spend some time with the Hernandez family, Ardyn goes with her, swapping out with his brothers. They each take one of the kids to the cafeteria to get them a snack, since the sun is now bright with a morning glow, and they are getting hungry and restless.

We watch as they all leave us, and Beau turns to me and says, "They seem happy." I nod, agreeing. "Would you be opposed to something like that? I know it's pretty unusual, but the more I think about it, the more it makes sense."

I give him a small smile and look back to the doors hiding Foxy from us and say, "I know exactly what you mean. I guess it's up to Foxy to decide at the end of the day, but I'm not against the idea."

Far from it.

'm alive.

The last thing I remember was bleeding out in the back of Beau's car as Theodore frantically tried to save me. I remember the panic, desperation, and love in his eyes as he begged me to hold on. Beau's shouts from the front asking if I was okay, as he drives like a madman, still ring in my ears.

But I'm alive. I know that before I even open my eyes because of the excruciating pain radiating all over my body. Every breath hurts like a mother fucking bitch, and I'm terrified to open my eyes in case it all gets worse.

I try to focus on the sounds around me to get my mind off it, the beeping of machines I'm hooked up to, heavy breathing, and a shuffling noise down near my feet. My eyelids squeeze tightly as the pain continues to intensify, and I give up pretending I can deal with it.

With a flutter, as I try to adjust to the sudden light, I slowly open my lids, holding in a groan of pain. It takes me a moment, but I eventually get them all the way open, apart from the pained squint.

I take in everything around me. There's a mask on my face helping me to breathe, and I quickly wiggle my finger and toes, making sure it all still works. With the unbelievable pain I'm in, it almost makes me wonder if I was hit by a truck a few times and just forgot about it.

On one side of me, Beau is face first in the bed, facing the opposite way but clearly asleep. On the other side, Theodore is close by my side, but with his arms crossed and head back, passed out and breathing heavily. It takes me an extra minute before I see Papi leaning against the hospital door jamb, watching me intently, with a deep frown on his face.

He sees me watching him and puts his finger to his mouth as he comes over to stand by my side behind Beau's sleeping form. "You had us worried, little one," Papi whispers to me, in an obvious effort not to wake the men by my side, and that confuses me because I don't know why they're here, or why he's letting them be here. "Mami and the boys are at home having a rest. We've been taking turns staying with you." He pauses and looks at Beau and Theodore with a scowl. "Except these two gringos, who haven't left at all other than to use the bathroom."

My eyes flick from one to the other, and then I flinch as my pain seems to rise again. A small moan slips out, and Papi quietly walks out of the room, coming in with a nurse that he quietly demands doesn't wake the guys up.

She comes over softly, telling my papi that it will send me back to sleep and to be quick if he has something to say.

While she does something at my side, Papi leans in and tells me, "Lo siento, mi princesa. I should never have gotten so mad at you, whatever you want, you have mine and Mami's support. Just rest now, you need to heal because there are a lot of people waiting for you. Te quiero."

He kisses me softly on my forehead as the room starts to slip away along with my pain, and I happily give in with his words dancing in my head.

I WAKE AND SLEEP AGAIN AS MY PAIN RELIEF KICKS IN several more times over I don't know how long. Every time I come to, even if it's for just moments, both Theodore and Beau are by my side. Sometimes someone from my family is with them either talking, laughing, scowling, sleeping, or arguing. It depends on who's there, but never once is either guy out of my line of sight, and it starts to be a comforting thing for me when consciousness reaches out to me.

Today as I wake up I feel a bit more aware and even though I'm still hurting everywhere, I don't have the instant desire to be knocked out because of it.

Alonzo looks down at me, and as I look around the room, I'm surprised to see my men missing for the first time. Well, not *my* men but Beau and Theodore.

"Don't Freak out, chiquita. I forced them to go home to shower. They fucking stink," Alonzo tells me with a knowing smirk. "They should be back any minute. Are you almost better because at this point I feel like you're just milking it."

"Shut the fuck-up," Papi growls at Alonzo, coming into the room with two coffees and handing one to him with a deep scowl of warning. "Leave her alone, she will take as long as she needs to. How are you feeling, Foxy?" he asks in a much nicer voice, sitting in the chair at my side.

I cautiously move my hand, it feels like lead and aches, but I manage to get it up to my face, slowly moving the mask on my face to the side.

"Don't push it," Papi warns, but I ignore him, knowing I'm doing exactly that.

I lick my lips, my mouth as dry as the Sahara desert, and swallow hard. Papi puts his coffee down, picks up a small glass of water, and leans forward to bring it to my lips, telling me to sip it carefully. With patience, I didn't know I had, I take my time trying out the cool liquid on my lips and after some trial and error, I manage to swallow a little bit of it.

My body feels heavy, pained, and foreign, with every movement I make more difficult than it should be. "How long?" I manage to rasp out, breathing heavily at the effort and pain it causes.

"You've been Sleeping Beauty for over three weeks," Alonzo tells me, with a way too happy voice as if there's a joke I'm not in on, and I squint at him trying to figure out what it is. "I always thought you were more like the Beast in Beauty and the Beast."

Papi gives him the hard stare we all know as 'stop talking, or I'll kick your ass' and Alonzo puts his hand and coffee up in a gesture of surrender but still lets out a dark chuckle.

"What? It's not like I told her she's pregnant and ruined the happy surprise?" Alonzo says with a grin, slowly backing out of the room, and he winks at me before disappearing into the hall.

That's not fucking funny. I think scowling at the empty doorway but when I look at Papi the guilty eye shift he does, has my heart pausing for what feels like a full minute, and I rasp out in between heavy breaths, "That's a joke right?"

Papi takes a sip of his coffee, looking over the lid at me the whole time like he's trying to pick his words carefully. My eyes widen and the intense pounding inside my chest tells me my heart is going for a different approach, the escape approach.

"Your Mami's going to kill that boy," he grumbles half to me and half to himself, but then sighs heavily, deciding it's too late to put the cat back in the bag. "It's true."

With excellent timing, Beau and Theodore come running into the room looking frazzled as fuck, skinnier than normal, and more than a little worse for wear and all I can think is, *I'm going to kill them!*

"Implanon?" I ground out, fighting the growing pain that's starting to get too intense for me to deal with again, as sweat starts to cover me.

The word has both men stopping in their tracks, figuring out pretty fast what we're talking about, and their eyes go from ecstatic that I'm awake to uncertain of whether I want them there. This gives me the impression that my family has informed them while I was out how much I have never wanted children.

"Apparently it didn't work," Papi grumbles getting off his chair and moving to leave, done with this conversation which I know is far out of his comfort zone. He stops next to Beau and Theodore, glaring at them, "This is the last time I'm saying it, and I'm making sure Foxy can hear me too." He looks back at me with raised eyebrows before he continues making his point very clear. "I don't care which one of you does it, but one of you will marry my daughter before this baby is born, whether she likes it or not. Not negotiable."

Papi leaves the room, and I gasp heavily in bed, unable to fight back, overwhelmed mentally and physically. Beau comes to my side and places the mask back over my face, seeing my discomfort, and he presses the button by my side to call the nurse.

"Don't stress about anything beautiful," Beau tells me, fixing my pillow and carefully tucking the blanket around me. "We have plenty of time for you to yell and tell us to go away. For now, just rest and let us take care of you."

Theodore comes around the other side, taking my hand into his and kissing the back of it sweetly before saying, "I'm sorry we left. We won't go again until you tell us to."

A nurse comes in and checks my vitals as I strain with the effort of just breathing. He tells Beau and Theodore that it's time for me to rest and does something that makes me feel weightless.

The nurse leaves, and I fall back to sleep. Both Theodore and Beau lean forward, kissing a cheek each, while holding my hands. I think I heard them say the L word, but that has to be a dream.

* * *

ANOTHER WEEK PASSES, AND I CONTINUE TO HEAL ONE day at a time, and the period of time that I manage to stay awake and speak only increases. It still hurts like crap, but I'm getting there. The doctor has come by and talked to me about my recovery and how I need to take it easy, especially until the baby comes. A baby I had no plans on ever having, but here I am, growing a person with a new appreciation for condoms that I should have had before. Assuming the Implanon was a reliable source of birth control was a mistake I'll never be making again.

Beau and Theodore leave my room after being kicked out by Allure. She then tells me that the guys have taken the guys away to have a 'sharing is caring' talk in the hopes that I can keep both. While she may think that's very sweet of them, I'd very much rather everyone mind their own business. I won't have them both stay with me just because they feel obligated to from all the outside pressure they're getting from my friends and family.

"Have you come to terms with having a baby yet?" she asks me, sipping on her latte with a smug grin. I flip her the finger, still refusing to even talk about it. "Seriously, Foxy, you can't just ignore it. No matter what you choose to do, you will always have my support."

I'm grateful that she said that because my mind has been turning over the options that my doctor has given me when we had a private talk a couple of days ago. He said it's not too late to abort if I really want to, but I need to choose as soon as possible. He also said that many people who aren't in a mental position to raise kids go for the adoption route instead, but no matter how I look at it, I only really have one option. This baby is mine now, and I never shrink away from my responsibilities.

I have a beyond large support system, money, and not one but two dads for this baby that have made it very clear that they aren't going anywhere and are happy about it. I may not have ever pictured myself as a mother, but the more I think about it, the more it doesn't seem like the worst idea. I just don't want to have to give up myself in the process because I'm not like Allure who's happy to stay at home and spend every waking moment catering to men and children. That makes her happy, but it sounds like hell to me. When I have this baby, I'm going to want to go straight back to work because I love my job and am not willing to give that up.

"I don't know who the father is," I tell her simply, but the statement is anything but simple in my mind because I know that when I find out who the dad is, I will have my choice between them made up and Papi will demand I marry him. This is another issue because I don't plan on ever getting married.

Allure just shrugs. "Does it matter? Seriously, does it? Why not just let it be like I do? I have no idea who is the sperm donor of the twins or of this little one, and I have no intention of finding out. They're all the Dads, so it doesn't matter."

"It's different for you though because you're all in a relationship. Whereas I broke up with Theodore and Beau, and Papi is going to make me pick one of them before this kid pops out," I complain, wiggling in the bed to get more comfortable, my pain a constant companion that I'm thoroughly over.

"You know I love your Papi, but this is none of his business. Do what you want, and why can't you have them both? Have you talked to them about it because the way I've seen them with you is nothing but love, hermana. I'm telling you, they'll be down for it," Allure says just before the door opens to the room and Beau's face pops in with a cheeky smile.

"Is it safe to come in or do you need me to come back later?" He waits for an answer, not taking another step to respect our privacy.

Allure waves him in, and he strides through with Theodore at his heels carrying fruit salad and closing the door behind him. He holds it up, smiling so that his dimples show, and says sweetly, "I got this for you. I thought you could use something fresh. Beau made it fresh, but I thought of it."

"I think that's my cue." Allure leans in and cuddles me gently. "Get better soon, and make sure you give me your new address." I raise an eyebrow, not understanding her meaning, and she winks. "You know, for when you move in with these two hotties."

Before I can refute her words, the door swings open and Callum comes striding in, sweeping Allure up in his arms with a frown. "There are no hotties but us. Bye Foxy, I need to get her out of here before she says something we'll all regret."

Allure kisses his cheek softly with a big grin. "I only see the Hunter men, baby, calm down. See you later, guys. Don't do anything I wouldn't do."

Beau laughs, leaning down to kiss the top of my head then takes a seat beside me, and Theodore gives me the fruit salad, tucking a rogue curl behind my ear and kissing the back of my hand. I look up just in time to see Allure giving me a knowing wink as she gets carried out the door. Maybe she's on to something after all?

"Where did you two go off to?" I ask, carefully picking out some of the small pieces of apple and chewing on them.

Beau tells me without batting an eyelid. "The Hunter brothers were telling us about how good it is to share somebody you love if it means their continued happiness and the benefits of having more than one father for kids, and I happen to agree with him. What about you, Tee?"

I almost choke on the fruit when Theodore agrees, stealing a piece of my pineapple. "Couldn't think of a better plan, actually." They both look at me expectantly, trying to act all cool, but they both swallow hard, showing that they're more than a little nervous about my response. Theodore takes a deep breath and holds it, asking, "Will you think about it?"

This feels a little too good to be true, but Allure's right about how well they take care of me together, and I've never once seen any jealousy from either of them. "What about who the father is?" I ask, needing to know the answer to that, more than I'd like to admit.

Theodore blows out the breath he was holding but shrugs. "Will it change things for you? Because we don't really care if we're going to be in it together anyway."

I take a moment to really think through what they're asking me, and they don't push me, giving me the space and time I need to process their words. By the time I know what I want to say, I'm finished with the fruit and ready to sleep again, feeling increasingly sore from sitting up and talking for too long.

"Alright, let's see how we go together, but if there's any jealousy or strain on your friendship, I'm out," I tell them quietly, using the bed remote to lower myself down. "Let's say we date until I'm twenty weeks along, and then talk about it again after that."

With shocked but surprisingly excited faces, they nod in agreement, and I close my eyes.

CHAPTER 32

FOXY

"What do you mean, you threatened them?" I question Mario as he drives me home from the hospital. I cringe a bit at my outburst, still not a hundred percent healed yet, even though it's been eight weeks since everything went down.

Alonzo chuckles darkly from the other front seat, spinning around and looking at me over his shoulder. "What did you expect? We had to sit them down and let them know exactly what our family business really is, and to be fair they took it pretty well considering. If we didn't remind them of the kind of death they'd experience if they told even one soul, what kind of brothers would we be?"

I roll my eyes, shaking my head and looking out the window at the scenery going by. "Is that all you said?" I question, waiting for the worst.

"I reminded them that Papi is expecting one of them to marry you, and you're running out of time," Mario explains. "You're fourteen weeks pregnant now, Foxy, and you need to make a choice before you get too big. As it is, you're showing already."

My hand rubs the small, round curve of my stomach, the surreal notion of someone being inside there is still crazy to me. In eight more weeks, I'll be able to find out what it is and have to decide if the shared relationship that the guys and I are trying is going to work in the long run.

I don't bother telling them that I'm not planning on marrying anyone because it's a conversation I need to have with my parents and my boyfriends. Ew, it sounds wrong to say boyfriends. It makes me feel like I'm in high school again.

"Of course, if you don't want either of them, I'm happy to help them fuck off. Just give me the word," Mario adds.

Alonzo turns back to look at me again. "Ignore him. I like them and think you should keep both of them." Mario starts going off at Alonzo, but he ignores his tangent. "They don't need to be strong and fearsome because you have us, and you. Just make them your bitches and get them to do all the shitty stuff, everyone has their place in the home after all, and you're obviously more of a man than those two clowns. But seriously though, they clearly love your psychotic ass, and I never thought you'd find someone that would put up with your crazy shit, let alone two of them. I say, keep 'em."

"What ended up happening with that other cartel?" I ask them, wanting to change the subject because they have no right to an opinion on it, but I'm not healed enough to fight them on it. "Did we get them or is there a turf war going on?"

I watch in fascination as Alonzo's eyes darken before he turns back to face the front and his words come out as cold as ice. "We killed every single one of them and anyone that we found connected to them in any way. It was brutal efficient, and we even got an apology from Mexico letting us know that it will never happen again."

Mario scoffs, "What Alonzo means is that when you got shot, he turned into a vengeful spirit and completely obliterated everything that even twitched. It was a fucking bloodbath and over quicker than anything I've ever seen before. I'm pretty sure he terrified all the international connections that he was going to fly there and skull fuck all their relatives before killing them slowly. Because we kept getting gift baskets and large sums of cash donations toward your recovery. It's the first time I've ever seen Papi completely okay with him being an utter psychopath."

"It was mass carnage. If it wasn't for worrying about you, I would have had a blast. Way to ruin the mood, chiquita." Alonzo laughs, once again showcasing how much control he has over his moods.

I relax a bit more in the backseat as we drive up the driveway, but as we reach the house, I see Beau's car and tense again. "What are they doing here?" I ask under my breath.

"We couldn't even get them to leave your side for almost two months, do you really think we could keep them away from the house when you got home?" Mario grumbles, clearly unhappy with the idea of them in his space.

We park and Juan comes over to my car door and opens it, obviously waiting for me to get home. "How are you feeling?" he asks with a worried furrow on his brow, reaching in his hand for me to take. I guess it's not so bad having a bunch of overprotective brothers at my beck and call. My baby will certainly be the best protected in all of Beastville.

"I'm alright, but I really want to lie down," I tell him honestly, letting him help me out of the car. This is how they know I'm serious because I normally wouldn't accept help from anyone.

Juan helps me into the house, carefully guiding me toward the staircase, when I hear Beau's voice coming from the kitchen. He sees where my attention went and puts his finger to his mouth in a shushing motion, changing our direction. I keep quiet and as we turn the corner I see why he wanted me to come in on stealth mode.

Theodore and Beau are dressed in Mami's aprons and are bent over the kitchen bench. Mami explains the process of working the pupusas with her hands and how to add the cheese mix in the middle, carefully folding over the sides and flattening it out to look like a savory pancake. They stare in fascination as they attempt to copy her movements with pupusas of their own.

"Like this?" Beau asks studiously, his pupusa looking surprisingly good for a first attempt, whereas Theodore beside him is making it look as hard as disarming a bomb.

Mami tells Beau he's doing a great job but makes Theodore try again and again until one looks semi-right. I find myself smiling at their patience and thoughtfulness, knowing that they're learning to make it after I told them it was my favorite food to eat.

Juan pulls me gently back to the staircase, picking me up at the bottom and carrying me all the way to my room. He carefully lays me down on the bed, the blankets already folded over and waiting for me.

As he tucks me in sweetly, Juan quietly says, "They aren't too bad, I guess, but I'll deny it if you tell anyone I said that." I cross my heart and swallow the pain relief medication he gives me, that I'm starting to need again. I can't wait to be back to my old self.

I'm so over being an invalid. I wasn't created to sit in

bed all day, it might be a day well spent for someone like Allure, but for me, it's like torture. I miss my morning workouts, working hard under a car, and getting my hands dirty with every part of life.

Juan leaves straight after, making sure my blinds are closed, my water is full, and the thermostat is at the right temperature. I just let him fuss around me like a worried old lady, knowing it'll never happen again.

A light tapping sounds on my door, and I tell whoever it is to come in, and to my delight it's Theodore, holding a pretty bunch of red roses in one of Mami's vases. Flowers aren't normally my thing, but I appreciate the gesture.

"Hey, pretty girl, I heard you were home and thought I'd come up and see you." Theodore put the flowers on my side table. "Beau picked these out. He always gets them when tough stuff happens because they remind him of his mum. He thought if she was here, this is what she would want him to do for you. Speaking of mum," he goes for a segue. "My parents would very much like to have you over for lunch when you're feeling better again. I've told them everything, including the baby and the shared relationship thing. Mom thinks it's all very exciting, and I've had to really contain her, so she doesn't come barging over with an intrusive amount of hugs and baby clothes." He shakes his head for emphasis, but she sounds like a decent enough person, and I can't blame him for wanting me to meet them. If it wasn't for the injury, I would have probably done it by now anyway.

"She sounds very understanding," I remark because not every mother would be as happy with their only child being stuck in such a complicated situation.

His dimples pop as he smiles sweetly, leaning in to kiss my cheek. "You'll find that my parents are very simple people. They may be billionaires, but the only things that they really ever care about is mine and Beau's happiness, each other, and soppy love stories. They're ridiculously romantic. It was really embarrassing growing up, but now I think it's kind of amazing. I'd love to know even half of the happiness that they do just by being with each other."

Looking into his eyes, I can tell that he's just as romantic as they are, and I have zero doubt that he will only ever treat me with love and respect. It might take some getting used to though because it's not exactly like I scream princess in need of a knight or any of that kind of shit. However, for these two guys who have given up so much of their time and energy over the last few months, they deserve for me to at least try.

"I'd love to meet them." My answer is surprisingly honest, but any people that managed to create such an incredible human being and take in and care for Beau when he needed love and support are worth getting to know.

He thanks me with hearts in his eyes, and I look up at his features, taking in every detail while wondering if the baby growing inside me will have his dimples, his strong nose, or his chiseled jawline.

Beau appears in the doorway with a wide smile. "Hey, sexy lady," he sings in the tune of the Gangnam Style song. In a more normal tone, he adds, "Did you miss us?" He comes in, leans down, and kisses my lips softly, and I have to hold back a moan at how nice he tastes.

My eyes flick to see Theodore's reaction to his friend kissing me like that in front of him, but as usual, he doesn't look the least bit fazed by it. Can these two seriously not feel any jealousy between them or ownership over me? I couldn't imagine it because if I saw either one of them kissing someone else, the carnage that Alonzo inflicted on the cartel would be nothing compared to what I would do in retaliation.

Theodore excuses himself politely, giving Beau some alone time with me, and I ask him, "Have either of you asked about my Papi's intense desire for a wedding?"

"We have, but we both agree that we will follow your lead. He's your dad, and we will respect whatever you need from us. Honestly, neither of us wants to unnecessarily worry about anything but getting better and cooking that little bean of ours." Beau places his hand on the blanket where my tummy bump is. "I love you, Foxy. I know I haven't said it enough, but it's because I don't want to overwhelm you or make you think it's just because of the baby. I knew I loved you before the incident happened, but I also knew that you weren't the kind of person who would've appreciated being told so early on in any relationship, and we weren't even official yet. Theodore feels the same way. That's why we were at your house that day. We'd arrived to tell you that our feelings were real, and we were going to fight for you, whether you wanted us to or not." Beau laughs, unconsciously rubbing his hand in small circular motions over my belly.

CHAPTER 33

BEAU

Sitting around the Hernandez family dinner table feels weird when Foxy isn't here with us. Obviously, she can't come down and eat with everyone else while she's still recuperating, but Theodore and I are a little out of our depth here.

Making matters even tenser, Mr. Hernandez turns his whole body to face us, putting down his cutlery halfway through the meal, and steepling his fingers. He then asks, in a very business-like tone, "Which one of you is marrying my daughter? You must have talked about it by now, and I want the answer, so I can start organizing something for when she is able to be on her feet again."

Tee chokes on his food, coughing harshly beside me, and I pat him on the back hard trying to buy time and figure out how to get the hell out of here.

When he clears his throat loudly after Tee gets his shit together again and has a long sip of water, I know there's no way out of this and turn to face him head-on. "Sir, we aren't sure what Foxy wants to do yet, but we've made it clear that whatever she decides, we'll support that decision."

"When will you be finding out who the father is?" Mr. Hernandez asks, getting straight to the next difficult discussion. "I asked the doctor, and they said that it's not a complicated test and people do it all the time."

I look pleadingly at Foxy's mum, who so far has been surprisingly on our side against the men of the family, but straight away I can tell that she also wants the answer to these questions and know we're on our own.

Deciding that it's worth risking their wrath, I take a deep breath and say, "With all due respect, sir. But this isn't a conversation we should be having without Foxy present, and I'm sure we can all agree on that. She is a strong woman who knows what she wants, and this is her body that we're talking about."

I can feel Tee tense beside me as we wait for some kind of retaliation. Usually, he's the one that deals with the tough talk while I happily lean on my sense of humor to alleviate tension, but today I think it's important to set boundaries. Our relationship with Foxy going forward will reflect how we handle situations like this with her family. We shouldn't be discussing this without her, full stop.

Alonzo snorts in between bites of his food and says with a mouth full, "Good answer."

Instead of going back to eat like Alonzo, Tee and I wait for Foxy's father's response. His mouth purses in thought, and then he slams one hand down on the table, making both of us flinch.

"It's settled then," he announces suddenly, standing up and pushing his chair back. "Let's go and talk to her about it. Food can wait, this can't anymore."

That's not what I meant. Shit. She's going to be pissed off.

Mr. Hernandez heads toward the chair with his wife

right behind him. Tee and I quickly catch up, not missing the laughter from her brothers at the table at our expense no doubt.

We enter Foxy's room and find her propped up in bed, playing with her phone, and when she sees the four of us coming into her room, her eyes darken, and she sends what seems to be a quick text.

"Are you talking to Allure?" Mrs. Hernandez asks, going to her bed and sitting on the side with a smile.

Foxy grunts and says, "Just telling her to wish me luck over whatever intervention this is going to be."

"It's not like that, don't be dramatic," her father says, but when she looks at us behind him, we give her 'I'm sorry' faces, telling her she's spot on, and please don't blame us. "We just came up to ask you two things, and I'm not leaving without proper answers. When are you finding out who the father is? And which one are you marrying because we need to let the family know when to come for the wedding?"

Tee and I freeze, waiting for an angry outburst that she's too injured to deal with right now, but to our surprise, she just shrugs like it's nothing and answers. "Okay. That's fair, I was going to talk to you all about it anyway, but it does seem unfair to the guys that they have to have this conversation in front of you when it's none of your business, but if they're cool with it, then let's get to the point."

They all turn to look at us and Tee says, "It's fine," and I happily agree. We're both pretty easygoing guys, and between the two of us, we've both already talked about it extensively and know what we want. Which is very much based on what will make her happy, but we are prepared to fight for her if she tries to push us away.

"Alright." Foxy ignores her parents, focusing solely on

us as she states. "I have no intention of finding out who the biological father is, especially if the arrangement we've all agreed on works out in the long run. But if something changes in the future, then I'm happy to talk about it again. For now, though, I'm happy the way it is. Is that alright with you guys because if you have some masculine need to know if your seed is working or some stupid shit like that, let me know now?"

I spit out a small laugh. "Nah, I'm good. I genuinely don't care and don't plan on letting you push me away even if you want to. Whether you like it or not, I'm going to love you and that baby, blood ties or not."

"Agreed," Tee adds. "We've already discussed it between us, and it doesn't matter at all. That's *our* baby with you, regardless of what any test says." He points to him and me.

She flicks a look at her parents. "There's your answer on that one. Now for your desire to see your little girl get married, you need to get over that." She looks back at us, an apology in her eyes. "I'm sorry, guys, but I don't want to get married." My heart drops. "I've never wanted to get married, I'm not a bride type of girl and don't see why I need some piece of paper to tell me who I can love. I'm not religious, and I'm not interested in the social structure of what a traditional 'marriage' looks like. Obviously, because otherwise, I wouldn't be sitting here with my own little harem, would I?"

I take in what she's saying, trying not to be offended, but instead accepting her words for what they are; her truth. Almost instantly I know I'm fine with that because the only thing that really matters to me is that she's in my life and a piece of paper won't change the way I feel about her.

Looking at Tee beside me, I can see clearly in his

expression of understanding that he's in the same place that I am, and I answer for both of us. "Whatever you want, gorgeous. The only thing we care about is you and our baby, the rest is just dressing we don't need. If you change your mind, we'll support that too."

"Absolutely not," her father bellows angrily. "You will not be having a bastard baby. Choose right now."

Mrs. Hernandez stands in front of him with her hands on her hips and a whole new level of fury burning out of her eyes at him. "If you push her away again, then I'm going with her. Do you hear me? We should be happy we're getting a nieto o nieta from her at all. Be grateful for that. I thought she would die alone and unloved, the way she pushes everyone away." She turns to her daughter. "Be happy. Let them love you. If you want this lifestyle, I will support you, but I want to see my grandbaby all the time."

"Fine, but it's the only one I'm having. Gracias Mami." Foxy rubs her belly unconsciously, and I make a mental note to accept that we're having an only child. This kid is going to be so spoiled! She lifts her head in defiance as she stares her dad down. "If you plan on having a relationship with this baby, you'd better get on board, Papi, and realize that this is our choice to make, not yours."

With a grunt that is as close to an okay as we're going to get, Mr. Hernandez waves his hand and walks out the door. Clearly, he's unhappy about it, but he's also choosing to come to terms with what she's telling him, and I'm mega grateful that I don't have to have this conversation with him again. After all, it's a woman's choice what she does with her body from procreation to marriage, no woman should ever be told how she should be doing it if she even wants to do it at all.

CHAPTER 34

FOXY

It feels like recovery is taking forever, but now that I'm seventeen weeks along, I'm finally well enough to go to Theodore's parents' house to meet them properly. Theodore has Facebook called them almost every time he's come over to visit, which at this point they live more at my place than at theirs, both bunking in our spare room together because they're so worried about hurting me.

Having them doting on me constantly is kind of awesome because I get everything I want. But as nice as it has been and all, I want things to go back to normal, not to mention I've been horny as hell the last couple of weeks. While it's great that they're being gentlemen, I need some dick. I made them promise to take me back out on a movie date after dinner, and then I want to stay at their place. I have some wicked plans, and it involves testing just how comfortable they are with sharing after all.

We pull up in front of a massive Greek-style mansion that has my eyes bulging out of my head. "I thought you said your parents own a clothes shop?" I question Tee as he opens the car door for me. "Are the clothes lined with crack?"

Beau laughs, getting out after me and jogging up the large front stairs that glimmer with marble. "You haven't seen anything yet. Wait till you see inside, it's gonna blow your mind."

"I told you that they own the Lumiere company," Theodore replies, looking a bit sheepish while he entwines my fingers with his, walking us up behind Beau. "To be fair, it's not my fault you don't know fashion."

Wide-eyed, I take in the styled hedges, enormous fountain, and gold trimmings everywhere. "Is it a well-known company or something?" I ask, completely overwhelmed by the wealth pouring off of every inch of this place. When they said his parents lived in Serenity, I knew they had money, but I was not prepared for this place.

Beau rings the doorbell and laughs again. "It's only one of the richest fashion companies in the world. Only the most elite people can afford Lumiere. It's a deluxe brand that only the best of the best from all over the globe wear. A little different from the overalls you tend to live in."

I smack the back of his head. "You said you like my overalls," I grumble, feeling way out of place and suddenly super conscious of my basic maternity jeans and t-shirt.

"One of the reasons we love you is because you're not superficial. Don't even worry about it, Mum and Dad know that you aren't into that kind of thing and couldn't care less. Their heads are in the clouds half the time, living in some whimsical land. You'll see, even their furniture looks like a fairy tale and over the top. They've always been like that, but they don't have a bad bone in their bodies," Theodore tells me as his thumb strokes the back of my hand in an attempt to comfort me.

The stunning Mrs. Bell flings the door open and straight away it's obvious that the camera did her no justice because this woman is freaking stunning, like a princess or some shit. It's a shame Allure's not here, she'd get a real kick out of this. Me, though, I'm a little worried that all the sweet and sugary is going to give me a cavity.

"Foxy," she cries out with her arms wide. Alright, she's a hugger. She pulls me in close but still carefully, and I stare at Beau's big smile at my discomfort and squint tightly at him for not warning me enough. "It's so lovely to finally meet our new daughter. Theodore has done everything to keep us from coming to your place, assuring us that we should wait. It's been hell." She pulls back and looks me up and down, putting her hands over my tummy, leaning down to talk to it in a baby voice. "Hello, little baby. I'm your grandmother, and I love you so much."

Okay. I can deal with this for Theodore and Beau's sake, I tell myself on repeat, and luckily the latter saves me. "Foxy's not much of a hugger, Ma, and she's still a bit delicate after her surgery. But I sure could use a squeeze." He pulls her away from me and into an embrace they both seem to genuinely enjoy. It's obvious that he thinks of Theodore's parents as a second set of his own, with love and admiration in his eyes.

"Thank you for having us for dinner, Mrs. Bell. It's nice to finally meet you properly," I say, determined to be on my best behavior. "Your home is really beautiful."

An older George-Clooney-looking guy comes through the door and says with a warm and inviting smile. "Please call us Mum and Dad, or at the very least Linkon and Jaelyn. We are family, after all." He reaches his hand out for me to take, and I happily return the gesture, grateful he isn't baby-talking my stomach as well.

"I'll stick with your names if that's alright, Linkon," I offer, wanting to be honest about my comfort zone. "The idea of the three of us doing this family thing is still kind of new for me, and I'm trying to still get used to the idea that soon there will be four of us. It's a bit daunting."

"Oh, I can understand that, dear," Jaelyn says, sliding her hand through Linkon's arm and looking up at him like he hung the moon for her. "Theodore is our miracle baby but becoming a parent is a big deal. Luckily, when you have someone to share it with that loves and supports you no matter what, it makes the whole thing truly magical." She looks between the guys and me, beaming a white-toothed smile. "And you have two men to love you. Aren't you all so lucky to have each other? It's so romantic."

Beau whispers in my ear, coming up behind me and sliding his hands over my growing belly. "Everything is romantic to them, you'll see." His little chuckle in my ear has goose pimples traveling down my spine. "You get used to it."

"Well, come on inside, you lot. Dinner is already on the table, and I'd hate for it to get cold," Linkon says, and I check the time on my watch to see if we are later than I thought. The sun is still dropping from the horizon, and we are exactly on time according to the time.

Theodore sees my confusion and takes my hand away, holding it sweetly instead. "This house has the magical ability to always serve food the moment someone arrives. It's pretty cool. Our family chef Chip is a magician, I swear."

"And wait till you try his cooking." Jaelyn does the kiss with her fingers as we walk inside. "Food will never taste the same again."

The inside of their mansion is exactly what Beau said it

would be. It's a mixture of what you'd see inside a medieval castle and a castle at the end of a Disney princess movie. All it's missing is singing birds and for the furniture to start dancing and twirling around the room. *Who the fuck are these people?*

We move into an oversized formal dining room with a ridiculously long table in the center lined with old-school candelabras and gold-lined table settings. Even the cutlery looks like it's gold, and I have to stifle a laugh, not wanting them to know how much I'm internally mocking them.

All the food and table settings are at one end of the table. We sit down in our places, with Linkon at the head, Jaelyn to his right, and the three of us on the left with me in the center of the guys. Theodore had told me that they were cool with our little arrangement, but I was expecting them to be this happy about it. The way they stare at the three of us is intense as if they're waiting for us to start singing a love song or some shit.

Beau picks up my plate, asking me what I want, and I just tell him a bit of everything. The massive dishes filled with roast beef, and vegetables all look and smell as good as Jaelyn said they would be, and I find myself salivating, the baby inside me all of a sudden demanding food. A little flutter of excitement has me stroking my bump and internally telling it that it's coming and to wait a minute more.

"Is the baby kicking?" Jaelyn asked me excitedly, looking down at where my hand is. "Bubba must be hungry. Make sure you eat as much as you like, you're eating for two, after all."

I hate that saying. It's not like there's a full-sized human demanding its own massive meal in there. Admittedly, I am definitely more hungry than I usually am, but not enough for two of me.

"It's more like a fluttering feeling than actual kicks," I tell her, picking up my fork and bringing the most mouth-watering roast I've ever had to my mouth. "Oh, my god. This is incredible," I moan rudely, shoveling in another big fork full.

The guys laugh at me, but I don't even care because holy shit, the meat melts in my mouth. Seeing that I'm publicly making love to my food, the others go on to talk amongst each other while I enjoy the moment, and I end up having a whole second plate after all, making my earlier inner monologue a moot point, but I'm not sorry. It's just too good.

"Have your parents decided what grandparent name they want?" Linkon asks me, folding his napkin up and placing it on the table beside him. "We're thinking of grandma and grandpa if it doesn't interfere with their names, of course."

It's kind of sweet how much they've thought about it and makes me relieved that when this baby does come it's going to be surrounded with so much love from every angle. At least that's one thing I don't have to be worried about.

I tell them that I love their choices and that my parents are going with the Spanish approach with abuelo and abuelita. We spend a great deal of time discussing how excited they are to be grandparents, and how wonderful they think it is that Beau and Theodore have found love in the same person. The unconventional nature of our relationship truly doesn't seem to faze them in the slightest.

After dinner finishes, Theodore excuses us, explaining to them that they owe me a movie date and want to go before it gets late in case I get tired. They practically usher us out the door, insisting we have a marvelous night, but not before Linkon fills Theodore's truck with baby clothes and accessories that they've been buying since they found out I was pregnant.

We watch some generic action movie that I immediately fall asleep in, more exhausted than I thought I would be at this time. But I decide I will need the nap if I plan on taking advantage of these men later on tonight.

"Wake up baby," Theodore says to me softly, and I come to, taking a second to figure out where I am, but when I do, I smile up at him and ask if it's over. With a laugh, he helps me up and both of them take one of my hands as we walk out to the car, getting more than one curious glance at our dynamic and my stomach. Yep, that's right nosey people, I fucked them both, aren't I lucky?

I let Beau help me into the car, and I excitedly do my seatbelt up, smiling and now wide awake, with my vagina waking up and ready to feast.

"What are you so excited about?" Theodore says, looking at my cheeky expression in the rearview mirror as we take off. "Do you want some dessert, beautiful?"

"Sure do, so we'd better get home sooner than later," I reply, looking out the window. "I have an insatiable appetite that won't be ignored anymore."

Beau turns in the front seat to look at me with confusion. "I don't think we have any food in the house, but we can take you somewhere else. What do you feel like?"

I look him square in the face and reply clearly, "Dick. Lots of dick." Can't say I'm not clear about what I want.

I watch with delight as his eyes widen, and he looks over at a very stiff Theodore in the driver's seat. That's right boys, tonight I'm testing the 'I'm fine with sharing' theory. I'm only three weeks off it being the time we gave this shared dating timeline, and I plan to use each day wisely, pushing every opportunity to see if it's something they really can live with. I don't want it to be a later problem when we have a kid in the middle of our situation.

The car ride becomes relatively silent for the rest of the way to their apartment, and I secretly love it. My mind flitters with all the things I want to do tonight, and half of them I have to veto straight away because I'm still not a hundred percent and don't want to injure myself or the baby.

Pulling into the garage, I find that my nerves speak up a little. If it doesn't go well, then it's all over, but I refuse to think about that possibility, reminding myself how important this is.

When we're out of the car, they each take one of my hands and hold it, quietly showing me that they understand the assignment, and we get in the elevator together. To my absolute delight, the old lady from the first night I stayed here steps into the elevator with us. She looks me over with distaste, taking in my rounded stomach and the two men holding my hand, and I wink at her conspiratorially.

"There was a two-for-one special," I tell her, pulling both guys closer. "Bargain right? The bun in the oven was just an added bonus. If you're interested, we could make some space for you."

To say that lady left the elevator in a massive hurry is an extreme understatement, and I lost my shit, laughing so hard that I almost pee myself.

Beau laughs next to me as Theodore asks what that was about and how I know Ms. Colfer. I explain in between fits of laughter that we almost had a thing once, but it didn't work out, making Beau laugh even louder.

Once we reach their level we hop out and head to the

door with Theodore looking more confused than ever and Beau one fit of laughter away from a stroke.

"Oh my god, open the door." I get out doing the wee dance, still laughing. "I'm busting, and I'm not going to be able to hold it."

I picture the look on her face again, and I have to bend over with my legs glued together as Theodore manages to get the key to open the lock. The second it opens, I practically run to the bathroom, Beau's hysterics behind me.

Making it just in time, I let out a relieved moan because that kind of satisfaction is almost as good as sex. Speaking of sex, I wash my hands and strip out of my clothes, leaving absolutely nothing to the imagination as I stroll with a confidence that would rival a priest entering heaven. With a little less virtue and a little more sin.

Two sets of eyes swing my way and hungrily devour every curve and crevice and since the last time they saw me naked like this I was definitely wearing one less curve. I rub my little belly and ask, posing, "How does it look? I'm sexy right?"

"So fucking hot," Beau growls, getting to his feet, striding toward me. "I can't wait to taste you. I've missed your flavor on my tongue." He picks me up in a bridal hold and starts carrying me into his room.

I look over his shoulder to see a conflicted Theodore standing in the lounge, and I call, "Are you coming? My ass won't fuck itself." Beau almost trips, and I laugh, but it gets Theodore moving, as he follows us in, a familiar hungry look in his gaze.

Beau lays me down on the bed, looking me up and down, and Theodore asks me, "Are you sure you're up to this?" I nod. "Alright, but the moment you start hurting, or it's too much, you have to promise to tell us."

I do the scout's honor sign and Beau sits at my feet, taking them into his hands and slowly massaging them. Theodore comes behind me, sitting me up and sliding behind me with one leg on each side of me.

Beau's massage begins to slowly make its way up my legs, and he parts my knees, gazing intently at what I know is his ultimate target, and the waiting drives me crazy but in a good way. He's always enjoyed playing with me.

Theodore goes for a more direct approach, which I knew he would, as his hands slip around to my front, kneading my heavy breasts and pinching my nipples the way he knows I like. I lean into him, letting myself get lost in all the sensory touch over my body.

Hands climb up my inner thighs, and I close my eyes, loving the feeling as my brain cries out for him to go higher. In a purely Beau move, he stops at the join of my body to my thigh and starts going back down. My eyes pop open, and I glare down at his cheeky face.

We both know what he wants and while I want to play back, my pussy clenches with the need for him to touch me and I cave, asking, "Please touch me, Beau."

Theodore starts kissing my neck, and I moan as Beau asks, "Where?" I might kill him.

"If you don't touch my pussy soon, I'm going to get Theodore to do it," I growl angrily, and Theodore chuckles on the sensitive skin of my neck, making me shudder.

Beau spreads my knees wide suddenly, crawling between my thighs, and lies on his stomach so close to my throbbing pussy that I can feel his hot breath fanning it. "You know the rules," he reminds me just before his tongue licks up my slit, and it takes all I have not to close my eyes.

I keep my gaze on him as he starts sucking, nipping, and licking at me like I'm the best thing he's ever feasted on.

And Theodore makes everything more intense by the way he kisses my neck and plays with my sensitive nipples.

A deep groan slips out of me, my climax only seconds away. "Don't stop baby. Don't fucking stop." And because he's a fucking God, he stays at the exact same tempo, not changing a thing until my head collapses against Theodore's chest, and I scream out in pleasure. I love a man that can take direction.

"Are you doing alright?" Theodore asks, lowering his hand to my baby bump while Beau backs up, looking at me for signs of distress. "This isn't too much?"

"You're not getting out of it that easily," I tell him with a satisfied chuckle. "We have a big night ahead of us. Why do you think I had a nap at the movies? Lie down, baby," I say to Beau. "It's my turn."

Like a good boy, he does what he's told lying on the bed beside me and Theodore moves back allowing me to straddle Beau's hips, enjoying the feeling of his hard dick sliding between my soaking lips. I raise myself up, grab his member with my hand and glide it to my opening, letting my wetness get us both ready.

Theodore sits beside me, watching what I'm doing intently and by the looks of his own hard cock he doesn't mind this one bit, which gives me a thrill. My gaze never leaves his as I start to slide down Beau's shaft, letting it stretch me open. He grabs his cock in his hand and starts to slowly pump it, getting off on his best friend spearing me to the hilt, and I couldn't be happier.

Finding it too taxing to bounce up and down, I go with the easier option and start grinding my hips instead, rolling back and forth, and enjoying the friction it causes. Theodore sucks on his fingers, then brings them to my clit, circling it and rubbing it in just the right way. I have to focus on keeping my grinding tempo because the pleasure building between the two different feelings is almost too much to handle.

"That's it, baby," Beau tells me, his voice strained with his own mounding pleasure. "That's so fucking sexy."

His words are enough to push me over, and I start to shake, cumming hard on Beau's dick. I lean over him, a hand on each side of his head as I slowly come down, but I never stop the grinding.

Theodore moves behind me, and I don't know what he's doing until I feel his tongue lapping at my back door, and I'm equally surprised and thrilled by it. His body lifts coming up behind me, and I feel his hard length between my heels as he says softly in my ear, "Last chance to change your mind."

Mierda, these two men get me hotter than anyone I've ever come across, and I smile at knowing I've hit the jackpot. "Give it to me, baby, just take it nice and slow," I tell him, pausing on Beau's dick so that I can relax enough to take Theodore too.

The head of his cock slowly and carefully nudges my puckered hole but because I'm a pro at this, it relaxes nice and easy helping him slide inside. I look down at Beau's features to make sure he's still cool with everything.

Beau's shoulders look tense, but he's panting as he says to me, seeing that I'm looking for answers. "It feels weirdly good. I like it."

"Fuck, you're tight like this, baby," Theodore groans, hitting the hilt.

They both stay still like that for a second, and I start to grind my hips again, needing movement and feeling so full. They moan simultaneously when I move, egging me on to keep going, and I do, but I only manage a few good grinds before they take over, moving in unison. In and out, in and out as my clit rubs against Beau's pelvic bone deliciously.

Sweat builds between our bodies and the tempo becomes more rapid and irregular as we all charge toward the finish line. As soon as my pussy clenches with another orgasm, Beau follows me, calling out my name wildly.

The second he stops coming, Theodore pulls out of my ass, lifts my hips so that Beau slips out, and then slams into my pussy hard. The wetness from both mine and Beau's combined climax makes it easy, and with only a few hard strokes of his dick he cums deep inside me, squeezing my hips with his fingertips.

Theodore pulls out and moves to the side, and I roll off Beau to the other side, and we all pant, staring at the ceiling together before we all start laughing.

"Well, I'd say that was a success," I chuckle. "Any objections?"

"Fuck no," Beau says without delay. "That was way more intense and hot than I was expecting. I was worried it was going to be awkward or gross having Tee's balls near me. Luckily, his balls are so small, it's not an issue."

Theodore smacks his chest. "Fuck off dickhead, my balls are epic, but I agree that went really well."

"Okay, so are we really doing this?" I ask, not wanting to wait for the twenty-week mark anymore, not now that I know how good it is to play nice with others. "The whole forever, with all three of us thing?"

"Sharing is caring and all that." Beau puts his fist up, and Theodore and I fist-bump him. "Guess I'm changing my last name to Hernandez."

I turn to the side, leaning up on my elbow. "What? Why?"

"Well, I want to have the same last as our kid, and I'd

never dream of making you choose between ours, so it only makes sense. You in, man?" He turns his head to Theodore, who nods easily.

"That's a great idea. Will your family mind?" Always the thinker. "I wouldn't want to do it without their consent."

"Fuck their consent, you have mine. Let's do this shit." I make up my mind on the spot, and the inner possessive beast in me purrs with contentment about having my name tattooed on them. It feels like they belong to me now, them and the baby. I like it.

CHAPTER 35

FOXY

The weird stick thing rolls around in the jelly on my stomach and the three of us stare at the black and white screen trying to figure out what is what. I'm pretty sure the big round thing is the baby's head, but it could be its ass.

"Okay, everything looks great," the ultrasound guy says to us. "The baby is a great size, the organs are all presenting within the right range and the heartbeat is nice and strong. Did you want to find out the sex of the baby today, or are you going for a surprise?"

Knowing how desperate both Beau and Theodore are to find out the sex, I say in a serious tone. "Please don't tell us. It will be nice to have a surprise on the day." Both faces flick to me with pleading eyes, and I can't keep a straight face. "Just kidding. What kind of problems are we looking at in the future, messy periods or wet dreams?"

"Really?" Theodore asks me, shaking his head at me.

I shrug. "What, it's a legitimate question."

The ultrasound guy smiles at my humor and moves the stick around again, stopping and clicking a few buttons.

"Looks like you better start saving daddies because girls are expensive."

Beau jumps up and starts whooping and hollering. "Oh, my god. I'm gonna be a girl Dad. We can have tea parties and make cupcakes, and I'm going to buy her every pretty glittery thing I can get my hands on."

Theodore laughs and says, "Unless she's like her mother, then you're going to have to get a mini tool kit and peewee bike instead." He scratches his head, looking bewildered, and leans in to kiss my cheek. "Holy shit. I'm having a daughter." His eyes fill with tears, and I roll my eyes at the two of them. You'd think they were the girls in the room.

"Well, Mami will be over the moon when we tell her," I say as the guy wipes off my belly and prints off some ultrasound pictures for us to take with us. "Maybe we should fuck with them and not tell anyone."

I sit up and pull my shirt down, watching as baby girl's daddies take the pictures and start cooing over them about how cute she is. I mean, she kind of looks like an alien at this point, but whatever.

My body freezes halfway off the bed when it all clicks into place. I can't have a girl, I don't know what to do with girls. I'm not ready for this. What was I thinking? Oh my god! I'm a mum!

"Breathe." Theodore rubs my back and I look up at him, feeling more than a little sick. "It's going to be alright because you're not alone and never will be. We've got you, every step of the way, and will never leave yours or her side."

Beau passes me a little picture and I can make out the outline of a little face. "This beautiful little girl is going to be the luckiest girl in the world because her mum is a strong, fierce warrior that is capable of taking on the world for her and when she needs a soft touch, she's lucky enough to have two dads that just so happen to love the mushy shit. Between us all, we've got it covered. Thank you for this gift. I love you so much." Beau's last words come out a bit shaky, giving away the level of emotion he's feeling.

I look between them both and blink rapidly, refusing to acknowledge that I'm about to cry like every other girl would. "Love you both, now feed us. Your girls are hungry."

"Our girls," Beau almost squeals excitedly. Yep, it's official, he's the girl in this relationship.

We start walking out of the room and just as we step into the waiting room, an uproar of sound bombards us. To my absolute shock and horror, it is packed to the brim with all the Hernandez family members, Theodore's parents, and Allure and family. They are all holding blue or pink signs in the air excitedly, and I want the ground to swallow me up as I apologize to the receptionist, who thankfully seems to find it funny.

"What is happening right now?" I cry, with my arms out. "¿Estan locos? This is not the place for this."

Mami, Jaelyn, and Allure all step forward, apparently the spokesperson for their families, and start asking what the baby is, completely ignoring my outrage at their public display.

Beau and Theo smirk beside me, trying not to laugh at my reaction, and I glare at them. "Did you know about this?" I growl, not at all impressed.

They both just shrug, but I don't believe them for a second. How else would everyone know the time and place of the ultrasound in the first place?

"Well, mija, what are we having?" Mami pleads, holding tightly to a pink sign in desperation.

Allure claps her hands excitedly with two signs, one blue and one pink. "Tell me, I've been out here dying of impatience. Is it a best friend for our little girl, or is it my future son-in-law?"

"Only you would be planning our kids' wedding before they're even born," I grumble at her, looking down at her bump that's a bit bigger than my own.

Her eyes widen in excitement at the same time that Mami's mouth drops open. Beau's hands go up and he calls out. "She didn't say it was a boy."

Jaelyn purses her lips, also holding a pink sign, and asks confused, "Wait, does that mean it's a girl? I don't get it."

Deciding to put them all out of their misery and me the fuck out of this building, I say, "It's a girl. Now can I go home?" I push past everyone, feeling overwhelmed as fuck as they all start cheering and congratulating each other as if they had something to do with it.

I am genuinely happy for them and us, but this was a lot, and it's not exactly in my comfort zone. Theodore comes up to me grabbing my hand and helps me escape the room, shuttling me to the car, and as soon as I sit down, I lean back against the seat, closing my eyes. Silence. Yay.

Theodore hops in the seat behind me, and Beau *eventually* gets into the driver's seat with a smile from ear to ear. I don't think I've ever seen him so happy, and this guy is always happy. "A bit excited, Beau?" I question, letting out a small laugh at how ecstatic he looks.

"Just a bit. Now put your seatbelt on because we have a present for you and our daughter." Beau's eyes sparkle with mischief, and my spider sense goes off that foul play is afoot.

"What have you done?"

He just switches on the radio and turns up the volume, singing away to the tune of 'She' by Elvis Costello. I didn't realize I was dating an old guy, hiding in an indie rocker body.

The drive we go on is much longer than I originally anticipated, as we go deeper South than we normally do, heading past the nothingness of Forevermore and the farmlands of Faith Plains. We head up to Mount Myth, and I figure we must be having a nice lunch up there or something.

We head up the beautiful mountainside and up, where the scenery is to die for. I've always told them how much I love it up here, it's one of my favorite places to go, and it means a lot to me that they remembered that and are doing something nice for me.

Before we get to the picturesque little village up here, they take a turn-off that I'm unfamiliar with. It's not long before they're pulling into a hidden driveway with a gate as big as the one at my parents' place but way prettier, with a more antique look instead of a we'll shoot you look.

"Where are we?" I ask, looking out the window, but I can't see anything behind the giant trees in the front of the yard. "Do you know who lives here?"

"Sure do," Theodore says from behind me as Beau presses a button on a little fob he pulls out of the glove department. "Pretty well, actually."

I scrunch my face, wondering why they'd bring me to a friend's place instead of out to lunch. And here I was thinking they were doing something thoughtful for me.

We start to slowly drive down the driveway and the trees clear away, showing off a large old stone house that's clearly been well taken care of. I find my nose almost squished up against the glass to take it all in.

"This is gorgeous." My voice is full of awe. "Can we have a look inside?" Just then Freja comes running around the side of the house barking at the car as we pull in. "What's she doing here?"

My confusion about what's happening grows when I open my door, and she happily asks for scratches, which I happily give her. This dog has become my best friend during my recovery. Allure had better watch out because if she's not lucky I'll start liking this bitch more. She never left my side and was always asleep at my feet, as if she knew that I needed help the same way she did when I found her.

"Good girl, Freja. What are you doing here?" I step out and watch as both Beau and Theodore walk toward the front door calling out asking if I'm coming.

I catch up easily enough and touch the stone wall, feeling the age with every bump. I marvel at the state of it as we walk through the front door, which they don't even knock on, might I add. There's not one note of disrepair anywhere, I notice as they give me a tour of the house. There's a state-of-the-art stone countered, dark wood finish kitchen, a massive garage that could easily house four big cars, and the basement has been done up as a huge at-home gym.

Where I really start to freak out is when we go upstairs, and they show me a stunning nursery next to the biggest master bedroom I've ever seen. The bed is almost double the size of a normal king bed, with a window wall that looks out over the valley below. There is a bassinet right beside the bed on one side and Freja's favorite bed on the other side which she lies on straight away.

My body does a slow spin and I turn to them with wide eyes, "What in the ever-loving Christ is going on?" Suspicion turns into confirmation when they beam giant smiles at me. "You didn't?" is all I can say, looking around the room again. "I don't understand." My eyes start to burn with unshed tears. "Tell me you didn't."

"We did," Theodore says, now looking a little nervous at my reaction. "Are you not happy? Did we fuck up?"

They most certainly did not, but I can't find any words as silent tears stream down my cheeks. Damn hormones. How could these two know me so well after such a short time and make me so fucking happy that I cry? Who even am I right now?

Beau approaches me cautiously with his hands up, "If you don't like it, we can find something else. Don't even worry about it. I'm sorry we didn't tell you, we just wanted to give you a nice surprise and save you from the stressful part of finding a place. Everything has gone so well with us, and I guess we got overexcited."

"If you're worried about not having your own space, you can have the room, there are plenty of others," Theodore adds, both of them looking upset on my behalf now. "It's just that our little girl will be here soon, and we thought it would be best if we all lived under the same roof."

I wipe my tears away and step between them, wrapping one arm around each of their necks, pulling them into me, and holding them close. "It's perfect." My voice breaks with emotion, and they hold me back, breathing out sighs of relief at my words.

"Do you want more surprises, or have you reached your limit for the day?" Beau asks nervously, still holding me close.

"Get it over and done with," I tell him, letting them go. "Just let me sit down first. I'm suddenly feeling very tired." I go to the bed and sit down on the edge, taking a breath. "Alright, shoot."

Theodore goes over to one of the side tables and pulls

out some papers, handing them to me. The first one has a picture of a garage, a lot smaller than my parents' one. "That is Foxy's Garage," he starts, and I almost drop the papers. "It was for sale, and it's the only one up here, so you will get plenty of local business. We've already filed the paperwork, and it's officially yours to do what you want with."

"What about the baby?" I was assuming that they'd expect me to stay at home and do what Allure does, which I secretly hate the idea of but feel bad for voicing it out loud, knowing how it will sound.

Beau runs out of the room suddenly, and Theodore laughs. "We've got that all covered for you. I was sure you would want to go back to work as soon as you can, yes? I've heard from your brothers, your dad, and Allure about how hard it will be for you not to be working and knee-deep in grease. So, we came up with a compromise we thought everyone would be happy with. In the meantime, keep looking at the papers." I turn to the next page and see a cute sandstone building with a big sign over it, 'Dr. Bell's veterinary clinic.' "That is for me. It's been a while since I've worked on something other than the dog, cat, or bird variety, but with the outlying farm and things around here, I'm pretty sure horses, cows and sheep are now on my list of patients."

"Is this something you want?" I ask, making sure that these choices aren't just being made because of me and what I want. If we are going to have a healthy future together, everything has to be equal.

Beau comes back in the room wearing a frilly white apron and holding a feather duster. "Are you kidding? It's his dream life, and as for me." He does a dramatic spin. "I'm going to be a househusband and stay-at-home dad. I was given a ridiculously large amount of money from my good-for-nothing father when he passed away, and ever since I've been trying to find what fits me best. I love having the shelters, which I will continue to nurture, but with managers to deal with the day-to-day duties. But I couldn't think of anything I'd rather do with my life than raise our daughter with the love, kindness, and support that every kid should receive from their dad. I will give her everything I never got and more. Plus, out of the three of us, I'm the only one who can cook and clean. You're both useless, no offense."

I stare between them stunned by how perfectly everything is falling into place, and I actually pinch my own arm, just in case. *Ouch.* Yep, this is happening. They are going to be getting the best head of their lives.

Theodore grins at me. "Who said it's a woman's place in the kitchen anyway. Make your own dreams, baby, and if that means you work full-time doing something you love, then do it. Are you happy?"

I stand up and drop to my knees in front of him, ready to show them both just how happy I am. I look at Beau as I take down Theodore's zipper, giving him a wink. "Keep on the apron."

EPILOGUE

FOXY

Allure and I clink glasses as we watch Jamee and Beau run around with tutus over their clothes, with our four-year-old girls Raven and Rose chasing them dressed as little fairies. Beau got to have the princess dream after all because Rose is as girly as they come, much to Mami's delight.

Rose Patricia Jaclyn Hernandez was named after all three grandmothers, with Beau's mum's name Rose the perfect name to go by. When I brought it up as an idea, he literally cried because of how happy he was. She must have been one hell of a woman to raise an incredible boy like him, and it's the least I can do to honor her memory.

"I'm glad they got over their little sulk," Allure says, laughing evilly into her wine glass. "To be honest, they took the whole thing better than I thought they would."

I laugh and take a swig of my bourbon and cola, thinking about their faces when Allure and I took all five men for a surprise vasectomy appointment. You'd think they were getting their nuts chopped off the way they bitched about it. We kindly reminded them of the horrific birth we both had to endure to push out their kids, which promptly shut them up, and now we don't have to worry about any surprises.

Our newbie puppy jumps up and down at my feet asking for attention, and I call Theodore, who comes outside. "What do you need, baby?" he asks, leaning down and giving me a sweet kiss.

"Can you check to see if the pup's water is full? I can't remember if I did it this morning." I only ask him because he's sitting right by the kitchen where he is playing video games with Callum, Ardyn, and the older kids. Allure's other daughter Starling is a little tomboy and would rather be inside playing video games and tech stuff with Jamee these days, than get all girlied up like Raven and Rose do. It really goes to show that every kid is different. Wren is the typical boy, though, covered in dirt half the time and stuffing his face with food the other half.

I look out at the valley below and the soft fluffy clouds and wonder how we all got here. Back when Allure and I were twenty and sharing a small square apartment in Sinhaven, there's no way I would have believed someone if they told me that this would be us ten years later. Having a drink, with our men watching our kids living our best freaking lives. Unique, filled with laughter, and perfect just the way we made them.

One thing hasn't changed though, and that's my love for this bitch by my side, and I can't wait to see where we are in another ten years.

The End!!!!!

THE SINNERS FAIRYTALES SERIES:

Book 1 - Gluttony by Kira Roman, a Red Riding Hood retelling
https://books2read.com/SFG

Book 2 - Sloth by AJ Blackburn, a Cinderella retelling
https://books2read.com/slothsins

Book 3 - Wrath by Jay Leigh Brown, a Sleeping Beauty retelling
https://books2read.com/wrathsins

Book 4 - Greed by J. Kearston, a Rumpelstiltskin retelling
http://mybook.to/GreedSinners5

Book 5 - Pride by Kris Butler, a Rapunzel retelling
https://books2read.com/pridesin

Book 6 - Lust by Alexandra K. Martin, a Golden Bird retelling
https://books2read.com/Lustsins

THE VIRTUE FAIRYTALES SERIES:

Book 1 - Charity by Alexandra K Martin, a Beauty and the Beast.
https://books2read.com/u/baBj2a

Book 2 - Temperance by EJ Everette, an Ugly Duckling retelling.
Live Release Only

Book 3 - Diligence by Jay Leigh Brown, a Peter Pan retelling.
https://bit.ly/DiligenceJLB

Book 4 - Chastity by Kira Roman, a Swan Maiden retelling.
https://books2read.com/Swanm

Book 5 - Patience by Mia Z Staysails, a Goldilocks retelling.
https://mybook.to/Patience_Virtues5

Book 6 - Kindness by Kady Monroe, a Bear retelling.
https://books2read.com/KDKindness

BOOKS BY ALEXANDRA K. MARTIN

<u>Series</u>

Rathe Chronicles (Epic Fantasy Paranormal Romance)

-Summer's Confine, Book 1 (RH)

https://books2read.com/summersconfine

-Janice's Entanglement, Book 2 (Menage)

https://books2read.com/Janice

-Havana's Hell, Book 3 (MF)

https://books2read.com/HavanaRathe

-Alice's Coalition, Book 4 (RH)

https://books2read.com/AlicesCoalition

-A Very Rathe Christmas, Novella Book 4.5 (RH/Coming Dec 2023)

-Nateesha's Awakening, Book 5 (RH/Coming 2024)

<u>Standalones</u>

-Broken Faun (Paranormal RH)

https://books2read.com/brokenfaun

-Hidden Fate (Urban Fantasy Menage/Coming Soon)

-Blood (Dark Erotic Horror/Coming Feb 2024)

<u>Collaboration/Standalone</u>

-Lust: A Golden Bird Retelling. Sinners Fairytales Collaboration, Book Six (Dark Contemporary RH) https://books2read.com/Lustsins

-Charity: A Beauty and the Beast Retelling. Virtue Fairytales Collection, Book One (Dark Contemporary Menage)

https://books2read.com/u/baBj2a

Soul Sisters Co-Write

-Dom X (MF Erotic Standalone Novella)

https://books2read.com/u/3JnMdX

-Releasing the Beast (MF Paranormal Horror Romance/ Coming 2024)

Visit my Linktree for more information on me, the characters, Rathe and other novels:

https://linktr.ee/alexandrakmartin

https://linktr.ee/soul.sisters.novels

Acknowledgments

Thank you to my family, friends, editor, designer/Formatter and street team. You are all amazeballs and appreciated so much.

To my alpha/beta team; your time, support and friendship has helped me to become a better writer with every story and I am forever grateful to each and every one of you. Thank you.

Lastly, but just as importantly, my incredible readers. Words can't describe how much your support has meant to me over my journey. I wouldn't be here without you and everything I do is for you.